TEMPTATION

She took a step backward as the big man closed the distance between them, stopping so near that she could feel the brush of his surprisingly sweet breath against her cheek as he said softly, "I'm not insinuating anything. I'm *telling* you. You're not going to find the kind of *protector* you're looking for in this hotel. My advice would be to take yourself down to the Seamont Hotel where you can find a man with better manners and a fatter wallet." His dark eyes drilled into hers as he added, "You're wasting yourself here."

"How dare you insinuate—?"

"I told you, I'm not insinuating. I'm telling you. Galveston survived a blockade that cost it dearly, and the people here are celebrating their freedom any way they can. If you don't want the same kind of fella knocking at your door again, get yourself out of here so you won't be a temptation to men who have suffered much and have little resistance to your kind of allure. There might not be somebody around to help you out next time."

HAWK'S PASSION

Elaine Barbieri

LEISURE BOOKS NEW YORK CITY

A LEISURE BOOK®

August 2006

Published by

Dorchester Publishing Co., Inc.
200 Madison Avenue
New York, NY 10016

ISBN 0-8439-5637-2

HAWK'S PASSION

Prologue

She awoke abruptly to the intense heat and blinding smoke of a fire. She struggled for breath, panicking as the din of crackling flames and the terrified shouts of other children in the dormitory grew louder. She stumbled through the searing flames toward her younger sister's bed in the infirmary. She called out her sister's name when she found the bed empty, but the sound was lost amidst the escalating chaos.

The fire raged hotter. The agonized cries of the trapped children grew louder. Her eyes were tearing and her throat was burning when a wall beside her collapsed unexpectedly, forcing her backward to join a group of children racing toward a window of escape briefly visible within the flames.

Bursting out into the open at last, she fell to her knees as the orphanage blazed behind her. She fought for breath as she searched the soot-blackened faces of the girls lying on the ground nearby.

Her sister was not among them.

The sound of her sister's frantic cries from within the inferno whirled her toward the fire with a gasp. Hardly aware that her shouted reply went unheard, she jumped unsteadily to her feet, and with a shuddering breath ran back into the burning building.

Disoriented, her lungs on fire, she dodged the voracious flames while calling her sister's name. She heard her sister's response, then glimpsed the younger girl's terrified expression through the blaze, only to watch with powerless anguish as a wall of fire surged up unexpectedly to consume her—the moment before a deafening crack of sound directed her own eyes toward a burning timber descending toward her—a timber that ended her torment in abrupt oblivion.

"I don't know if this was wise, dear." Smartly dressed in gray traveling attire that unobtrusively marked her as an Easterner of considerable means, Ella Huntington glanced at her husband as he drove their rented buggy steadily forward. She continued softly, "The tragedy last night …" She shook her head, and tears filled her eyes. "The beloved matron of an orphanage and her staff gone … so many of the children killed and burned beyond recognition … the manor house that was their home destroyed—this community has suffered a catastrophe of monumental proportions. The smell of smoke and death still permeates the area. With most conscientious citizens actively involved in fighting the fire last night, or now tending to whatever survivors were found, you can't really expect Mr. Richardson to be of a mind to discuss business this morning."

"Ella ..." began Wilbur Huntington, the male counterpart of his striking wife, "I know what you're saying, but I have business to discuss that can't wait. The members of the board will expect a detailed report on my recommendations as to the extent of financial support that our bank should extend to businesses in this area—and rightfully so, in view of the unsettled political situation in Texas. Time is of the essence. However difficult the circumstances, Mr. Richardson will understand my need for haste so I may return to New York City."

"We're strangers here, Will. No one really knows us. Surely your intention to press business matters in the aftermath of such a terrible occurrence will be considered heartless."

"Perhaps, but I don't think so. I think Mr. Richardson will understand."

Her response was aborted by the unexpected appearance of a small, soot-stained figure that stumbled out onto the roadway. Ella exclaimed, "Watch out!" at the same moment that Wilbur drew back strongly on the reins.

Gasping as the child collapsed onto the ground, Ella jumped down from the buggy the moment it shuddered to a halt. She ran toward the girl, her breath catching in her throat as she drew nearer. The child's face was blackened; her clothes hung in singed rags. The girl strained for breath even as she lay unconscious, and as Ella stroked back a strand of scorched hair from the unnatural heat of the child's forehead, she saw a bloody wound on her scalp.

Ella glanced at her husband as he knelt beside her. She said shakily, "She must be one of the children from the orphanage fire. She must've escaped and wandered off before anyone arrived to help. She has a fever and a head wound—and she can't seem to breathe properly. She's so little, probably not more than ten or eleven."

Wilbur did not immediately respond.

"Will?"

Still no response.

Stunned at his unexpected reaction, Ella gasped, "She's badly hurt, Will. She may be dying!"

"Of course we'll help her." Appearing to snap out of his momentary trance, Wilbur ended his silence by adding, "My heart hasn't hardened to the extent you seem to believe, Ella. Mr. Richardson will have to wait."

Running ahead of him to spread her shawl on the backseat of the buggy as Wilbur lifted the child up carefully into his arms, Ella felt a familiar distress surge to life inside her.

The child was so small, so terribly injured … and so helpless.

The fire burned hotter. The flames surged higher. She couldn't breathe in the dark, heated torment that surrounded her. She struggled to escape, but she was trapped.

She was hot … hotter than she had ever been before. There was no relief to assuage her.

But … what was that … the soothing voice filtering through the sound of raging flames … the touch that cooled her burning brow?

"You'll be all right, dear; you'll see. Your breathing will ease and your wounds will heal … and I'll stay right here beside you until they do. I promise you that. I'll stay right here beside you."

She listened acutely to the soothing whisper that had become familiar to her through her pain. Still straining for breath, she struggled to open her eyes. She wanted to see the person who was speaking. She wanted to be sure the voice was not just another part of the dreams inundating her mind.

"She's trying to open her eyes, Will. She's regaining consciousness."

"Don't get your hopes up, Ella. The child is badly injured. She may not survive."

"Don't say that!"

She tried harder to raise her heavy eyelids. She wanted to see the woman with tears in her voice. She wanted to reassure the woman that she would survive. She wanted to tell her that she must survive … she must because … because …

A sliver of light filtered into her confused semiconsciousness as she forced her eyes open. She was lying abed in a strange room, and the woman was seated beside her. The woman was slender. Her face was pale, her hair streaked with gray, and there were tears in her weary brown eyes as well as in her voice.

5

Elaine Barbieri

She wanted to reassure the woman. She wanted to tell her she would be all right.

"She's awake! Thank God … thank God. It's been two days."

A tear slipped from the corner of the woman's eye, and she brushed it away as she leaned closer to whisper to her, "You'll be all right, my dear. You escaped the fire and you're going to be well. I know you are."

But the woman was shaking, and the girl knew the woman was afraid for her. She didn't want her to be frightened. Fear was an enemy. She would not allow it into her mind; she would not let the woman suffer because of her.

"Can you speak, dear?"

The woman's lips trembled as she brushed a strand of hair back from her heated forehead. She spoke coaxingly.

"Try to speak … just say a word … your name. I so much want to know what to call you."

Her name.

She tried to remember. She tried to reply. Both efforts failed as she continued to strain for breath.

The woman's hand dropped back to the bedside, and the girl's frustration mounted. She could not remember her name. It had slipped away into the vast void in her mind now filled with fiery nightmares and the difficult effort to breathe.

But the woman was suffering.

She struggled for the strength that had seemed to desert her.

With a supreme effort, the girl inched her hand forward.

6

She felt the warmth of the woman's long fingers as she covered them with her own.

She heard the woman gasp.

She saw the woman's tears.

They were tears of joy … as the girl's consciousness slipped away.

"I'm sorry, I can't answer your question. I can't really say if the girl will survive."

Ella stood rigidly still beside her husband in the anteroom outside the bedroom where the child lay. Almost a week had passed since the fire that had taken the lives of so many. The survivors of the fire were few, but their conditions were so critical that the sympathetic people within the community caring for them were taxed to the full extent of their ability.

Ella was only too aware that the same could be said for the child who lay in the bed beyond the door behind her, the girl whose bedside Ella had not left since Will and she had driven the child back to their quarters in town to care for her.

Now this statement by the overworked doctor that the girl might not survive …

Ella glanced at her husband before looking back at the doctor. "But her burns don't appear too bad, and her head wound is healing well."

"It's her breathing that concerns me." Dr. Johansson paused to wipe his wire-rimmed glasses before continuing sympathetically, "I'm sorry, Mrs. Huntington. I dislike saying this as much as you dislike hearing it, but I think the girl's lungs may have been affected. I'm afraid they may have been seared by the fire, and if they have …" He shook his head.

"No … I'm sure the condition of her lungs is only temporary." Ella looked back at her husband for support that was not forthcoming. Tears sprang into her weary eyes as she then said in a softer tone, "Surely there's something we can do."

"There's nothing *I* can do. Unfortunately we don't have the kind of equipment that might make a difference for the girl. Only specialized facilities have the equipment and breathing apparatuses that can treat the girl's lungs properly."

"Specialized facilities?"

"In large hospitals."

"Like they have back East?"

Dr. Johansson shrugged. "Otherwise, we'll just have to watch and wait … and pray." He repeated, "I'm sorry."

Ella watched as the portly doctor pulled the hallway door closed behind him. She turned back slowly toward her husband.

His even features tight, Wilbur Huntington shook his head. "No, I don't want to go through this again, Ella. I *can't* go through it again."

Ella took a shaken breath. The ordeal of their dear daughter's death three years earlier was still fresh in her mind. Lydia's prolonged illness had nearly cost Ella her sanity, yet it was Will who now seemed unable to come to terms with their loss.

Ella said softly, "The girl needs immediate care if she is to survive, and she can't get it here."

"No. We can't take her back East with us. We don't even know who she is."

"Neither does anyone else. All anyone seems to know is that she's one of the orphans Mrs. Kingsley took in. Whoever she is, though, that much is clear. She's an orphan. It's also clear that she won't survive if we don't provide her with the chance she needs."

"She may have some distant relatives around here who will come looking for her."

"Do you really believe that? The orphanage burned down, the matron and her staff were killed, and all the records were burned. If the child had a relative anywhere nearby, he surely would have come to her aid by now. Even if the girl had a chance of finding a relative through her records when she grew older, that possibility went up in smoke, along with her chances for a normal future. She'll have no future at all if we fail her."

"It's not a matter of failing her."

"What is it, then?"

"I just don't know if we should invest our hopes and dreams in another child"—she saw her husband shudder as he continued—"another child who may never reach maturity."

"Oh, Will!" Closing the distance between them in a few steps, Ella slid her arms around her husband and pressed her lips to his. She held him close as she looked up into his tear-filled eyes and whispered, "She's an orphan who stumbled into our lives. She has no one, and we're alone, too.

Perhaps we were meant to be traveling on that particular road the day after the fire. Perhaps she was meant to stumble into our path."

Wilbur shrugged.

"Perhaps it was divine intervention that brought her into our lives."

"Ella …"

"Perhaps we should be grateful to be given this opportunity … this chance to regain even a small part of what we lost."

"Dear—"

"Perhaps we were destined to have a second chance."

A sigh.

"Perhaps she is the answer to our prayers."

"Stop."

"W-what?"

"Don't waste your breath saying anything else."

Ella went silent.

"You win."

Ella did not immediately respond.

"I said, 'You win.' " Drawing back from his wife, Wilbur continued softly, "Divine intervention or not, and as much as the uncertainty of the girl's future frightens me, I know you're right. I tried to deny it, but we accepted responsibility for this child when we picked her up off the road, and we can't abandon her now."

Ella took an unsteady breath.

"Yes … we have no choice but to take her back home with us."

"Thank you, Will. You won't regret it. I know you won't."

Her heart filled with the sincere goodness of the man she had married, Ella slipped her hand into his and drew him back to the bedroom where the girl slept, still struggling for breath. She leaned lightly against his side, aching at the sight of the child. She was such a lovely little girl, even with her blond hair severely singed, her skin blistered from the fire, and her wide hazel eyes often unclear.

Her throat momentarily too tight for her to speak, Ella looked up lovingly at Wilbur. She managed, "She'll get better, Will. You'll see. She'll grow up strong and healthy, and she'll be beautiful when she grows up, too—even more beautiful than she is now."

"You haven't mentioned the most important reason for taking her back with us, Ella—the fact that you've already begun loving her."

"Yes, I have."

"Or that you would not have been able to leave her behind."

"No, I wouldn't."

"And that it doesn't make any difference to you that the child is so badly hurt, she can't even remember her name."

"Her name? Oh, Will, that will be the easiest hurdle to overcome." Looking back at the child, Ella said with a tremulous smile, "We'll call her Elizabeth—Elizabeth Huntington."

Chapter One

Galveston, Texas, 1866

Elizabeth Huntington entered the Easton Hotel and glanced around her in silent despair. Surely there was some mistake. Surely the carriage she had hired at the train station had brought her to the wrong Easton Hotel. Surely the dependable Thomas Biddlington, Esquire, her adoptive mother Ella's family attorney, could not have arranged for accommodations for her in this ... *place!*

Elizabeth walked across the shabby hotel lobby toward the registration desk, a stiff semismile on her lips. She had been warned not to expect too much, that Galveston, Texas, had suffered greatly during the war, both from a brief occupation by Union troops and from a blockade that had held the port hostage after Union troops were driven out. She had been told that Galveston would probably be unlike any city she could remember—surely different from New York City, where she had lived for the past eight years of her life with her adoptive parents, Ella and Wilbur Huntington. Yet she had dismissed that concern as inconsequential. The death of her dear adoptive father two years earlier had triggered a return of the nightmares that had plagued her for as long as she could remember. Those frightening dreams had made it no longer bearable for the first years of her life to remain a mystery, and she had been more driven to put the mystery to rest. She had told herself that since Texas was the place where her adoptive parents had found her, Texas was most likely the place of her birth, and she could never feel uncomfortable there.

Wrong.

Elizabeth glanced around her. Galveston left her feeling as unsettled as the appearance it presented. Union soldiers freely walked streets where only months earlier the same uniforms had been scorned. Buildings and thoroughfares damaged by cannon fire and neglect stood side by side with new construction that appeared hasty and haphazard at best. The hotel's deteriorated exterior had also been a disturbing sight as she had approached it on a street still bearing the scars of cannon bombardment, yet the interior lobby left her stunned. Drab and gloomy, a step above a shambles with its mismatched furniture and worn carpeting, it had the look of a place long past its prime.

Disturbing her even more, however, were the occupants of the lobby. They were male, poorly dressed and unkempt, outfitted in all manner of

Western dress. They appeared to be either indolently passing the time of day relaxing with a smoke, or leaning against a bar visible through an open doorway nearby with half-empty glasses in their hands. They made no attempt to hide their interest in her appearance, and were even bold enough to follow her progress across the room with snickers and whispered comments that left no doubt as to their opinion of a woman who would be registering at that hotel by herself.

For the first time, Elizabeth regretted bidding good-bye to her traveling companion, Agatha Potter, the sour-faced, cynical, middle-aged woman hired by her mother's attorney to travel with her in her adoptive mother's absence. Mrs. Potter had not been shy about voicing her opinion of the journey *after* leaving New York. She had said that Elizabeth was borrowing trouble with the hopeless dream she was pursuing, and that the sizable sum she was being paid to accompany Elizabeth barely made the journey palatable. The abrasive woman had declared more often and with more vehemence than Elizabeth had been able to abide that she would be only too happy to "leave the lawless state of Texas and return home to the civilized city of New York," and Elizabeth had taken the first opportunity to accommodate her.

She could now see that had been a mistake.

"Can I help you, ma'am?"

The hotel clerk's question was polite, even if his gaze, as it assessed her from the top of her sensible brown hat to the tip of her equally sensible leather shoes, caused her to stammer, "Yes … well, I believe … I think you have a reservation in my name?"

"You must be Miss Elizabeth Huntington then. I figured you had to be her, because there ain't nobody else who would bother with a reservation for a room here." The fellow did not wait for her reply as his toothless grin flashed and he continued, "But you was supposed to share a room with another lady."

"Mrs. Potter won't be coming."

"You're paid up for two weeks in advance. The draft came with your reservation, and your room is ready, so that's all right with me. If them's your bags over there, I'll have a fella carry them upstairs for you."

Uncertain how to react to the clerk's statements, Elizabeth said simply, "Yes, those are my bags."

"Hey, Charlie!" Startling Elizabeth, the clerk called out sharply, "Where are you, old man?"

"I'm right here, and I'm a step ahead of you."

Elizabeth turned to stand eye-to-eye with a scruffy, white-haired man who appeared at her side with her bags in hand. His back curved with age, his hair sparse, and his legs bowed, he said gruffly, "Follow me, lady."

When she did not immediately react, the old man said harshly, "Did you hear me? I'll lead the way."

The buzz of comments in the lobby heightened as Elizabeth started up the stairs behind the grizzled old fellow. She attempted to discount the heated gazes that followed her, and she raised her chin higher. She told herself that it didn't matter how poor her present accommodations had turned out to be, or what any one of those men thought; she was a woman with a mission, and she wasn't about to leave Texas until she had accomplished it.

Jason Dodd stood near the doorway of the Easton Hotel. He watched as the young woman climbed the worn staircase to the second floor, aware that he was one of many watching the sway of her narrow hips. It also occurred to him that his watching her was probably exactly what she wanted. Unfortunately, he'd seen too many of her kind since the blockade had been lifted. They had arrived in increasing numbers, along with Yankee speculators hoping for a quick profit at the expense of Galveston residents. Women like her usually fit into one of the following categories: Yankee women hoping for an alliance with one of the wealthy speculators; Southern "ladies" raised in a genteel manner—women who had lost everything but had learned nothing about the changes war had brought to their way of life; or women who had had no loyalty to either side and who were as willing as some of their male counterparts to profit from the suffering of those less fortunate. All were women willing to trade on their physical assets, or to do whatever they must to support a lifestyle they felt they deserved.

Jason admitted to himself a moment's regret when the young woman disappeared from sight.

This woman was particularly clever. She hadn't arrived dressed to attract attention; the sober brown traveling outfit she wore modestly covered her curves. She appeared to be smart enough to realize that there was no need to embellish the simple beauty of honey brown hair that shone with a glow of its own, of dark brows complementing incredibly long fans of lashes framing wide hazel eyes, or a faultless complexion set off to perfection by small, delicate features. The picture she presented was that of a demure, unworldly young woman on her own for the first time in her life—a young woman in desperate need of a protector strong enough and wealthy enough to keep her safe.

The only problem was that if she had come to this particular hotel hoping to strike up that kind of a liaison, she had come to the wrong place.

It was true that the Easton Hotel's reputation had been sterling many years before the war. Like other locations in Galveston, however, it had suffered greatly since it was built, and even more greatly during the war. In short, it was no longer a meeting place for the affluent.

The only thing the Easton Hotel now had to recommend it was its proximity to the rail yards. As a result, it was now the choice of an occasional businessman, but more often of stragglers representing the city's current mix—men desperately hoping to improve their situation, those who were uncertain which way to turn, and those who had given up trying.

Jason glanced at the clock on the lobby wall and

frowned. He was only too aware that he fit into one of those categories somewhere—actually one of the former, determined never to become one of the latter. For that reason he had come directly to the hotel after long days on the trail with the knowledge that he was already late for a meeting. He could not afford to sacrifice timeliness to either comfort or convention. He was equally aware that his appearance was lacking. His dark hair curled in an unsightly manner at the collar of his sweat-stained shirt, his firm chin was covered with three days' growth of beard, and his strong features were marked with lines of strain. His clothing also showed the effects of long days spent in the saddle, from a hat and bandanna still layered with dust, to pants and boots liberally spattered with dried mud—but all that mattered very little to him at present.

Approaching the registration desk with a long, fluid stride that bespoke cool resolve, and with a powerful stretch of shoulders denoting years of physical labor, Jason halted to tower over the squinting desk clerk. "A man by the name of William Brent should have arrived sometime late yesterday or early today. I'm supposed to meet him here."

"Mr. Brent … yes …" The clerk assessed his appearance for long moments, leaving Jason uncertain whether he would be forced to state his case more strongly, before the fellow continued abruptly, "Mr. Brent arrived this morning. He said he was expecting somebody, only I figured maybe that somebody would be female, more like the woman who just registered. I guess I was wrong."

"I guess you were."

"He said to send his visitor right up."

Jason waited.

"Mr. Brent looked like he might be a railroad man. I figured he was here on some kind of business." The clerk winked. "I ain't the kind to talk about what kind of business that might be—legal or otherwise. I figure that's none of my affair."

Jason glared at the nosy clerk. He was tired and irritable. He knew he looked less than professional, but he didn't like the fellow's assumption that he had come on business that would be considered shady—or the fact that the clerk appeared only too happy to tolerate it.

His patience short, Jason responded coldly, "That's right: it's none of your business—and Mr. Brent's room number is …?" When there was no immediate response, he added more forcefully, "Or do you want me to pound on every door in this *establishment* until I find the right one?"

"No, sir!" The clerk took a spontaneous step backward. "That would be room number eight up them stairs. Like I said, he's probably expecting you."

Jason turned in the direction indicated. With a last deadening glance at the clerk, he headed up the stairs.

Elizabeth stood stock-still inside the doorway of her hotel room. Her bags on the floor beside her, she stared around her with dismay. The room was small and spare. A single window covered by a lopsided shade and limp curtains overlooked the street; faded wallpaper hung tenuously from the smoke-darkened walls; and a threadbare rug that had long since lost any hint of its original color covered the floor. Crammed into the space between door and outer wall was a bed, a nightstand sporting an oil lamp, a dresser with a mottled mirror, and a wooden chair with one leg obviously shorter than the others. She hadn't expected much as she had followed the old man carrying her suitcases down a hallway of nicked and stained doors bearing numbers that appeared to follow no particular sequence, and discolored walls marked by years of wear and deliberate abuse; yet she supposed she had hoped for more.

She was spoiled; that was the problem. Her dear adoptive mother and father had given her the best they could afford from the day they had rescued her. The best included a speedy trip home to their Park Avenue mansion in New York City, medical treatment guided by their personal physician at the best hospitals the great city could offer, and recuperation in a large, airy, sun-filled room that she was able to call her own.

Elizabeth sighed as she recalled those days. She had been protected from everything with her new parents—everything but her own nameless fear. That fear had nagged at her during endless nights while nightmares of a raging fire assaulted her; while terrifying images within the flames awakened her time and again to the darkness of her room.

The shifting shadows in the night had then

worked to accelerate a fear that rose to the point of hysteria in her mind, only to be controlled at last by a faint echo ringing in the back of her mind: *Fear is an enemy. Don't let it win.*

Strangely enough, she had been told time and again as an adult that she was fearless. There was no task she would not tackle, no question she would not challenge, no individual too big or too brash for her to confront. She was proud of that facet of her personality, and she'd been forced to exercise it occasionally within her adoptive family.

There was an aunt who took every opportunity to attempt to discredit her in her adoptive parents' eyes. Firm in her rebuff of all Aunt Sylvia's unfair insinuations, Elizabeth was always civil to her, but she had long since given up trying to change the situation. It was a mystery to her how Aunt Sylvia could possibly have given life to a son as gentle and kind as Trevor, who often suffered abuse from his mother in her defense. Although at first concerned at Aunt Sylvia's concealed animosity, she no longer gave it much thought, because she knew her adoptive parents were proud of her and of the way she had handled things.

It was her silent humiliation, however, known only to herself and her dear adoptive mother, Ella, that as fearless as she was in most aspects of her life, she had not yet totally conquered her fear of the dark. Instead, she had learned to control her fear, and she had told herself that would have to do.

Still standing inside the doorway of her room, Elizabeth silently berated herself for her reaction to the austere quarters. She walked a few steps farther and scrutinized the bed linens as she folded them back. They were spotlessly clean and fresh. She then noted that the oil lamp sparkled with cleanliness, the rug on the floor had obviously been swept, not a trace of dust marked any visible surface in the room, and resting on the dresser was a small glass in which a few wildflowers, obviously freshly picked, had been artlessly placed.

Elizabeth swallowed hard against the lump that rose unexpectedly to her throat. Someone had made an obvious effort to present the room in the best possible manner.

It was equally obvious that someone had memories of a time when the Easton Hotel had been more than it presently was—and she envied that person. Memory was a gift ... a treasure to hold forever in one's mind. Her own limited memories had been tenderly cultivated by her adoptive parents—yet she was haunted by the void in her past where memory had been consumed by the same fire that had almost taken her life.

Almost overwhelmed by familiar sadness, Elizabeth sat on the side of the double bed. She reached into the neckline of her traveling dress and withdrew a delicate oval pendant emblazoned with an elaborate crest. She had no idea how she had gotten the pendant or what it meant. It was all that remained of a past buried somewhere in the shadowed reaches of her mind—yet she was certain it was the key to the who and why of all she had forgotten.

She studied it, caressing its raised surface with her

slender thumb. It was beautiful. Daintily wrought
on a gold base in subtle shades of blue enamel, it
pictured a sailing ship on a sea of white-crested
waves. The image of a hawk in flight was outlined
by a red rising sun. Below the ship, on a banner
garlanded with a vine of orchids, were the Latin
words *Quattuor mundum do*; and on the bow of the
ship, in minuscule letters that had been almost too
small for her to identify, was inscribed the name
Sarah Jane.

She had no idea how an orphaned child had
come to possess what appeared to be a meaningful
symbol of the past. She knew only that her adoptive mother told her she was wearing the pendant
underneath her torn and scorched dress when
she escaped the fire; that she had stirred from the
pained semiconsciousness of the days following
the fire only when someone inadvertently touched
the pendant; and that the pendant was—for a reason Elizabeth could not quite define—her most
cherished possession.

After Elizabeth's subsequent recovery from her
injuries in New York, her adoptive mother attempted
to discover more about her origins, but the fire had
done its work too well. Ella had learned by having
the Latin translated that *Quattuor mundum do* meant,
"To four I give the world;" yet Elizabeth's perspi-
cacity was responsible for deciphering the minuscule letters that formed the name Sarah Jane on
the bow of the ship. A relentless search of ships'
registries in the time following revealed several
ships named *Sarah Jane,* but only one registered in

Texas—in Galveston. That was when the idea of making her present journey was born.

Tears briefly clouded Elizabeth's vision. Years had passed since that moment of discovery. Her adoptive mother and she had intended to make the journey to Galveston together, but her adoptive father's unexpected illness and his three-year struggle to survive had put it on hold. Wilbur finally slipped away, but his extended illness had already affected Ella's health adversely. When Ella Huntington suffered a stroke, Elizabeth knew she had no choice but to remain by the side of the dear woman who was the only mother she could remember.

The mystery of her past was never forgotten, however. It interfered with the progress of her life. Aaron Meese, a handsome, sincere young man who was heir to his father's fortune, loved her—but she had been unable to make a commitment. Another sought-after bachelor, Gerald Connors, made similar intentions known, but her answer was the same, that she could not commit to the future while her past was shrouded in darkness.

Helpless against nightmares that grew in frequency as time passed, Elizabeth had no choice but to agree when her adoptive mother insisted that she delay her search no longer. She knew Ella would be disturbed when Agatha Potter returned prematurely and she realized Elizabeth was alone in her search. She suspected Aunt Sylvia would do her best to place harsh blame on her for Agatha's return, but Elizabeth also knew she could not allow either thought to hinder her. She was in Texas, the place of her birth, she hoped. This was her last chance to unearth the mystery of her past and to halt the nightmares that plagued her. She knew—

Elizabeth's pensive moment ended abruptly at the sound of a knock on her door. Uncertain, she approached it slowly and asked, "Who is it?"

"It's me, ma'am. I figure you was waiting for me."

Waiting for him ...?

Had someone recognized her? Could her search have ended successfully and so quickly?

With a shaky smile on her lips and her heart pounding, Elizabeth pulled open the door—then went stock-still at the sight of the bearded, grinning cowpoke swaying in her doorway. She took a step backward as the smell of whiskey and stale perspiration reached her nostrils. She said stiffly, "I think you made an error when you knocked on my door, sir. Perhaps you should try another room."

"No, sirree, you're the one I was looking for." The man's grin widened, allowing a broader view of uneven, yellowed teeth. Elizabeth suppressed a grimace when he reached into his pocket with hands that were less than clean and pulled out a wad of greenbacks as he said, "I got the money to pay for a good time, and you're the one I want to spend it with."

As he attempted to enter the room, sudden fear closed Elizabeth's throat. Reacting spontaneously, she shoved hard at his chest, knocking him a few steps backward, but she was not quick enough to halt the hand that grasped the door as she attempted to slam it. She was still struggling to force the door closed when the cowpoke pushed it open with a sudden thrust and said harshly, "Think you're too good for me, huh? Well, you ain't, and it looks like I'm going to have to prove it to you."

Elizabeth responded in as firm a tone as she could manage, "You've made a mistake, and I'm asking you to leave. If you don't leave, I'll call the manager of this establishment and have you thrown out."

"The *manager*?" The cowpoke's burst of laughter was halted abruptly by a deep voice from behind him saying, "You heard the lady, partner. You made a mistake, so put your money back in your pocket and go back where you came from."

Elizabeth restrained a gasp when she looked at the big man standing behind the drunken cowpoke. Bearded, disheveled, and decidedly unclean, he was a much larger version of the man he was displacing.

Making contact with the hard, dark-eyed gaze that turned briefly in her direction, Elizabeth swallowed. No, she was wrong. This man wasn't drunk— and unless she was wrong, he wasn't someone who would be turned away easily, either.

What had she gotten herself into?

The big man's gaze did not falter as he stared at the shorter fellow and pressed, "Did you hear what I said?"

The drunk looked up at the man standing behind him. His expression hardened for a moment. Then, he said abruptly, appearing to reconsider, "All right, I ain't so drunk that I can't see you're bigger than I am and steadier on your feet—so you win. She's all yours. As far as I'm concerned, she ain't worth the trouble she'd cost me, not when I can go to Miss Sadie's place and get me a woman who's more willing."

"That's good thinking. Miss Sadie's is the right place for you today."

The drunk was staggering back down the hallway when the big man turned toward Elizabeth and said unexpectedly, "I hope you learned a lesson here today, *lady.*"

"I beg your pardon!" Insulted by his tone, Elizabeth continued, "If you're insinuating—"

She took a step backward as the big man closed the distance between them, stopping so near that she could feel the brush of his surprisingly sweet breath against her cheek as he said softly, "I'm not insinuating anything. I'm *telling* you. You're not going to find the kind of *protector* you're looking for in this hotel. My advice would be to take yourself down to the Seamont Hotel, where you can find a man with better manners and a fatter wallet." His dark eyes drilled into hers as he added, "You're wasting yourself here."

"How dare you insinuate—"

"I told you, I'm not insinuating. I'm telling you. Galveston survived a blockade that cost it dearly, and the people here are celebrating their freedom any way they can. If you don't want the same kind of fella knocking at your door again, get yourself out of here so you won't be a temptation to men

27

who have suffered much and have little resistance to your kind of allure. There might not be somebody around to help you out next time."

"Help me out? Is that what you think you did?" Elizabeth was incensed. "I'll have you know that I could've handled that fellow on my own. I didn't need your interference, and neither will I ever need it again! And for your information, my room here has been paid up two weeks in advance, and I don't expect to lose any part of that sum, your *advice* notwithstanding!"

"Suit yourself."

"I will do exactly that!"

The big man's dark eyes drilled into hers a moment longer before he dismissed her without a word and headed on down the hallway.

Catching herself staring after the fellow—at the self-possessed way he walked, with his head high and his broad shoulders squared, as if he knew where he was heading and no one was going to stop him— Elizabeth strode back into her room and slammed the door closed behind her. She was breathing heavily when she turned back to twist the key in the lock. She glimpsed her face unexpectedly in the mottled mirror. Her kind of allure? What was it about her that had made either of them assume …?

Preferring not to finish that thought, Elizabeth picked up her suitcase and placed it on the bed. So she should go to the Seamont Hotel, where she could find a protector with better manners and a fatter wallet, huh? She gave a short laugh. Better manners, maybe, but she didn't need a fatter wallet *or* a protector.

Elizabeth withdrew a small derringer from her suitcase and slipped it into her handbag. She had made a mistake packing away the small weapon that her adoptive mother had insisted she carry— but the truth was, she hadn't thought she'd need it. But then, neither had she thought lessons on the small gun's care and usage were necessary when her adoptive father had insisted on them years earlier.

Wrong twice.

But she *had* learned a lesson a few minutes earlier, even if it wasn't the one the dark-eyed derelict had intended. She would never be caught unawares again.

The face of her unlikely savior returned unexpectedly to mind, and Elizabeth frowned. He had been angry when he left and had looked as if he regretted having halted the advances of the fellow who had appeared at her door. His advice to her had been caustic, and his obvious assumptions were insulting. In addition, the intense heat of his dark eyes when he had looked at her had made her uneasy in ways she could not clearly define.

The conclusion was apparent. She needed to avoid him—and she would. She had more important things to do.

Jason strode down the hallway, his jaw tight. He had walked away from the foolish young woman without any further comment, knowing anything else he had to say would be a waste of time. She had confirmed the truth of that notion when she slammed her door closed indignantly behind him. She obviously hadn't expected to attract the kind of fellow who had come knocking on her door, but she had been too stubborn to admit it.

Actually, he had been sorely tempted to walk on past when he saw her arguing with the drunken cowpoke in her doorway. It was his thought that any woman foolish enough to put herself in such a position deserved what she got; yet there had been something about her that had forced him to stop. He supposed it had served him right to have the woman look at him the way she did, as if he were no different from the drunk he had driven off.

But he *was* different.

That thought kept Jason scanning the numbers on the doorways he passed, his determination firm. The war years had been as long and difficult for him as they had been for Galveston. A lively port city with a great future, Galveston had been unexpectedly abandoned by the Confederacy. It had then been overrun by the Union army and subsequently recaptured by the Confederacy—only to be left virtually undefended when the Union fleet blockaded it afterward.

Now that the war was over, it would have been just as easy for him to abandon Galveston for greener pastures, but he hadn't. His reason could be stated in two words.

Simon Gault.

Jason's stern expression flickered briefly. Yes, the war was over, but he knew he would not be able to rest until he obtained the evidence he needed in order to prove that Gault had secretly collaborated with the Yankee blockade commander. Gault had ensured his own ships' safety when running the blockade by revealing the shipping plans of other blockade runners—at the cost of many of their lives. His own best friend, Captain Byron Mosley, was among that number.

Jason's thoughts slipped back farther into the past as he remembered the day before the war, when he'd arrived in Galveston with a herd slated to be shipped from that point. The drive had been lengthy and difficult. He had been tired and ready for a change when he met Byron Mosley, a young, affable ship's captain who was long on experience and short on cash. He had been impressed by the stocky seaman's intelligence and foresight, and with the captain's ambitious plans for the future. An immediate bond was struck between them, and Jason made the impromptu decision to use funds from the sale of his herd to form a partnership with Byron.

With the purchase of a schooner, the *Willow,* they had embarked on an adventurous undertaking that was aborted abruptly by the declaration of war.

It had been natural for Byron and Jason to turn to blockade running when Union forces blockaded Galveston. If asked to declare the reason for that choice, Jason supposed he might have said it was necessary in order to remain solvent, yet he had known down deep inside that Byron and he shared a common aversion to allowing any port in their home state of Texas to be held hostage. Their success in moving Confederate cotton and bringing back necessities for the residents of Galveston was limited, however, due to the depredations of the Union fleet.

Jason recalled with simmering anger that already slim profits suffered dramatically when the blockade situation worsened abruptly, with Union gunboats seeming to anticipate the activities of blockade runners. When it appeared not to matter how carefully blockade runners planned their voyages or how secretive they were, Jason knew that Byron and he weren't alone in their suspicions that the Yankees had been notified in advance to expect them.

It seemed significant to both Byron and him that Simon Gault's ships escaped the blockade with only token resistance offered by the Union fleet each time they made their runs; yet Gault was so kind, so generous to those in need, so willing to lend a hand to a worthy cause, that not a word was allowed against him.

It was rot, all of it!

Jason felt a familiar surge of angry heat. Byron and he had both known the truth, and they were determined to expose Gault for the collaborator that he was. They came close to confirming their suspicions the night a sailor from one of Gault's ships let it slip, after indulging too freely at a local saloon, that Simon Gault did indeed have an arrangement with the Yankee blockade commander—and that he could prove it.

It was particularly significant to both Byron and Jason that the sailor "disappeared inexplicably" the next day, and was never seen or heard from again.

Meanwhile, the *Willow* managed to continue eluding Yankee gunboats, but not without swamping of cargo and damage to the ship that almost negated profit. Strangely enough, however, neither Byron nor he ever considered that the price paid for their final escape would be Byron's life.

Jason breathed deeply as memory conjured up images of a starless night filled with gunsmoke, of Byron breathing his last shuddering breath, the victim of a Yankee bullet that turned the deck of the *Willow* red with blood.

Jason lost heart for shipping after his friend's death. He sold the *Willow* when the war ended and returned to the occupation he knew best. Yet with each herd he drove to Galveston, his determination to see Simon Gault brought to justice deepened.

Jason slowed his pace and dismissed his memories as the hotel room he sought came into view. It was time to turn his mind to the business at hand so he could bargain intelligently with the cattle buyer waiting for him inside. He knocked on the door and waited.

Emerging from the hotel room as the afternoon shadows lengthened, a bank draft in his pocket and his stomach warmed by the drinks they had shared, Jason shook the cattle buyer's hand and started back down the hallway. His silent concern at the outcome of that meeting became a frown as the door closed behind him. The cattle buyer had not blinked an eye when notifying him that all future herds must be driven to Houston for shipment instead of Galveston. Momentarily stunned into speechlessness, Jason had launched a vociferous protest that he subsequently realized was pointless.

Jason squared his shoulders with determination. The handwriting was on the wall if he couldn't change the present situation in Galveston.

Jason's steps slowed, his thoughts reverting to his angry exchange with the indignant young woman as he neared her door. He saw light flickering underneath the door frame, and then saw a shadow as the woman walked past on the opposite side. He cursed softly at the responsive tug somewhere in the area of his groin that the mental image of her provocative expression evoked. He silently admitted to himself with a trace of discomfiture that a part of his angry reaction to the woman's situation stemmed from the fact that if not for his previous appointment with the cattle buyer in room eight, he might have been the fellow who had come knocking on her door.

Causing him even further discomfort was his realization that although he would have been received the same way as that fellow, the temptation still remained.

And he didn't even know her name.

Jason frowned at the thought, telling himself he had been saved from making a mistake. The haughty beauty was apparently looking for a "special protector," and he didn't fill the bill.

Scowling as he passed her door, Jason shrugged.

Well, he hoped she found what she was looking for.

Chapter Two

The sun had risen on a bright, if uncomfortably warm morning as Elizabeth adjusted the collar of her simple green gown. She frowned at her reflection in the mottled mirror and tilted the brim of her small straw hat to a more sedate angle. She had tightly bound her hair in an effort to appear more dignified and mature. She supposed the shadows under her eyes could not be helped, since she had not slept particularly well. Thoughts of the dark-eyed stranger who had "rescued" her had returned with annoying frequency during the night. The gall of the man to suggest that she was present in Galveston for ... for *untoward* reasons simply because she had registered at the hotel alone!

Admittedly, he did not appear to be the only one who'd made that assumption. She had been met with similar reactions as she had walked through the hotel lobby to find a place to eat the previous evening. In the absence of suitable facilities at the Easton, she had finally settled on a small restaurant a few doors up the street, where the clientele was less than desirable. She had eaten in a rush and retired to her room in a state of mental exhaustion.

She had retained only enough energy to compose a lighthearted letter to Ella, whom she was certain would begin to worry about her after Agatha Potter returned to New York prematurely.

Elizabeth frowned at her certainty that *dear* Aunt Sylvia would take the opportunity to make her adoptive mother even more worried about the situation. She was not sure why Aunt Sylvia resented her so. Although she doted on her only son, Trevor, Aunt Sylvia could not seem to comprehend that Ella and Wilbur Huntington still had a similar love to give after the death of their own daughter. Nor could Aunt Sylvia accept that Elizabeth's advent into their lives as a lost and ailing child had partially filled that aching void.

Elizabeth reconsidered that thought. It was not that Aunt Sylvia *could* not comprehend her adoptive parents' love for her. More likely she did not *want* to comprehend it.

Elizabeth knew that Aunt Sylvia had often tried to convince her two generous and loving adoptive parents that her love for them was insincere. The woman had actually gone so far as to intimate that Elizabeth's desire to uncover her past proved that point. Fortunately, her adoptive mother did not agree; yet Elizabeth suffered no illusions. Despite Aunt Sylvia's pretended concern about her sister-in-law's ill health, she would not hesitate to remind the dear woman that only Trevor was truly capable of carrying on the Huntington bloodline.

But a new day had dawned, and Elizabeth was determined not to allow concerns or annoyances to defeat her, even though the moist air persisted in curling tendrils at her hairline, while causing little beads of perspiration to line her upper lip. Brushing them away impatiently, she finally shrugged in acceptance: Her appearance was not going to be all she'd hoped today. She needed to concentrate on accomplishing—

Elizabeth jumped at the sound of an unexpected knock on her door. She turned toward it and called out in what she hoped was a confident tone, "Who is it?"

"It's me … Charlie."

Charlie?

Momentarily stumped by the response, Elizabeth belatedly identified the voice as belonging to the old man who had carried her bags to her room the previous day. She smiled tentatively as she drew the door open and said, "Did you want to see me, Charlie?"

Gray brows knit over his rheumy eyes, Charlie looked at her silently before saying, "I was wondering if there might be something I could do for you."

Elizabeth paused, uncertain how to reply.

The old man's face colored unexpectedly as he produced wildflowers previously held behind his back and said, "I figured them flowers I put in your room before you arrived would be dead by now, and you might want to replace them with these that I picked fresh this morning."

"Oh ... thank you ... that would be nice."

Elizabeth felt her own face grow warm as she accepted the flowers and stepped back to place them in the glass on the dresser. The old man continued with sadness tinging his voice, "There was a time when fresh flowers was in every room in this hotel, but there ain't been no need for them these past few years. I figured you had to be different when your reservation came with payment in advance and all, and that you deserved a little better than most."

At a loss for words at the old man's unexpected thoughtfulness, Elizabeth remained silent as he continued with a frown, "But I got to admit I wasn't figuring you'd be so young and pretty, and that threw me for a loop at first. I figured you might cause more problems for this place than its already got. It took me a little while to reason that even if that turned out to be true, it wouldn't be your fault. I also reckoned you might be needing a little help this morning. Even a right proper young lady like you needs a hearty breakfast, and I reckoned you might want to eat it in a place where you won't be bothered by some of the trash that lives in this hotel."

"You guessed right, Charlie. I would appreciate being pointed in the right direction. I think I made a mistake in the place I chose to eat last night."

"If you're talking about Barney's place a few doors down, you sure enough did. You need to get yourself a carriage ride to a street where businessmen will tip their hats to a lady like you and you'll be able to eat in peace."

Elizabeth swallowed past the lump unexpectedly forming in her throat as she replied, "That would be lovely."

"The Seamont Hotel is a right nice place. They serve good meals there, so they say—almost as good as they used to serve here in the Easton's heyday— and the doorman will be happy to get you a carriage to take you wherever you want to go from there."

"The Seamont …" Her savior's reference to that hotel the previous day returned to mind, causing her to stammer, "Good meals, you say?"

"That's right. You might ask for one of the cooks working in the kitchen there if you get a chance. Her name's Fanny Bigelow. I talked to her last night about you. She'll do her best to set you on the right track." When Elizabeth did not immediately reply, Charlie shrugged. "Like I said, it ain't often a lady makes a reservation in this hotel anymore."

"Thank you again, Charlie. That will be very helpful. I have a big day ahead of me."

Charlie added, "I figure you came to Galveston for a good reason. Nobody like you ever comes here anymore without something definite in mind."

"I do have a good reason, and I suppose it's no secret." Suddenly realizing that Charlie might be just the person who could fill in some of the blank spots in her mind, she said, "I'm looking for … for some kind of information about my family. We lost touch with one another quite a few years ago, and

I'm hoping to find some news of them around here."

Charlie nodded. "There's been a lot of that going on since the war ended, but I got to say the name Huntington don't ring a bell in my mind, and I've been around here for a while."

"That isn't the name of the family I'm looking for. Actually ..." Elizabeth hesitated. She scrutinized the old man's expression a moment longer but saw in it only honest concern. "I was adopted and took that name. I don't know my real family name. All I have is this pendant." Carefully withdrawing her pendant from the collar of her dress, she said, "I was hoping someone in Galveston could help me identify this crest."

Elizabeth held her breath.

She released it disappointedly when Charlie shook his head and said, "I ain't never seen anything like that before. I spent most of my life on horseback until an accident in the rail yards dropped me off here. Except for the Yankee blockade that kept everything in short supply during the war, I don't know nothing much about ships. But if you're looking to find somebody that might be able to tell you more, you might do better down by the harbor. We got plenty of ships there, and lots of traffic, too, since the war ended." He paused again. "But I'd make sure it was daylight when I went. It's safer that way."

"Thanks again, Charlie. I appreciate your advice." Elizabeth paused before continuing, "I wish there were some way I could show you my appreciation in a more material way."

"If you're meaning money, I don't want none of yours." Charlie shook his head adamantly. "I figure you'll probably be needing it more than me if you plan on staying awhile. I'll do my best to look out for you, but this ain't the easiest town to get along in if you don't know nobody here."

"That's very kind of you, Charlie, but I'm sure I'll be fine. Somebody is bound to recognize my pendant sooner or later."

His expression doubtful, Charlie shrugged his curved shoulders. "Maybe, but the war hit Galveston hard. There's been a lot of changes around here in the past few years, so I wouldn't set my heart on it if I was you. Anyways, you'd better get yourself out on the street so you can get yourself a carriage before the tables at the Seamont fill up—it's that popular, you know." Charlie added reluctantly, "And if I was you, I'd pay no mind to what the fellas in the lobby say when you walk through downstairs. Some of them ain't too polite."

"I know."

Snatching her reticule off the bed, Elizabeth pulled the door closed behind her and turned the key in the lock. She turned back, surprised to see Charlie already heading down the hallway.

Jason entered the Seamont Hotel and paused inside the doorway to look around. The luxurious lobby with its European elegance boasted heavily tufted chairs, mellow wood, and crystal accessories. Its luxury belied the difficulties other parts of the city were experiencing; yet he supposed he should have expected as much. Galveston had been a cosmopolitan city before the war, where residents rode in fine carriages down clean, spacious streets lined with palm trees and oleander. Shops along the thoroughfares were filled to bursting with luxuries of every kind; churches and market houses were abundant; town hall, municipal court buildings, and adjunct offices were easily found; facilities for higher education were readily available; and residents as well as visitors dined well at American, German, and French hotels constructed in fine taste.

The Seamont Hotel had always been, and seemed destined to remain, typical of that scene, with the sophistication of its columned entrance portico, spacious lobby, extensive facilities, and graceful architecture. It was an example of a recovery that had not reached other areas of the city, where streets still bore the scars of war, where deterioration was painfully obvious, and where the harsh sounds of reconstruction grated on the ear.

Jason walked across the lobby toward the hotel restaurant. His meeting there that morning was imperative to his own future as well as to the future of Galveston, and he was dressed accordingly. Making good use of his time since arriving back in Galveston the previous day, he had visited the barbershop and the baths, and had emerged from the quarters he rented in a conservative area of town bearing little resemblance to the hardworking Western cowboy of the previous day. Admittedly, he was more comfortable in his Western attire than he was in the dark suit coat and trousers he wore today; yet he knew that his appearance, including the finely starched linen shirt and string tie, the subtle brocade of his vest, and the dark, broad-brimmed hat he wore down low on his forehead, gave him an air of credibility necessary to the success of his meeting that morning.

Jason stood briefly in the restaurant doorway. He shrugged off the assistance of the *maître d'* when the man he was looking for waved him toward his table.

Willard Spunk's designation as a city father signified far more than the words implied. Short, balding, his expanding waistline unaffected by the shortages the city had recently experienced, he was well dressed and perfectly at home in the elegance of Galveston's favorite restaurant. The stellar reputation he enjoyed had been earned by years of devotion to Galveston's welfare, and Jason knew that the gentleman's pride in the resurgence of the city was sincere. Jason was also aware, however, that Spunk was one of a group of entrepreneurs who controlled the wharves, railroads, and most of the business that moved through the city; and because of that control, he and others in his association ultimately controlled the future of the city and all its residents. Jason knew that Spunk and his associates were heavily influenced by a man of sterling reputation who had no sincere interest in the city beyond the accumulation of his own personal wealth; a man who would stop at nothing, including the deaths of supposed compatriots, to achieve his ends; a man whose munificent exterior shielded cold-blooded avarice.

That man was Simon Gault.

Jason smiled as he approached Spunk's table and shook his hand warmly. It was fortunate for him that his blockade running had elevated him in Willard Spunk's estimation. The fact that Spunk actually liked him, and that Spunk had a pretty, unmarried daughter whom he wanted Jason to court, did not hurt.

Jason smiled sincerely as Spunk spoke an effusive welcome. Actually, Elvira Spunk was a nice girl. He liked her, but that was as far as it went—for either of them.

Jason sat down and ordered while indulging in the niceties of conversation that were a prelude to the more important conversation he had in mind.

A short time later Jason was lingering over a breakfast of steak and eggs that had been presented by the French chef himself as he continued, "The truth is that railroad men and important speculators have banded together to turn Galveston's trade toward Houston. In their opinion, the city of Houston, despite its unattractive surroundings, is better situated to serve as a base for both rail and sea transportation than Galveston."

"Nonsense, my dear Jason." Spunk's round face creased into a patient smile. "The combined advantages of Bolivar Pass and Galveston Bay afford a natural Texas trade route. I've already discussed this matter with fellow businessmen prominent in our association. We are all agreed that the threat you speak of poses no real danger to us."

"Really? I was notified when I arrived with a herd yesterday that all further herds must be delivered to Houston to be shipped."

"A small setback, Jason." Spunk patted his hand. "Don't worry about it. We'll take care of it. As far as you personally are concerned, Galveston is aware of the contribution you've made to its welfare in the past. Our city won't desert you."

"It's not my welfare I'm primarily concerned with, sir. I have a ranch upstate that was recently left to me. It can provide me with a reasonably secure future when I decide to take advantage of it."

Frowning for the first time, Spunk inquired, "And the reason for your attention to Galveston then is ...?"

Jason paused before responding succinctly, "I have business here that involves Byron Mosley. It's important to me to see it settled satisfactorily."

Spunk nodded, then wiped his mouth with his linen napkin before replying thoughtfully, "I understand. I know Byron and you were close friends. This issue is important to you, and if it's important to you, I will give it the attention you feel it deserves." He paused again, then said, "I'm having a soiree this weekend—a get-together of some business associates and friends. Everyone concerned in this matter will be there, and you'll be able to discuss your concerns in a relaxed atmosphere. Come. Bring a friend if you're so inclined. We'll enjoy your company."

Obviously satisfied that the matter had been momentarily handled, Spunk flashed a smile. "So, finish your breakfast. I have to be leaving for a meeting soon, and we have personal matters to catch up on." He winked. "You're not married yet, are you?"

Jason could not restrain his smile—a smile that faded abruptly at the unexpected appearance of a stunningly familiar young woman in the restaurant doorway.

Elizabeth stood stock-still in the entrance to the elaborately equipped restaurant. Linen, crystal, silver, dutiful waiters … She took an astonished breath. She had been startled when her carriage had drawn up in front of the magnificent Seamont Hotel, so amazing was its contrast to the humble quarters where she was staying; yet the interior left her speechless.

Take yourself down to the Seamont Hotel where you can find a man with better manners and a fatter wallet.

Her savior's words returned again to haunt her.

Elizabeth felt a responsive heat rise to her cheeks when the maître d' approached her with a cautious expression and said, "May I help you, *mademoiselle?*"

"Yes, you may. I'd like a table, please."

"You are Mademoiselle …?"

"Mademoiselle Huntington."

"You are expecting someone to join you, Mademoiselle Huntington?"

"No. A table for one will be fine."

The maître d' assessed her boldly from head to toe, then said with a revealingly stiff smile, "May I see your key, *s'il vous plaît?*" And when she did not immediately reply, "*Pardon, mademoiselle.* It is not the custom of this hotel to serve unescorted ladies unless they are residents here."

Annoyed, Elizabeth responded, "Unfortunately I was not aware of your policy—as archaic as it is during these changing times—but since I am here now, I would like to be seated so I may have breakfast."

"That will be impossible, *mademoiselle.* This hotel discourages traffic that might adversely affect its reputation. It would be best for you to leave."

"Traffic that might adversely affect ..." Elizabeth's eyes widened at his outrageous presumption.

His tone betraying open disapproval, the maître d' continued more softly still, "I suggest that you try another location, *mademoiselle.* There are any number of places where you will be more easily received by gentlemen responsive to your needs."

"Are there!" Her cheeks hot with anger, Elizabeth said in a carefully modulated tone, "My *needs,* however you seem to regard them, will be met just fine in this restaurant this morning, so I suggest you turn around and escort me to a table, unless you want to personally escort me to the door, in which case I will—"

Elizabeth's angry retort was cut short by a deep, unexpected voice from behind her that said, "There you are, darlin'! Howard asked me to express his apologies because he isn't here to meet you. He said to tell you he was called to a meeting but he hopes you'll be available for him to express his personal apologies later."

Elizabeth turned toward the handsome, dark-haired stranger smiling down at her so warmly. Something about him struck a familiar chord as he continued, "In the meantime, Howard asked me to escort you personally to a table in the hope that you'll be able to enjoy your breakfast in his absence."

That voice … those dark eyes …

Sudden realization struck Elizabeth.

No, it couldn't be!

The maître d's small mustache twitched with mortification. "My sincere apologies, *mademoiselle*. All friends of Monsieur Dodd and Monsieur Meecham are welcome here, of course. I will be only too happy to seat you, *s'il vous plaît*."

Elizabeth attempted to resist as the tall, dark-haired stranger slipped his arm under hers and turned her firmly to follow the maître d' across the floor. Continuing to hold her arm fast, the stranger whispered in a tone meant only for her ears, "I'd consider myself lucky to survive this incident without further embarrassment if I were you, lady. When I advised you to come to the Seamont, I didn't expect that you'd be fool enough to walk in here like you owned the place!"

"So it *is* you!"

"Right." His haunting dark eyes turned toward her as he said with a grunt, "It seems to be my destiny to rescue you from awkward situations."

Unable to pull free of his grip without causing a scene, Elizabeth responded hotly, "Rescue me? You are mistaken again, *sir*. I could have handled this situation just as easily as I could have handled the situation yesterday."

"No doubt."

Replying to his scarcasm, Elizabeth snapped, "That's right—*no doubt!* I'm not the helpless, weak-minded woman you obviously think I am."

"That thought never crossed my mind."

"Nor am I in need of protection!"

Another glance from those dark eyes spoke silent volumes.

"I'm quite capable of handling this sort of thing, whether you believe it or not!"

Their whispered exchange was interrupted by the maître d' as he stopped beside a well-situated table and said apologetically, "I hope this table will do, *mademoiselle*." At her stiff nod, he pulled out the chair and said courteously, "It will be our pleasure to serve you."

Elizabeth sat down heavily and glared at the maître d' as he walked away. She drew back defensively when the dark-eyed stranger leaned down to whisper, "Behave yourself! Whether you know it or not, you're the guest of Howard Meecham this morning. Howard is a very important man, but knowing him as well as I do, I'm sure he'd be happy to oblige in this situation."

"By that you mean …?"

Again that knowing glance.

Exasperated, she snapped, "I don't need—"

"I said, behave yourself! You'll never find what you're looking for with that attitude."

"How do you know what I'm looking for?"

"You don't really want me to answer that question, do you?"

Elizabeth bit back her reply as the stranger straightened up to his full, towering height and said, "I'm going back to my table now. You'll be all right if you don't cause any more problems." He added as if in afterthought, "And … don't bother to thank me."

"I won't."

"I didn't figure you would."

Elizabeth did not allow herself to reply as he turned with a frozen smile and left.

"Who is she, Jason?"

Jason saw the gleam of interest in Willard Spunk's eyes when he resumed his seat at their table. Spunk scrutinized the young woman as she sat tight-lipped, staring at the menu. He mumbled, "She appears to be on her own, which makes me believe she's unattached and available for the right compensation … and she is a beauty, isn't she? She has an innocent look about her, with that clear complexion, those large eyes, and those perfectly shaped lips."

Jason hesitated to respond. He recognized the look on Willard's face. As respectable a family man as Willard was, he had an occasional appetite for the ladies. Elise, his lovely wife of twenty-odd years, turned a blind eye when necessary, as did most others who knew him. Having formerly counted himself among that number, Jason felt a knot of unidentifiable emotion twist tight in his stomach at the thought of Willard's interest.

Jason took the opportunity to respond with the name he had overheard the young woman speak, replying, "Her family name is Huntington. I can't say I really know her first name." He added, "Howard refers to her as 'darling.' "

"Oh, so that's the way it is." Appearing disappointed, Willard shrugged. "I was hoping ... but I don't suppose it would do to try my luck, with Howard being interested in her and all. He is a single man, after all."

"Yes, he is."

"Not that it makes much difference in his case, since Howard is such a womanizer."

Jason did not reply.

Appearing to have lost all taste for further conversation, Willard consulted his pocket watch, then said, "I'm sorry, Jason. Time seems to have gotten away from me. I'm expected at the office, so I'll have to leave. Please stay to finish your breakfast." He added, "And don't forget the soiree at my house this weekend. I'll be expecting you."

"I won't forget."

Standing as Willard left, Jason shook his hand, then resumed his seat. His steak was cold, his appetite was gone, but the interest the male patrons evinced in the solitary Mademoiselle Huntington kept him glued to the spot. He wondered absentmindedly if her intention had been to register at the hotel, as he had advised. It appeared that she would not have to wait long for an opportunity to better her situation if she did.

Uncertain why that thought bothered him, Jason

dawdled with a third cup of coffee until Mademoiselle Huntington patted her mouth with her napkin, stood up, and walked toward the restaurant exit with interested gazes trailing her.

Following at a distance, Jason saw her hesitate, then turn toward the registration desk, where she spoke to the clerk in a lowered tone. He was still watching when a flurry of movement at the hotel entrance turned him toward the startling couple who walked boldly through the doorway. He frowned at the whispers of disapproval that susurrated across the lobby and saw the flicker of acknowledgment that moved across the woman's face as she turned toward the restaurant.

The hypocrisy of those whispers struck Jason forcibly. Chantalle Beauchamp ran the most discriminating bordello in town, and most of the men present in the lobby were her customers. Her card games were honest; the liquor she served was never suspect; she took good care of her employees, whether they worked in the upstairs rooms or in the kitchen; and she was discreet and honest in the services she supplied. There was not a man present in either the lobby or the restaurant who was not familiar with Chantalle in some way, yet she went unacknowledged by every one of them.

Jason suppressed an angry snort. What most did not know about the striking middle-aged madam was that while many residents of the city had been unable to afford the high prices blockade runners like himself were forced to demand, Chantalle could. As a result of her generosity, the employees in her house lived well, if not extravagantly, and her customers did not suffer deprivation of any sort. Unknown to most, too, was the great abundance of foodstuffs and necessities that Chantalle contributed anonymously to the many churches and hospitals in the area in order to supply those who might have otherwise suffered. Nor were most people aware of the many situations that might have ended in tragedy if not for her anonymous intercession.

Jason watched as Chantalle neared the entrance of the restaurant with her companion, Captain Joshua Knowles. Captain Knowles's liaison with Chantalle was legend in the city. He was a good man, but the sober suit coat and trousers he wore for the occasion could not hide the man's seafaring swagger, nor the unconventional queue in which he wore his white hair.

Jason glimpsed the expression of the maître d' as the couple approached, and he turned spontaneously in their direction. He reached them just as Captain Knowles's gray brows began knitting over his fiercely blue eyes when the maître d' pronounced that there were no tables available.

"Chantalle … so nice to see you again."

Chantalle's smile was spontaneous, as was her raised brow as she quipped in her husky tone, "I wasn't sure you would remember me here, Jason."

Jason responded with a smiling glance at her gown, a purple silk garment more conservative in the neckline than her usual attire despite its rather gaudy gold trim. "You look lovely, as usual, Chantalle, but you don't look that different." He turned toward the captain and extended his hand. "And you don't look much different in that handsome suit, Captain."

The maître d' lowered his eyes toward his reservation book as Captain Knowles responded with a grunt. He then looked up with a stiff smile to say, "*Pardon, s'il vous plaît!* I see I am in error. We most certainly have a table available for *madame* and *monsieur.*" The maitre d' glanced at Jason and said pointedly, "Any friend of Monsieur Dodd is welcome here."

The maître d' turned to pick up the menus as Captain Knowles mumbled begrudgingly, "He had better find a table for us."

Chantalle responded with a wink, "Not to say that I didn't warn you this might happen, but you heard the man, Joshua. Any friend of Jason's is a friend of his. I suppose we need to remember that the next time we attempt to dine at such an exclusive place."

Captain Knowles was still mumbling when Chantalle bid Jason a short *adieu* and started toward their table.

Jason's responsive smile faded as he turned back toward the registration desk to see the mysterious Miss Huntington looking at him with a tight-lipped expression. He frowned as her gaze dismissed him and she turned toward the door.

Responding to impulse, Jason asked at the registration desk when her carriage pulled away, "Was Miss Huntington inquiring about a room?"

"Miss Huntington …?"

To the young clerk's vague response, Jason responded flatly, "The young woman you were just talking to … the *pretty* young woman you were smiling at a few minutes ago."

"Oh, Elizabeth Huntington."

Jason barely nodded in response.

"No, she just wanted to drop off a letter to be posted and to ask about the office locations of various shipping companies."

"And she told you her name?"

"She identified herself, of course. She left the address where I could send her any information I might be able to gather about ships berthed at the Galveston docks twenty years ago. I told her I didn't know of anyone who might be of help to her because of the changes that have affected Galveston recently." He grimaced. "She's staying at the Easton Hotel. I told her it wasn't a very good place for a lady like her to reside, even temporarily, but she said she was committed." The clerk leaned closer to whisper, "I have the feeling that her funds were limited and she couldn't afford the rooms here. That is unfortunate, to say the least."

"To say the least."

"If you like, I could try to contact her for you—"

No longer listening, Jason turned toward the street. So she was interested in a particular ship that was berthed in Galveston twenty years ago....

And her name was Elizabeth.

Chapter Three

Elizabeth walked slowly along Galveston Harbor as the unrelenting sun neared its apex. She was wearied to the bone by what she saw. It was obvious even to her untrained eye that an effort had been made to clean up the docks after the federal blockade ended; yet also obvious was the fact that success had been minimal.

She had been surprised by the condition of the water lapping at the docks. She had not expected that it would appear so muddy as to seem unclean or polluted. Nor had she expected to see a lonely ship's mast protruding above the water in the distance, silent testimony to the vessel lying at the bottom of the bay, a victim of Yankee gunboats. Startling had been the deplorable state of disrepair visible in every direction, with rotting wharves and cannon-pocked buildings wherever she looked.

Elizabeth took a deep breath of salty air and pushed a stray lock of hair back from her damp forehead. She supposed she should remind herself

that the sound of building—or repair—echoed from
every quarter, and that she had been informed during her inquiries that the muddy water was not a
consequence of neglect or assault; it was simply the
result of the rush of water that the island's geogra-
phy produced. She supposed her present low spirits
could be partly attributed to the fact that the long
morning had not been particularly productive. Her
inquiries at different shipping companies about
a ship named the *Sarah Jane* had produced blank
looks, and inquiries about the crest on her pendant
had been met with suspicious glances and insulting questions as to her true intentions.

In other words, a woman alone in Galveston was
suspect.

Incomprehensible. Archaic. Downright frustrat-
ing!

Elizabeth looked up at the position of the sun in
the cloudless sky. She was tired and hot, and she
was beginning to get hungry, as well. It had been
a long morning since she had left the Seamont
Hotel in a mood that could be described as less
than pleasant. She supposed her foul mood had
also been caused by her reception at the Seamont
Hotel restaurant—yet she knew blame could more
precisely be placed on her meeting with the abominable Mr. Dodd. To think that she had actually
begun to feel a semblance of gratitude for his intervention at the restaurant! It had taken only one
glimpse of his similar intervention when a matronly
woman of obviously questionable virtue attempted
to enter the same restaurant for her to realize,

first, that the offensive Mr. Dodd had put her in the same category as the woman with the outlandish red hair; and second, that he appeared to be too friendly with the redhead for their relationship to be casual.

It had been a totally embarrassing experience, made all the worse by the registration desk clerk when he whispered the woman's name and rolled his eyes in a way that said her opinion of Madame Beauchamp was correct.

Elizabeth looked up at a warehouse in the distance bearing the sign GAULT SHIPPING & EXCHANGE. Two-storied, it appeared to be an office as well as a warehouse. With its steep roof and white stone construction, its wide steps and brass railings leading up to a first floor set high off the ground to avoid the possibility of flooding, it dominated the dock at the far end and was the most elaborate building on the street. As she neared, she realized it appeared miraculously untouched by the federal barrage that had otherwise left its mark on other buildings along the wharf.

Elizabeth paused to catch her breath and to prepare herself for yet another disappointment as she reached the top of the stairs. Taking a moment to wipe the perspiration from her brow and upper lip with a handkerchief that was limp with moisture, she did her best to improve her appearance by smoothing back errant wisps of hair and affixing a smile to her face as she pulled open the door.

Pleasantly surprised by the rush of cool air that welcomed her as she entered the lobby and crossed the black-and-white mosaic floor, she drew open the office door. She approached the clerk's desk, walking silently on a green-and-yellow patterned rug that was a bit too gaudy for her taste. She halted abruptly when the bespectacled man at the desk inquired in a tone offensive to her battered sensibilities, "Do you have some business here, madam?"

Elizabeth gritted her teeth, forcing a courteous reply. "My name is *Miss* Elizabeth Huntington. I'm here to make an inquiry about a ship named the *Sarah Jane* that I believe sailed out of this port at one time."

The clerk's eyes narrowed in a way she'd seen countless times earlier that morning. Silently despairing, Elizabeth pressed, "My reason for the inquiry is that my family and I have lost contact with one another and I'd like to find them if I could."

The clerk asked rudely, "This ship you're inquiring about—what did you say the name was, the *Sarah Jane*? What does it have to do with your story?"

Your story?

Increasingly annoyed, Elizabeth restrained her desire to tell the slight, gray-haired, man with the obnoxious manners that it was none of his business, and that she wanted to speak to someone in authority who would treat her with the respect she deserved. The vulnerability of her situation, however, precluded that response. Yet, unwilling to give him the satisfaction of showing him her pendant, she replied, "The *Sarah Jane* is the name of the ship on a crest I'm hoping to identify. It's my only connection to the family I'm looking for. I came to Galveston because a ship called the *Sarah Jane* was registered in Galveston years ago, and I thought someone might have information about it."

The clerk's eyes narrowed further as he replied, "I've never heard of any ship called the *Sarah Jane.* You came to the wrong place."

"Really." Her patience short and her smile stiff, Elizabeth said with acid sweetness, "Maybe someone else can help me ... your *superior,* perhaps."

"There isn't anybody in Galveston that's my *superior,* lady, and my boss isn't available to speak to you."

"Is that so?" Elizabeth felt her face flame as she continued, "Well, the fact is—"

The sound of movement at the doorway to the inner office turned Elizabeth toward a well-dressed man who emerged unexpectedly to say, "You must forgive my clerk, my dear. Bruce is so protective of my privacy that he sometimes overextends himself."

Offering his hand politely, the gentleman said with a smile, "How do you do? My name is Simon Gault."

Simon Gault emerged boldly into the outer office. Supremely fit despite middle age, he was a womanizer who did not recognize age as a boundary. Vain to the extreme, he kept his hair dark and his body carefully maintained, in line with a taste for youth in the opposite sex that was still lasciviously active. He had been unable to hear the full exchange between Bruce and the young woman standing in the outer office, but her youthful beauty had been enough to bring him immediately to his feet. Sensing an opportunity when he listened to her inquiry and realized she was alone, without any apparent male guidance or protection, he felt the stirring of a familiar excitement.

The possibility of ingratiating himself with the young woman, and the thought of his eventual reward in exchange for a few hours of attentive listening, caused Simon to add politely, "Can I help you in some way?"

The young woman turned hazel eyes sparking with anger toward him. "I'm afraid your clerk didn't feel my business was worth your time."

"I am always available to someone with an honest inquiry, and I can tell just by looking at you that you fit into that category. How may I help you?"

Bruce interrupted, "She came here looking for information on a ship and she—"

Simon turned sharply toward his clerk. "The young lady can speak for herself, Bruce." Turning his attention back to the young woman, he said, "I'm sorry … what did you say your name was, my dear?"

"Elizabeth … Elizabeth Huntington. I explained to your clerk that I was separated from my family years ago and I am hoping to find some information about their whereabouts."

Separated from her family … ideal.

Simon smiled more broadly. "I'm afraid the Huntington name doesn't ring a bell in my mind."

The clerk interrupted again: "She isn't looking

for anybody named Huntington. She's looking for a ship called—"

Increasingly annoyed at Bruce's persistent interruptions, Simon snapped, "I repeat, Miss Huntington can speak for herself."

Simon ignored the angry flush that transfused Bruce's narrow face as he continued, "Why don't you step into my office, Miss Huntington? We'll be able to talk more comfortably there."

Watching the sway of her narrow hips as the young woman preceded him into his office, Simon turned toward Bruce to snap, "I don't want to be disturbed for any reason. Do you hear me, Bruce?"

"I hear you, all right, but she—"

"I said I don't want to be disturbed!"

Bruce's mouth snapped closed.

Following the beauteous Elizabeth into the office, Simon closed the door gently behind him and offered her a seat. He assumed a chair beside her instead of taking his position behind his great mahogany desk, making his first inroad into intimacy as he smiled into her eyes and said, "How may I help you?"

Only half listening to Elizabeth Huntington's ardent reply as she explained her recent arrival in the city, her loss of memory, and the consequent adoption, Simon marveled at the clarity of her smooth skin, at the perfection of her small features, at the visual impact of honey brown hair that shone with gold highlights and eyes that glowed with sparks of green and amber. He speculated with growing heat whether his somewhat deviant sexual preferences would excite her. He wondered if her flesh would be yielding to his unconventional persuasion and if she would enjoy having his hands wander roughly over the tight, slender body underneath her modest dress.

His body beginning to react predictably to the stimulus of his thoughts, Simon struggled to clear his mind and forced himself to listen intently as she continued, "… and I wondered if you might be familiar with the crest on this pendant—which is the only link I have to my past."

Simon watched with increasing interest as Elizabeth reached into the neckline of her dress to withdraw a dainty pendant that had rested against her firm, young breasts.

His mind freezing, Simon struggled to maintain his smile as Elizabeth displayed the crest emblazoned on her pendant.

No, it couldn't be!

Had another Hawk come back to haunt him?

Simon struggled to control his reaction as the young woman pointed out the familiar ship bearing the almost indiscernible name, the *Sarah Jane*, the Latin words *Quattuor mundum do* inscribed in the banner underneath, declaring, "To four, I give the world"; and the unusual garland of orchids surrounding the dainty script.

His mind raged, *I should have known!* The startling appearance of Whit Hawk, the eldest son of Harold Hawk, a few months earlier should have been a warning! He should have realized then that the information claiming the four Hawk siblings had died in an orphanage fire was flawed.

Simon struggled against the sneer threatening to twist his lips as he recalled the day so many years earlier when Harold Hawk had bought his seemingly worthless California gold mine from him. He had been elated to be rid of the empty hole, but his elation had turned to disbelief when Hawk struck it rich only yards from the place where Simon had prospected without results for four long, back-breaking months. Simon's anger deepened at the memory of Hawk's unconcealed delight at having struck it rich, at the man's ecstatic ramblings about going back to claim his children and restore to them what they had lost.

Simon recalled with satisfaction the moment when Harold Hawk turned away from him momentarily, when he picked up a shovel lying close by and struck Hawk across the head with all his might. He remembered his fury as he hit Hawk again and again, even after the man had stopped breathing. He recalled dragging Hawk's lifeless body into an abandoned shaft, and the relief he'd experienced when he blew up the shaft, bringing the mountain down on top of Hawk to seal him forever in his secret tomb.

Simon remembered the care he had taken when he briefly assumed Hawk's identity in order to sell the claim and reap the profits.

Yet brightest of all in Simon's memory was the moment when he found Hawk's journal. In it, he'd read with envy Hawk's careful chronicling of the phenomenal success of Hawk Shipping in Galveston, Texas; the christening of his ship, the *Sarah Jane*, named after his wife, the beautiful Sarah Jane Higgins of Baltimore, Maryland; the subsequent births of their four children, Whit, Drew, Laura Anne, and Jenna Leigh; and Hawk's supreme egotism in designing a crest celebrating his success, which would adorn rings and pendants for himself, his wife, and each of his children at their births.

Simon recalled his glee when he'd read the story of Hawk's abrupt change in fortune in the years following: the emergence of Hawk's gambling habit, which finally bankrupted Hawk Shipping; the foreclosure on the elaborate residence he had maintained for his family; his descent into homelessness and debt; and most delicious of all, Hawk's heartbreak when his wife and the mother of their four children ran off unexpectedly with another man. He read with great interest that Hawk, then ashamed but still determined, took his children to live with his sister before going West to "strike it rich," so he could restore his children's lives to their former glory—a goal Hawk was destined never to achieve.

Simon scoffed when comparing Hawk's suffering with his own: at his being born the illegitimate, despised son of wealthy Daniel Gault's mistress; at being forced to endure the miserable hovel his mother tolerated while emotionally bound to that man; the beatings and the deprivation they both suffered at his hands; the demoralizing harangues his father heaped upon them both; and his own final humiliation at being turned out by his father after his weary, abused mother died.

Simon's bitterness swelled anew as he recalled his determination to achieve final victory over Harold Hawk, the man who had sought to cheat him of his triumph despite his father's predictions of failure. Harold Hawk had paid for that effort with his life; yet successfully impersonating Hawk in order to sell the gold mine and reap the fortune that was meant to be his had not satisfied his need for revenge. It was then that Simon had realized that the pièce de résistance would be to put the Gault name on the same shipping company that Hawk had lost, and to assume in Hawk's stead all the prestige and luxury that the dead man had hoped to reclaim.

Simon controlled a grunt at the sudden blurring of that perfect picture. His mistaken belief that the Hawk progeny had all expired in an orphanage fire had relieved him of any thought of future retribution. It was somehow ironic that Whit Hawk had shown up unexpectedly in Galveston a few months ago at the height of Simon's success, when his power and the confidence of the so-easily-duped citizens of Galveston were at their height. His personal conflict with Whit Hawk had proved painful and was not yet avenged, but he consoled himself with the knowledge that the eldest Hawk son had left the city without discovering the truth about his father's entombed death. Simon was resolved, however, that Whit Hawk would not escape him.

With those thoughts in mind, Simon considered the possibility that he was now faced with another Hawk's return.

Simon stared at Elizabeth Huntington as she continued speaking.

If it were true, she was a truly vulnerable Hawk.

He wanted to smile at the abrupt realization that although he'd temporarily failed to gain vengeance on Whit Hawk, he had been given the perfect retaliation for Harold Hawk's intention to steal his success—the seduction of his only remaining daughter! And she was so lovely, so ripe for the picking. He would enjoy gaining her trust by pretending to help her; then he would seduce her and crush her little by little, until she remained only a shadow of the woman she pretended to be.

When he was done, he would dispose of her and add her pendant to his collection of Hawk treasures—all before she could lay any claim to the empire he had built on the wealth Harold Hawk had intended to take from him.

He was aware, however, that to achieve full and true satisfaction, he needed to be certain Elizabeth Huntington was indeed a Hawk.

Simon smiled as Elizabeth finished speaking. Drawing out his gold pocket watch, he checked it and said casually, "I'm getting hungry, and I'm sure you are, too. If you agree, I'd enjoy having you join me for lunch, so we may continue our discussion at leisure."

Pleased when Elizabeth's hesitation was brief before she responded, "That would be lovely," Simon stood up and slid Elizabeth's hand onto his arm. He smiled at the thought of the very pleasurable vengeance that might soon be his—a thought he conveyed to Bruce with a flicker of his dark brow as they walked out the doorway.

Jason walked along the familiar harbor, his destination the shipping firm of Johnson and McGruffy. Samuel Johnson was an old friend and an influential member of the consortium that controlled the future of Galveston. He was keenly aware that if he could get Sam on his side about the threat Galveston faced from Houston, he would be a step ahead when he attended Willard Spunk's soiree that weekend.

Jason felt a familiar discomfort at the thought of Spunk's party. Simply put, he wasn't the partying type; he never felt comfortable at the extravagant parties that the Galveston affluent chose to give. More at home in Western gear that included cotton shirts and comfortable trousers, well-worn boots, and a wide Stetson to protect himself against the burning rays of the sun, he found formal wear uncomfortable. Also uncomfortable was his realization that he would be thrown together with Elvira Spunk, the unfortunate victim of her father's matchmaking. His only consolation was knowing she would be as uncomfortable with the situation as he.

The thought of the sweet but determined Elvira inexplicably restored to mind the image of the haughty and unappreciative Elizabeth Huntington. Her claim that she could have managed the angry drunk who had attempted to break into her room the previous night, and could have secured herself a table at the Seamont against the maître d's wishes, astounded him. Yet the look in her eye when she made those ridiculous claims might have convinced him—if he hadn't noted an almost imperceptible quiver of her bottom lip.

Also impossible to strike from his mind was the lingering thought that her lips had been soft, full, and compelling.

His thoughts halting abruptly as he approached the Johnson and McGruffy warehouse, Jason stared at the two figures walking down the long staircase from Gault Shipping. Simon Gault was unmistakable even at a distance from the superior cut of his stylish clothes, from his mature and carefully preserved physique, and from the polished, insincere smile he flashed so easily, baring teeth as carefully maintained as all other aspects of his physical appearance.

Yet it was the woman walking beside Gault who stopped Jason cold.

Pausing, Jason waited until the two had stepped down onto the wharf before deliberately catching Elizabeth Huntington's eye and tipping his hat to her with a hard smile. She flashed him a tart smile in return, and then looked up at her companion when Gault nodded coldly to him in greeting.

The meeting was brief, but the impact of it burned hot inside Jason.

So, he now knew the reason for Elizabeth Huntington's inquiries about Galveston shipping companies. She obviously had done her homework in seeking out a "protector" and had set her sights on one of the most affluent shipping company owners in Galveston. It wouldn't have been difficult for her to obtain the information that Gault was unmarried and that he was attracted to young, beautiful women. What she would not have learned, however, was that Gault's benevolent facade hid a darker side. If Jason did not miss his guess, she was getting in over her head.

That thought dug down deep inside Jason as Elizabeth Huntington turned with a haughty air toward the carriage that Gault motioned toward them. He hesitated at the doorway of Johnson and McGruffy shipping as Gault helped her into the carriage and sat beside her, then lifted her hand to his lips.

Sickened at the sight, Jason entered the warehouse and slammed the door shut behind him.

Jason recalled that his original reaction to the beauteous Elizabeth Huntington was that he hoped she found what she was looking for.

Well … it appeared she had.

Elizabeth could not help being amused at the maître d's stunned expression when she approached the restaurant at the Seamont Hotel on the arm of Simon Gault. Actually, she almost felt sorry for the poor man as he scrambled to accommodate the very aristocratic Mr. Gault and to pay inordinate attention to her comforts. She saw Simon glance between the maître d' and herself, and was not surprised when Simon commented after they were seated, "It seems Pierre is especially taken with you, Elizabeth. He appears to be doing his best to please you."

"He is very accommodating, isn't he?" Preferring not to mention her earlier visit to that same restaurant, she continued, "I suppose he wants to make all newcomers feel welcome here."

"Yes, and such a lovely newcomer at that."

Elizabeth smiled in response to Simon Gault's flattery. The man was charming, and so interested in helping her. It had not taken them long to progress to a first-name basis as they exchanged pleasantries in the carriage, and she was relieved. Formality made her uncomfortable—almost as uncomfortable as the assumptions that Jason Dodd had obviously made when he saw Simon and her together.

As if in response to her thoughts, Simon said, "I couldn't help noticing Jason Dodd's salute to you when we emerged from my office, Elizabeth. I didn't realize you two were acquainted."

"We met briefly … unfortunately."

Elizabeth did not miss the smile that twitched at Simon's mouth as he said, "Unfortunately? It appears you weren't fooled by Dodd's appealing manner."

"His appealing manner?" Elizabeth responded

with a touch of angry heat. "I didn't find his manner at all appealing. As a matter of fact, I found him to be arrogant and extremely rude." She paused, frowning as she said, "I'm sorry if he's your friend—"

"Jason Dodd is no friend of mine!" Simon gave a short laugh. "He's an acquaintance, and not a particularly favorable acquaintance, I might add."

"Really?"

Uncertain why she was somewhat distressed to hear Simon's reply, Elizabeth remained silent as he continued, "I suppose it would be better if we could all forget the adverse deeds done during the war, but ... " Simon shook his head. "But there's something about unpatriotic behavior that I can't seem to dismiss."

"Unpatriotic behavior?"

"Jason Dodd's actions during the war may not be considered unpatriotic to someone who wasn't a resident of Galveston while the federal blockade was in effect, but collaborating with the Yankee fleet commander against the suffering people of the city—"

Elizabeth went cold. "He did that?"

Simon said softly, "His collaboration is responsible for the deaths of several of my friends. I have no proof of his crimes, of course, but that doesn't change the facts. Still, I don't normally talk about something I can't prove. If you hadn't mentioned your reaction to him, I probably wouldn't have said anything about it. In a way, I'm already sorry I spoke out. I hate to malign anybody's name."

Elizabeth responded confusedly, "But he appears

to command a great deal of respect in some quarters of the city."

"The truth is either unknown or ignored by some people, but there are a few of us who are privy to information unavailable to others."

Elizabeth did not respond.

Waiting only until the smiling waiter placed their lunch before them, Simon changed the subject by saying, "But we didn't come here today to talk about things that make us both uncomfortable. Actually, I admire your determination to discover your roots, and I would be pleased to hear more about your search."

Elizabeth was relieved that they would no longer discuss Jason Dodd, but she was suddenly reluctant to begin her tale.

Simon smiled stiffly as Elizabeth glanced down at her plate, appearing hesitant. He wondered at the young woman's reaction to the story he had fabricated about Dodd. She appeared to dislike Dodd immensely, and he had taken advantage of her antipathy to say just enough to keep her away from a man who might prove dangerous to his plans.

Losing patience with her hesitation, Simon urged, "Elizabeth?"

Elizabeth looked up at him, her clear-eyed gaze suddenly direct as she said, "I really don't know how much more I can tell you, other than that the years prior to my being adopted are a total blank to me."

"You're sure you originally came from Texas?"

"I'm as sure as I can be." At Simon's raised brow, she explained, "The morning after a fire swept the local orphanage, I staggered out, badly injured, in front of my adoptive parents' carriage as they were riding through the Texas countryside north of here."

Simon's heart began a slow pounding. "A local orphanage ..."

"A small manor house where a woman took in orphaned children."

"The other children at the orphanage—there was no one who could identify you?"

"The matron and her staff were all killed, and the dead children were burned beyond recognition. The few who survived—if they recovered at all—were apparently taken to different locations and became impossible to trace."

"What about the records?"

"According to the information my adoptive mother was able to obtain, all the records were lost in the fire—gone without a trace."

"Leaving only your memory."

"I had no memory, only terrifying images of a fire that still haunt me. The only key I have to my past is the pendant I was wearing underneath my smock when my adoptive parents found me." Elizabeth touched her breast as if to confirm that her pendant was still there as she continued, "The name of the ship on my pendant—the *Sarah Jane*—is what brought me here. My adoptive mother and I believed it was the best place to begin my search. She originally intended to make the trip with me, but when she became ill, she didn't want to hold me back any longer."

Simon remained silent as the import of Elizabeth's tale registered in his mind. The fire, the damned crest that haunted him as persistently as it haunted her—as naive as she was, she had just confirmed beyond doubt that her name was Hawk.

Simon said with feigned concern, "The *Sarah Jane* ... I wish I could help you there, but that name isn't familiar to me." He paused deliberately, then said, "If I could see your pendant again ..."

Simon watched as Elizabeth reached underneath the collar of her dress for the gold chain. She continued, "As you can see, there's very little else about the crest that gives a clue as to what it represents."

Simon leaned toward her and said softly, "If I could see the pendant more closely ..."

Without waiting for her response, Simon took the pendant into his palm, drawing Elizabeth closer as he did. The pendant was warm from the heat of her flesh, and Simon resisted drawing Elizabeth closer still as he said, "It's beautiful, obviously crafted lovingly. I can see why you cherish it. I only wish I could tell you more."

Forcing himself to release it, Simon drew back. He noted the flush that had transfused Elizabeth's face, and he added, "However, I think I'm in an excellent position to make inquiries that could turn up information for you. There are many ships sailing from this port, and many seamen returning here every day. I'm sure I can find someone eventually who'll remember the *Sarah Jane* and who will be able to tell you more about it."

He noted the protective manner in which Elizabeth tucked her pendant back out of sight as she responded, "I would appreciate that, Simon. I've learned to be patient about the mystery of my past. I didn't expect to have immediate success in uncovering its secrets when I came here."

"Which means, I hope, that you expect to stay in Galveston."

"For a while, yes."

Simon said earnestly, "I'd be very pleased to help you in your search if you'll allow me to, Elizabeth."

Elizabeth's flush darkened. "You're a busy man. I don't want to burden you."

"It's my pleasure."

"Of course, then … and I appreciate your interest."

Elizabeth dropped her gaze back to her plate, and Simon drew back. He needed to be careful not to overwhelm her. Show an interest, make her feel safe, close in gradually, and then …

Simon signaled the waiter to refill their glasses. He was going to enjoy this.

Gaslights lit the street beyond her window at the Easton Hotel as Elizabeth prepared for bed. Exhausted, she glanced around her shabby quarters as the noise in the lobby below reverberated up into her room. Shrugging, she sat down on her bed and reviewed the long first day she had spent in Galveston.

Strangely, Simon's confidences about Jason Dodd continued to resound in her mind. She speculated on the accuracy of Simon's assertions, and then asked herself why she cared. She wondered at the cold look in Jason Dodd's dark eyes when he had tipped his hat to her as she walked beside Simon at the docks, and then questioned why his displeasure continued to disturb her.

The irony of the fact that Simon had shown as much displeasure as Jason Dodd when he discovered where she was staying had not escaped her. It appeared both men, however deep their distrust of each other, agreed that the Easton Hotel was not the right place for her—even though the reasoning behind their judgments was vastly different.

Frowning, Elizabeth lowered the lamp on the nightstand and lay back against the pillow. The door was locked, she had placed the rickety chair under the doorknob just in case, and the small derringer that she had carried in her reticule was safely tucked under her pillow.

She was safe—she supposed.

At any rate, it appeared Jason Dodd had left an impression on the hotel clientele when he drove off the drunk the previous day. A few comments from the desk clerk ... whispered remarks when she walked past loungers in the lobby ... knowing smiles of cowpokes who made no move toward her despite their interest—all led her to believe that Dodd's protection continued to work in her favor.

Elizabeth unconsciously shrugged. She supposed she had that much to thank Jason Dodd for.

She had far more reason to thank Simon Gault, however, and she was sincerely grateful. Having such a prominent man take an interest in her was flattering.

So, why did she feel so … unsettled?

Ungrateful, that was what she was. Despite her protests, she was becoming more and more aware that she would need all the help she could get to obtain any credible information about her past. Time was her enemy. Her dear, adoptive mother's health was too uncertain for her to stay away from New York long, and there were so many intangibles for her to consider.

Namely, she hoped her letter had relieved some of the concerns the dear woman was sure to have experienced because of Agatha Potter's premature return.

She regretted the opportunity she had afforded Aunt Sylvia to bedevil Mother Ella.

She worried that she wouldn't be able to uncover the secrets of her past quickly enough to bring the information back to her adoptive mother—because Elizabeth knew that whatever her search uncovered, her adoptive mother wanted more than anything in the world for her to be complete and whole again.

Elizabeth fluffed her pillow with renewed determination as the din from the downstairs lobby grew louder.

Jason Dodd's disapproving, dark-eyed gaze flashed unexpectedly before her, and Elizabeth fervently wished that she would never have to see him again.

* * *

Simon walked down the luxuriously carpeted hall-way of his home as twilight shadows turned into evening, anxious for the task that he had waited all day to perform. He had entertained Elizabeth Huntington royally for as long as he dared. He had instructed his carriage driver to take them both on a short tour of Galveston and had delivered a history of the city as they rode. He had smilingly denied that the time he was so generously spending with her was taking him from his busy work schedule. He had described his company's success in the most modest terms while extracting from her whatever further information she could provide—which had proved to be little, indeed. He had flattered and cajoled her while making sure not to overextend himself or concern her with his interest in any way.

He had then returned Elizabeth to the seedy hotel where she was staying, had expressed his concern at her residence there, and had offered to find her more favorable quarters. She had refused his help, stating she was "previously committed," and he had said he understood. Yet he had been secretly enraged at the possibility that some drunken cowpoke on the prowl might interfere with his very elaborate plans for Elizabeth's seduction.

Arriving at the doorway of his study, Simon entered and pushed the door closed behind him. He approached the great, carved desk dominating the center of the room, paying scant attention to the bookcases filled with leather-bound volumes that

crowded the shelves behind him, the deeply cush-
ioned wing chairs that faced his desk like soldiers
awaiting command, and the armchairs grouped in a
deceivingly casual manner beside a fireplace screened
by a massive brass fan shipped at great expense
from India. He didn't stop to fill his glass with the
imported brandy from the crystal decanter on the
sideboard, or to choose one of the costly cigars in
the humidor nearby. He didn't even glance at the
great standing globe of the world that displayed
the success of Gault Shipping & Exchange by trac-
ing the shipping lanes his vessels followed across
the ocean. All were trappings of success that Simon
deeply valued; yet they were far less valued by him
than the item he urgently sought.

Simon paused at his desk, smiling as he withdrew
a key from his vest pocket and unlocked the bottom drawer. He sat down and removed the ragged
journal that had brought him so much pleasure.
He read Harold Hawk's name, inscribed in the arrogant man's own hand on the first page, and then
turned quickly to the entries he had added in his
own hand since taking the journal from among his
victim's possessions.

It had given him joy beyond measure to write in
Harold Hawk's journal, recording each major step
he had taken since the day he had assumed Harold
Hawk's identity and claimed the gold mine that
was rightfully his. He had recorded on those pages
secrets known only to the journal and himself. It
was his way of laughing in the face of Harold Hawk,

81

of demonstrating to the man even after death that he could and would outdo Hawk in every way.

Simon frowned as he read his most recent entries. He had recorded the day that Whit Hawk returned to Galveston, and he had also written down his vow to make the eldest Hawk son pay in the same way his father had paid for his treachery against him.

Simon's frown faded as he composed his next entry. He needed to write the date of Elizabeth Huntington's appearance in Galveston and of his identification of her as yet another Hawk. He needed to state his intentions toward her—the joy he anticipated in toying with her. He needed to describe the exhilaration he would feel when he brought her to her knees. He needed to list his objectives clearly so that when he wrote of his success, he would further negate whatever achievements Harold Hawk had previously set down in the journal. Reducing Harold Hawk's descendants to the lowest level possible before destroying them was essential to Simon. It emphasized his triumphs— so he could read them over and over again.

Valueless, was he?

Not worthy of the Gault name, was he?

Destined for the gutter like his mother before him, was he?

Simon's face flushed as he scribbled his thoughts viciously in the tattered journal, then sat back abruptly and slapped his pen down on the desk in front of him.

There, it was done. He had again prepared to

refute in writing his father's predictions for his future. All that was left was the pleasure of following through.

Poor, unsuspecting Elizabeth.

He had so much to look forward to.

Chapter Four

Sylvia Blair Huntington stood stiffly beside Ella Huntington's bed. She turned toward her twenty-three-year-old son, Trevor, as he hesitated near the doorway of the Park Avenue mansion bedroom, a familiar anger blotching her sagging cheeks. Her sharp features tightened into a shrewish visage and her matronly figure stiffened with disapproval as she sought his eye. He was biting his fingernails again, a repulsive habit that he had practiced since early childhood. Unfortunately, her only progeny had always been a nervous sort, totally unlike her side of the family, which had gumption to spare. She had always maintained that if she had been born male instead of female, the sky would have been her limit. Instead, she had used her youth, her then-pleasing features and voluptuous proportions, to best advantage, and had settled for marrying the malleable older son of a wealthy man. She had thought that her future was thereby secured.

She could never have been more wrong.

Sylvia could not count the times she had cursed her failure to take into account that *malleable* in her husband's instance would translate into *weak*. Drinking, gambling, every manner of vice had been his crutch until his wealthy father had despaired. It was not until David Huntington Senior died, however, that she learned how deep her father-in-law's disapproval had gone. In his last will and testament, David Huntington Senior left everything he owned—with the exception of a house for his elder son's family to live in, an allowance that barely sustained them, and provisions for the education of his grandson, Trevor—to his younger son, Wilbur.

Sylvia restrained the twitch of her lips that the memory evoked. She recalled the day when the will was read, as a stunned Wilbur Huntington turned to his older brother and expressed his dismay at the terms. She remembered Wilbur's offer to share the proceeds of the will with David. She knew she would never forget her drunken husband's refusal of that offer, as well as his response that their father had done the right thing, that he had provided adequately for his family, and that his eldest son could get along very nicely with what was left of his allowance—as long as he had a bottle of his favorite cognac to console him.

Her unrealized dreams had been shattered that day.

Sylvia knew in her heart that if her husband hadn't done her the favor of getting killed in a drunken venture shortly afterward, she might have managed the deed herself, so angry had she been at his reaction to the terms of his inheritance. But done was done, and no amount of pretended grief at his death had changed her circumstances.

Until ...

Sylvia remembered the day that she learned Wilbur's only child, Lydia, would never recover from her illness. She had silently celebrated, aware that Ella could not have another child, and that Trevor had finally reached the status of heir to the Huntington fortune.

Wrong again.

With the introduction of Elizabeth Huntington into the family, and then Wilbur's death and Ella's quickly deteriorating health, Sylvia and her son stood ready to lose a second time.

Not that she hadn't done her best to shed the poorest light possible on the nameless waif that Ella had adopted. She had been constant in her subtle criticisms of the girl; she had been tireless in her clever derision of the girl's achievements; she had been indefatigable in her attempt to direct the child onto paths that would put her in disfavor; yet her efforts had failed.

Standing beside Ella's bed, where the woman lay presently dying, Sylvia knew opportunity was quickly slipping through her fingers. If she did not act quickly, the Huntington fortune would soon belong to the young woman who now bore her adoptive parents' name.

Finally catching Trevor's eye, Sylvia mouthed an obscenity that snapped his hand to his side. She then looked back at the pale woman clutching a carefully written letter in her trembling hands.

Sylvia's long face was transformed into a smile when Ella looked up unexpectedly and said with tear-filled eyes, "I can't thank Trevor enough for bringing this letter directly to me when it was delivered in the post. I was so concerned."

"Yes, that was considerate of him, wasn't it? If not for him, that letter might have been directed to your attorney along with all the other items to be sent there. It might have lain in his office unread for days."

"Elizabeth writes that she is doing quite well in Galveston," Ella continued. "She explains that Agatha Potter was homesick and expressed a desire to return, so she sent her home." Ella smiled. "Elizabeth always was sensitive to the moods of others."

"Really? That isn't what Agatha claims. I believe she said that Elizabeth dismissed her abruptly."

"I suppose it appeared abrupt to Agatha, but Agatha was exceedingly happy to be home when I spoke to her. She said Texas was wild and uncivilized, totally unlike New York. It's my thought that Elizabeth sacrificed her own convenience for the woman's comfort. That is like her, you know."

Sylvia could not make herself reply.

Ignoring Sylvia's lack of response, Ella continued in a voice quavering with emotion, "Elizabeth said she has settled into the hotel Thomas arranged for her, and that she's quite comfortable there."

Sylvia's brow tightened in momentary confusion. That would be the Easton Hotel that she had recommended to Thomas Biddlington, Esquire, the old fool who was Ella's solicitor. The naive fellow had taken her at her word, believing that the Easton Hotel was the preferred place to stay in Galveston, while Sylvia knew the truth was just the opposite. She had done considerable research to find the most run-down hotel in the most undesirable neighborhood in the city. So ... what was Elizabeth talking about?

"Elizabeth said an old man who works at the hotel has befriended her, that he very kindly brings fresh flowers to her room every day. She says she's also met a young man who has gone out of his way to provide protection for her there."

"Of course. I'm sure there are any number of men who will be"—Sylvia paused for effect—"willing to help a lonely young woman."

Appearing not to have heard Sylvia's response, Ella clutched the letter against the bodice of her white nightdress as she said, "Of course, Elizabeth hasn't uncovered any information as to her family name yet, but someone will certainly recognize the crest on her pendant sooner or later. I confess that I hope it's sooner." Ella leaned back weakly against her pillow. "I miss her dreadfully."

"Yes, don't we all." Sylvia covertly signaled Trevor toward the bed and watched out of the corner of her eye as the young man walked reluctantly toward them. She continued, "Trevor was just saying yesterday how quiet things seem here without Elizabeth. There were always so many young men around when she was here."

"Yes, she is such a lovely girl." Pride flashed in Ella's eyes.

"And so ... accommodating to young men."

"Sylvia!" Ella gasped, shocked at her comment. "You certainly aren't implying—"

"Of course I'm not implying anything." Sylvia leaned down to adjust Ella's coverlet as she continued, "Young men are drawn to Elizabeth—a fact—isn't that so, Trevor?"

"Yes, Elizabeth does attract men ... b-because she's beautiful."

"And she's kind and considerate."

Sylvia could not resist a shrug. "I do admit to being surprised, though, that she chose to leave you alone in this big house while she chased after a will-o'-the-wisp."

"I'm not alone here. I'm very well taken care of with Molly, Helga, and Rufus at my beck and call. And she isn't chasing after a will-o'-the-wisp." Ella frowned and clutched the letter tighter. "I told her to go, because I wanted Elizabeth's past to be restored to her before ... before more time elapsed."

Sylvia said coldly, "She certainly didn't hesitate. Truthfully, I don't know why she didn't wait for you to recover enough to make the trip with her."

Ella's pale face moved into a wan smile. "Why do we play this game, Sylvia? We both know I'm not a well woman and that I may never regain full strength. To deny it would be a waste of time."

"I don't like to hear you talk that way." Taking her opportunity, Sylvia pressed with a forced smile,

"We, in this room, are all that's left of the Huntington family, you know. And dear Trevor …" Sylvia glanced at her son lovingly, "Dear Trevor is the only one left to carry on the Huntington name."

"That's true to an extent, I suppose."

"It's *completely* true, and you know it." Adamant, Sylvia continued, "What do you suppose Elizabeth will do when and if she discovers what her true name is and where she came from? She'll start looking for relatives; she'll make herself comfortable there; she'll start a new life for herself and forget about all of us here."

"Elizabeth would never do that."

"No? You were always too trusting for your own good, Ella. The girl has lived very well at your expense all these years, but that obviously hasn't satisfied her. She's determined to find out what the world has to offer her."

"You're wrong, Sylvia. Elizabeth has suffered from the void in her past. She needs to remember."

"That's if she really lost her memory."

"Sylvia!"

"You must admit that it's implausible she should have no memory of an incident as tragically memorable as a fire. I wouldn't be surprised if she has chosen to forget because there was something *to* forget. Difficulties with the matron, perhaps, or with the other children; complaints that were registered against her that she doesn't care to have come out … there could be so many reasons for her pretense."

"She isn't pretending, I tell you!" Growing breathless, her skin taking on a gray pallor, Ella said, "You didn't spend time with her after the accident. You didn't hear her screams when her nightmares returned night after night."

"She had nightmares about her past … when she says she can't remember her past?"

"Nightmares about the fire! The heat … the flames … the screams of the dying. She was terrified."

Aware that Ella's breathing was growing labored, that her color continued to fade, Sylvia ceased her verbal assault. It wouldn't do to have Ella die just yet. The payment of a particularly large sum to the right person in the right place had confirmed her suspicion that Ella's will left the bulk of her estate to Elizabeth Huntington, with a painfully small allowance that was supposed to secure Trevor's and her future.

Determined that the entire proceeds from the Huntington estate would soon be in her hands, Sylvia changed her demeanor abruptly. Her tone concerned, she said, "I didn't meant to upset you, Ella. We're family, and I just want what's best for you."

Ella struggled to catch her breath.

Turning sharply toward Trevor, Sylvia ordered, "Bring me some of Aunt Ella's tonic from the sideboard."

Trevor hastened to put the tonic into her hand. She poured it carefully into a glass from the nightstand as she instructed, "Drink this, Ella. Dr. Whittier said it would calm you down when you become breathless. It'll make you sleep for a while, too, which is good, because you need the rest." Watching as Ella drained the glass, Sylvia tucked the coverlet more firmly around her and said, "Give me the letter. I'll put it on the nightstand for you."

"No, that won't be necessary. I may want to read it again before I fall asleep."

"The letter obviously agitated you, Ella. It would be best if you put it aside for a while."

"No, you're wrong. The letter calms me. It's ... it's almost like holding Elizabeth's hand."

Going momentarily still, Sylvia then turned abruptly toward her son to say, "Aunt Ella needs some rest. We should leave now."

Trevor walked closer to the bed and said timidly, "Sleep well, Aunt Ella."

"Trevor and I will be leaving for a while. We'll come back later, but I'll tell Molly to watch out for you in the meantime."

Ella nodded weakly, and Sylvia drew the door closed.

Aware that Trevor followed close at her heels, Sylvia walked a few steps down the hallway before she turned back toward her son and imitated mockingly, " 'Sleep well, Aunt Ella.' Stupid! Why did you bring her that letter? Can't you see we had the opportunity to make it look like Elizabeth forgot about her if we held it back?"

"I ... I didn't think about it." Trevor swallowed and raked his thinning hair with a nervous hand.

"I knew she was waiting to hear from Elizabeth and—"

"All right, what's done is done. There's no going back. Your aunt will cling to that letter until she receives the next one, no matter how long it takes."

"You know you're wasting your breath, don't you, Mother?" His small eyes intent, Trevor ventured, "There's nothing you can say to turn Aunt Ella against Elizabeth."

Sylvia looked at her son with burgeoning disgust. To think she had actually believed for a while when he was younger that he would turn out to be a *real* man. Instead he was mediocre in every way— medium height, common features, nondescript coloring, thin, pale, and jumpy as a cat—but he was still her son and a Huntington, and she was determined that they would both receive the financial reward that was their due.

She needed to remember, however, that Trevor was like his father. That said it all.

"You're right, Trevor," Sylvia said. "There's nothing I can say that could possibly make Aunt Ella see Elizabeth in a true light. I'm just wasting my time."

The gratification in Trevor's expression turned her stomach. She started down the hallway, aware that he followed at her heels. Weak … like his father. She would have to take steps that he didn't have the courage to take for himself if she were to save him from the common existence that was otherwise destined to be his future.

Trevor's footsteps echoed behind her, concurring

with her thoughts as Sylvia's mind jumped forward to the only alternative left to her.

Simon's carriage pulled to a stop and Elizabeth stared up at the grand mansion ablaze with lights. She was unacquainted with the more affluent residences on Broadway, and she was stunned at the building's sumptuousness. A grand staircase curved up to the broad front porch of the stone residence adorned with curved porticos, marble facings, and floor-to-ceiling windows through which music drifted into the star-dappled evening.

Accepting the hand Simon offered her, she stepped down from the carriage, shook out her amber gown, and nodded to the servant who greeted them and ushered them up the staircase. Her sense of unreality deepened at the splendor of palm trees rustling overhead in a warm breeze scented with the fragrance of tropical flowers. They approached the front door, where smiling, uniformed servants waited to take their wraps and direct them to the ballroom.

Elizabeth was aware, however, that Simon was not similarly affected by the grandeur of the scene. She had sensed his worldliness the moment she walked out of her hotel and saw him waiting beside his carriage, appearing totally at ease and exceedingly debonair in his magnificently tailored evening attire. She had originally refused Simon's invitation to the party, partially because he had mentioned that formal apparel was required. She had explained that she had packed sparingly for her trip and wasn't prepared for the occasion. His response had been to offer to advance her the expense of a gown, explaining that she could pay him back whenever she was able—which she had refused. He had stressed that attending the affair would be important to her, that she could make essential contacts that would serve her well in her search. Finally convinced, she had agreed to go. Yet she had not fully realized that the small island of Galveston was capable of such luxury.

Approaching the ballroom with Simon at her side, Elizabeth passed through a room complete with crystal chandeliers, sparkling silverware, glasses filled with the glowing colors of exotic wines, and a buffet table so lavishly set as to briefly set her head spinning. She was momentarily taken aback.

"What's wrong, Elizabeth?" Simon looked at her with concern. "You look upset."

"Upset? No. I'm stunned at the sheer magnificence of this home."

"Are you? It has suffered a bit as a result of the blockade. Willard hasn't been able to bring it back fully to its former standard yet, but I'm sure he'll be happy to hear your praise."

Strangely, the same sense of uncertainty that had caused her to hesitate at Simon's invitation again crawled up her spine. She was frustrated by her reaction. Simon had been so kind during the few days she had been in Galveston. He explained that her direct inquiries about her pendant left her vulnerable to the ploys of less principled individuals in the port. He told her she should be more cautious about showing her pendant to people, and he gave her a list of the men to contact who might be able to help her uncover information about the crest and her family. Grateful for his direction, she followed his advice to the letter and had shown her pendant only to the people on the list; but as yet, she had received only negative responses.

Simon had urged her not to despair. He had been extremely considerate of her in every way, going so far as to have his carriage pick her up at the Easton each evening so she would not have to dine alone. She could not understand why it bothered her that Simon should send his carriage for her instead of presenting himself at the Easton to pick her up on those occasions. He had explained that the pressure of business affairs made that arrangement necessary. She did not fail to note, however, that he dropped her off at the Easton each evening and drove directly on, as if he did not wish to have anyone see him there. And when he'd arrived with his carriage to pick her up that evening, he had sent his driver inside to inquire for her. The fact that he would not enter the Easton Hotel—as if were beneath him—struck a sour note in her mind.

Having had time to study the residents of the hotel more closely, she realized that aside from the few men who were obviously malcontents or drifters, others appeared to be merely former Confederates down on their luck after the difficulties of war. They were men who had lost much, were still disconsolate, and who had yet to find a new direction; or simply businessmen connected with the railroad who valued proximity to their work over a more fashionable temporary residence. She wondered if members of her own family might have been included in that mix somewhere, if they might have been men such as those—common, honest men who still deserved to be regarded with respect despite their unfortunate circumstances.

A deeper discomfort nudged her when Elizabeth recalled the almost imperceptible familiarities Simon had recently introduced into their exchanges: the grazing of her lips as he brushed her cheek with his kiss on greeting and departure, the subtle caress that seemed to have crept into his touch, and an occasionally proprietary manner that was growing increasingly difficult to ignore.

"Oh, there he is."

Brought abruptly back to the present by Simon's comment as they reached the ballroom doorway, Elizabeth suppressed a gasp. Crystal chandeliers flickered above a polished oak floor where extravagantly dressed couples whirled to music provided by an accomplished orchestra. Groups of laughing guests gathered around the dance floor, lingering with drinks in hand and conversing animatedly while servants circulated among them with trays, guaranteeing that their glasses remained filled. Other guests lounged on luxuriously upholstered settees lining walls decorated with silk fabric that rose to a magnificently vaulted ceiling on which a breathtaking mural was painted. The opulence in every quarter put her in mind of a French château pictured in one of the books she had studied on European architecture. Although the room was stunning, the scene left her somehow sad to see luxury in such sharp contrast to the austerity some good people in Galveston still suffered as a result of the war.

"Willard, how are you?"

Elizabeth turned toward the short, balding, meticulously dressed gentleman approaching. She smiled as Simon shook hands with a broad smile and said, "Elizabeth, I'd like you to meet our host, Willard Spunk." He continued smoothly, "Elizabeth is visiting our city, Willard, and I was certain you'd welcome her and agree that her outstanding beauty would be an asset to any occasion."

"Yes, I do agree." Willard Spunk's gaze was a bit too intense for Elizabeth's comfort as he took her hand and continued, "I'm very pleased to meet you at last, Elizabeth. I missed my first opportunity to do so at the Seamont Hotel a few days ago because of pressing business demands, but I'm delighted to have been provided with another chance." He winked unexpectedly. "I think you will find a few familiar faces here tonight. Howard Meecham's, for one. There he is in the corner of the room, conversing with Emily Dunham. He is such a gregarious fellow. And, of course ..."

Elizabeth turned in the second direction Willard indicated, her breath catching in her throat when she met the dark-eyed gaze of the tall, conservatively attired man standing apart from a laughing group. Her heart went still as he raised his glass in her direction with a sardonic smile, and Willard added, "There he is ... your friend Jason Dodd."

Elizabeth was saved from a reply as Simon said tightly, "Elizabeth met Jason in passing, but I wouldn't say he was a friend. I must admit that I didn't realize she knew Howard."

Turning her back on Jason Dodd's irritating salute, Elizabeth regained her composure and said, "I'm afraid I don't know Mr. Meecham, but I'm sure if he's a friend of yours, Mr. Spunk, he's well worth knowing."

"Call me Willard, please, my dear." Appearing charmed by her response, Willard turned with annoyance toward the servant who appeared at his side and whispered in his ear. He looked back to say, "Excuse me, please. There is evidently an emergency in the kitchen, and my dear wife needs my assistance. Enjoy yourselves. Until later ..."

Waiting only until Willard began working his way through the crowded floor, Simon asked, "Why do you suppose Willard had the impression you knew Howard?"

"I have no idea, but it really doesn't matter, does it?"

Somehow annoyed, Elizabeth turned with a stiff smile toward the gray-haired couple approaching, grateful for their intervention.

Jason's smile grew tight as the beauteous Elizabeth Huntington turned away without acknowledging his greeting. He sipped from his half-empty glass, struggling to restrain his reaction to her unexpected appearance, then chiding himself for his surprise. Simon Gault's preference for beautiful young women had served the lovely Elizabeth well—and the fact that she was lovely could not be denied. The amber silk of her gown emphasized the gold highlights in her hair and enriched the warm tone of her faultless skin while highlighting the perfection of her delicate features. The conservative cut of her gown had obviously been carefully chosen to allow only a glimpse of firm young breasts while drawing attention to her minuscule waist.

So demure, yet deliberately eye-catching.

Perfect.

And she was on the arm of an obviously pleased Simon Gault, who did not seem to realize she had deliberately sought him out. Jason wondered, however, how long it would take for the inevitable to occur—for Gault's true nature to emerge. Elizabeth would then realize how great a mistake she had made in choosing him.

He also wondered if Elizabeth's realization would come too late.

"Jason, there you are!"

Jason turned at the sound of the familiar female voice. He smiled with true warmth at the young woman approaching him. Dark-haired with even, if not memorable, features, Elvira Spunk was a pretty young lady who appeared momentarily harried. Accepting the hand extended toward him, he squeezed it lightly and said sincerely, "Elvira, it's always a pleasure to see you."

"Really? I admit to being a bit worried about

that. My dear father …" She grimaced. "He means well, I think, but he has no compunction about attempting to run people's lives—mine in particular, since I'm his only child. He thinks this house and all the prestige it represents will make any man feel flattered to be pursued as a son-in-law. Unfortunately, he doesn't seem to trust my ability to attract a worthy husband on my own."

"Your father's greatest mistake."

"I agree! I'm seventeen years old, hardly a spinster yet, although that thought seems to be my father's greatest fear. He also fails to take into account how uncomfortable his handling of the situation makes me feel. Actually, Jason, you're the only single man present at this party whom I feel safe talking to, because I can be honest with you—or at least, I think I can be."

Sensing more behind that statement than Elvira originally intended to reveal, Jason inquired, "Meaning?"

Elvira sobered. "I *can* trust you, can't I, Jason? We have similar interests, namely avoiding my father's matchmaking attempts."

Jason replied, "You're a lovely young woman, Elvira, and I'm flattered that your father—"

"Yes, yes, I know all that. I suppose I should be grateful that Father hasn't looked in Simon Gault's direction as a potential son-in-law."

Jason did not respond, and Elvira laughed. "No comment, huh?" She glanced at Gault, who stood at the edge of the dance floor talking with Trina and Elmore Little. She shrugged. "I don't know why

I should feel that way, considering all Mr. Gault has done for Galveston, but he gives me the willies. I'm lucky he doesn't consider me pretty enough for him."

"I agree—that you're lucky, not that you're not pretty enough."

"Always the gentleman, Jason." She added, "It's obvious to anyone with eyes that Simon and you aren't exactly friendly; which, incidentally, only makes me respect you more. So ..." Elvira fluttered her stubby eyelashes and said, "Would you mind dancing with me so I may satisfy my father's immediate concerns and avoid his eye for a while?"

Jason studied Elvira's bright expression before replying with a hint of suspicion, "Somehow I have the feeling there's more to your invitation than you presently choose to say. I don't know what you're planning, but whatever it is, I hope you'll remember that your father doesn't miss much."

"That's very true, Jason. My father knows you went to see Samuel Johnson and that you're waiting for Uncle Samuel to arrive so you two can provide a united front when you bring up your concern about Galveston's future."

"W-what? How did you know that?"

Elvira winked. "I'm smarter than you think, I'm more in touch with Galveston's affairs than my father realizes, and I *definitely* have a mind of my own—so, can I count on you?"

Wary, Jason said, "To do what?"

"To dance with me, of course!"

"I intended to do that anyway, if you were willing."

"And to pay enough attention to me to satisfy my father until you need to tend to the real reason you came."

"Elvira … something tells me you're still leaving out an important element here."

"Maybe"—Elvira's eyes twinkled—"it's because I have my eye on somebody else present here tonight, a fellow I'd rather not call to my father's attention until I'm ready."

"Maybe," Jason could not help teasing, "you could tell me the name of the fellow you have your eye on so I'd feel safe helping you."

"That's easy. It's Edward Kroller. There he is, standing in the corner. He's shy, but I know he likes me. He's also smart and has a budding business on the Strand—leather goods. Father abides him but doesn't consider him a likely candidate because he's a merchant."

"While I'm just a former shipowner and am presently an unemployed cattle drover."

"But you're a man Father trusts." She sobered. "Father knows about all the good works you did during the blockade, Jason. He knows how you suffered the death of your best friend, and even if he doesn't totally agree with the reasons you came here tonight, he believes you have Galveston's best interests at heart."

"He's right in that respect."

"Unfortunately, Father is right most of the time.

He's just dead wrong with every candidate he chooses as a future son-in-law."

"Elvira … I think you just hurt my feelings."

"Oh, pooh! You don't want Father picking and choosing for you any more than I do." Elvira turned her back abruptly on her father's approaching figure and whispered, "Oh, here he comes, heading directly for us. It's now or never, Jason."

Taking her arm, Jason whispered with a smile as he swung her out onto the dance floor, "Just remember to look like you're enjoying yourself."

"Oh, but I am, Jason." Elvira laughed aloud. "I most definitely am!"

For the life of her, Elizabeth couldn't understand why the burst of laughter from the dark-haired young woman in Jason Dodd's arms annoyed her so as they danced past!

Directing her attention back to Elmore Little as the gray-haired gentleman whirled her with surprising expertise to the lilting music of the waltz, Elizabeth said truthfully, "You dance very well, Mr. Little. I don't think I've ever had a more competent partner."

"Elmore … please, Elizabeth. And thank you for the compliment, my dear, which just goes to prove that although there may be frost on the roof, there can still be fire in the hearth." At Elizabeth's startled expression, he added, "Music and a beautiful woman appeal to a man at any age, which is the reason I spirited you away from Simon while I still had the opportunity."

Feeling obliged to explain, Elizabeth said, "I think you misunderstand the situation between Simon and me. I'll be in Galveston for a limited time, and Simon is very generously helping me to … to locate family that I've become estranged from."

Elmore frowned. "The war caused similar difficulties for many." He continued sincerely, "But you certainly have found the right man to help you in Galveston. Simon is highly respected here."

"That's obvious from the way everyone treats him, and I can certainly understand why he is respected. Simon has been selfless in helping me in my search, and he hardly knows me."

"My dear, your youth and beauty are the only identification you'll ever find necessary in order for able men to volunteer their assistance."

"Now it's my turn to thank you for a compliment … I think."

Laughing somewhat uncomfortably as the music ceased, Elizabeth allowed Elmore to take her arm and usher her off the dance floor. He delivered her to the location where Simon stood speaking to a young man who turned toward her with an expansive grin and said, "At last an opportunity to meet the elusive Miss Elizabeth Huntington." Taking her hand, the round-faced blond young gentleman raised it to his lips, continuing, "In case I haven't already been pointed out to you, my name is Howard Meecham. I say that because you've certainly been pointed out to me this evening. Our names have been mistakenly intertwined since your arrival in Galveston, but it's my sincere pleasure to finally meet you."

"And my pleasure to meet you, Mr. Meecham."

"Howard, please. And I'll call you Elizabeth." He winked. "We're old friends, after all."

Elizabeth was conversing easily with Howard when Simon said abruptly, "I don't think your purpose in coming here tonight includes idle conversation, Elizabeth. If you'd like me to make some necessary introductions, I suggest we start now."

Elizabeth's smile dropped away as she replied candidly, "You're right, of course, but I don't think simple courtesy should be forgotten in the meantime."

Simon responded apologetically, "Of course not, Elizabeth, but I have the feeling that the inevitable political groups will begin forming soon and we'd be better off taking the opportunity to circulate freely while we can. I'm sure Howard understands."

Obviously miffed, Howard replied, "I suppose I'll have to understand." His smile returning, he said to Elizabeth, "But I do want to reserve a dance later, once your business is taken care of."

"I look forward to it, Howard." Waiting only until Howard began making his way back across the crowded floor, Elizabeth turned toward Simon and said thoughtfully, "I'm sorry. I didn't take into account that you might have business to conduct tonight, too, or that I might be stealing valuable time from you. I certainly appreciate the time you're taking to help me."

"Elizabeth … it's my pleasure. But I do think we

should make an appearance on the dance floor first." He smiled. "Willard expects it."

Elizabeth forced a smile as Simon took her arm possessively and led her out onto the floor. His hand was warm and moist against her waist as they started to dance, and Elizabeth felt a nudge of discomfort that flared to annoyance at another burst of laughter from the same dark-haired girl dancing again with Jason Dodd.

She forced her smile even brighter at the thought that the young woman was almost as annoying as Jason Dodd himself.

"Jason ..." Elvira laughed as Jason whirled her out of her father's sight on the dance floor. "You're such a clever fellow. Sometimes I really wish you weren't too old for me."

"Too old ..." Jason's mouth curved in amusement. "I suppose a man in his middle twenties does seem old to some people."

"Definitely." Elvira leaned toward him and whispered, "I happen to know for a fact that Edward Kroller is in his *early* twenties, that he took over the family business at the age of nineteen, and he's considered to be an excellent businessman with a promising future."

"A perfect candidate."

"I wish my father thought so."

"Well—"

Jason's thoughts came to an abrupt halt as Simon Gault danced Elizabeth Huntington past him.

"Jason, you're frowning."

His attention snapping back to Elvira, Jason responded, "Am I?"

"She is beautiful, isn't she?"

"Who?"

"Jason, please ..." Elvira shook her head. "Neither you nor any other man in the room has been able to take his eyes off Elizabeth Huntington since she walked through the doorway—with the exception of Edward, of course."

Realizing subterfuge was useless, Jason responded, "Yes, she's beautiful; and yes, Edward has eyes only for you." When the music ended opportunely, Jason suggested, "I could just happen to leave you off beside where Edward is standing so you could strike up a conversation."

"That's a good idea. Edward is beginning to look restless. I have the feeling he'll be leaving early and I'll miss my chance if I don't just happen to approach him before he does."

"And you say I'm clever."

Glancing back at Simon, Elvira commented, "It doesn't look like you'll get the same chance with Elizabeth Huntington, though. Judging from appearances, Simon isn't going to let her out of his sight any more this evening."

"Really?"

Not expecting a response, Jason led Elvira to the edge of the dance floor near the spot where Edward Kroller stood uncomfortably with a half-empty glass in his hand. He left her with a polite bow and noted out of the corner of his eye that Elvira wasted no time striking up a conversation with the shy fellow.

Jason was momentarily amused, but his smile dropped away as he made his way deliberately across the crowded floor.

Elizabeth felt a hand on her arm a moment before she heard a deep, familiar voice say, "I think this is our dance, Elizabeth."

Elizabeth turned toward Jason Dodd and said with a stiff smile, "I don't remember making that promise."

Jason's hand remained firm on her arm as he replied, "Oh, but I do."

Realizing that the only way she could elude his grip would be to make a scene, Elizabeth gritted her teeth and said, "In that case, I'm sure Simon will excuse me for *one* dance."

Elizabeth noted Jason Dodd's cool dismissal of Simon's nod as he led her onto the dance floor. Ignoring the tremor that moved down her spine when he curved his hand around her waist to hold her firmly, she whispered hotly, "You and I both know I didn't promise you a dance, just as you and I both know we wouldn't be dancing right now if you hadn't forced the issue. So my question is, why would you want to put us both in a situation that is mutually disagreeable?"

"Speak for yourself, Elizabeth." Jason did not smile. "I'm enjoying myself."

"Really? I'm sure there's not a person in the room who would believe it, judging by the look on your face—but aside from that, I have a feeling dancing with me isn't what you're enjoying. You don't like Simon, and Simon doesn't like you. You just enjoy getting the upper hand with him."

"You're very observant."

"Observant? I'd have to be blind not to see that you don't like each other."

"And outspoken."

"Right, so you'll understand when I say I don't like being used as a pawn in what looks like an ongoing war between you and Simon, Mr. Dodd."

"My name is Jason … and you're dead wrong if you think that's the only reason I wanted to dance with you."

Elizabeth hesitated to respond. She attempted to ignore Jason's unexpectedly heated perusal of her face, and the fact that his gaze ended on her lips.

"The trouble is," he went on, "I don't think you know exactly what you're letting yourself in for."

"Oh … I suppose that means I'm going to get more of your *sage* advice."

"I wouldn't be so flippant about what I'm telling you, Elizabeth." His expression darkened suddenly as he continued, "Look, I can understand the situation you find yourself in. You're young, lovely, obviously accustomed to the better things in life, and even more obviously alone in the world—no parent, relation, or man with an ounce of grit would have let you to come to a strange city without an escort."

"I have good reason to be here."

"I know what your reason is, and you've made a mistake if you've chosen Simon Gault as your benefactor."

"I suppose it wouldn't occur to you that you could be mistaken about my reason for being in this city."

"Not when I see you on the arm of one of the richest single men in Galveston."

Beginning to tremble with ire, Elizabeth replied, "You advised me to look for a man with a fatter wallet, didn't you? You should be pleased that I followed your instructions."

"This isn't a laughing matter, Elizabeth."

"That's good, because I'm not laughing."

Glancing around them abruptly, aware that their angry conversation was gaining the attention of couples dancing nearby, Jason waited only a moment before sweeping her out through the French doors onto the subtly lit terrace. Startled, Elizabeth gasped as Jason gripped her hand and pulled her into the shadows, where he turned around to face her and said roughly, "Simon Gault is more than you can handle—more than any woman can handle."

"Simon offered to help me, and I—"

"Did he tell you what his help will cost you?"

"He didn't ask for any payment."

"Not yet."

"What's that supposed to mean?"

"Simon Gault is a notorious womanizer."

"Simon is well respected in Galveston!"

"One thing doesn't necessarily cancel out the other."

"To my mind it does."

"But not to the minds of most influential men in

the city, who tend to consider that part of his personality admirable."

"But not you ... you don't look past it."

"I've ignored it in most cases. I figure most women who get involved with Simon Gault know what they're doing and are getting what they asked for, one way or another."

"So?"

Jason pressed closer. The flickering lights of the ballroom within were reflected in the depths of his dark eyes as he said, "I don't think *you* realize what Simon has in mind. Doesn't it seem strange that he's so attracted to you—a woman half his age—and that although he has so much to offer, he's still not married?"

"He's not attracted to me. He's just helping me."

"Liar."

"Don't call me a liar! Simon has been a complete gentleman."

"So far. But you didn't answer my question. I suppose you haven't wondered why a rich, influential, well-respected man like Simon isn't married."

"I haven't given it much thought. It's none of my business ... or yours."

"Maybe it wouldn't be my business if Simon's secret life hadn't caused so much damage."

"I don't know what you mean."

"I mean that Simon Gault is a man without principle. It may not mean much to a Yankee woman that he collaborated with the federal blockade during the war, but it means a lot to me."

"Simon collaborated?" Elizabeth was astounded

at his claim. "Don't you mean *you* collaborated with the Yankee blockade?"

"That's a lie!" Jason snapped, "If it were true, would I be welcome here tonight?"

"You're just as welcome here as Simon is."

"Maybe ... but I'm not one of the richest men in Galveston. And I don't own a large shipping company that makes me influential in city affairs. I'm just a former blockade runner and an unemployed cattle drover who proved his loyalty to the city during the war."

"Who proved his loyalty—just like Simon?"

His hands tightening on her arms, Jason pulled her so close that his warm, sweet breath brushed her face as he said, "What do I have to do to make you understand that Simon's intentions are dishonorable? He'll use you just like he used Melanie Wakefield, who stumbled innocently into the city a few years ago, was befriended by Simon, and then seemingly left the city without a word to anyone and was never heard from again. Then there was Judith Agar, who was befriended by Simon and supposedly left Galveston so abruptly because she had an ailing brother."

"Very commendable of her."

"An ailing brother who didn't exist!"

"This is ridiculous!" Elizabeth attempted to pull her arms free. "If Simon had anything to do with any of those women's disappearances, someone would have proof against him."

"Simon is very good at eliminating proof."

"Eliminating ..."

"Anyone who gets in his way."

Elizabeth gasped. "That's enough! I won't listen anymore."

"You'd better listen." The hard wall of his body was warm against hers as he held her fast and asked, "Why would I be telling you all of this if it weren't true?"

At a loss for a quick response, Elizabeth jumped when Simon unexpectedly stepped into view beside them and responded in her stead, "I don't know what he's been telling you, Elizabeth, but I think the answer to that question is obvious." Turning toward Jason, Simon said tightly, "Whatever your intentions are toward Miss Huntington, Dodd, I advise you to take your hands off her right now, before I'm forced to put the first touch of tarnish on the sterling reputation you enjoy in this household."

"My conversation with Elizabeth is none of your business, Gault."

"The fact that I escorted Elizabeth to this affair makes it my business."

Unable to speak, Elizabeth felt Jason's grip on her arms tighten as he said warningly, "This is a private exchange between Elizabeth and me, which means—"

"Which means, gentlemen"—thrusting his portly figure between the two men, Willard Spunk continued with a touch of amusement—"that your conversation has begun gaining the attention of some of my guests. My dear ..." Willard offered Elizabeth his hand. He waited for Jason to release her before he drew her out of the shadows and said, "Elizabeth will be returning to the ballroom to dance with me. I suggest that you two friends of mine save whatever you have to discuss for another time and place."

Aware for the first time that she was trembling, Elizabeth allowed Willard to draw her toward the terrace doors. He looked back to add for the benefit of the two men standing silently behind him, "Please remember that you're my guests, gentlemen, and although I understand that a beautiful woman can sometimes affect a man's judgment, I would not appreciate having the evening brought to an unfortunate end because of it."

Willard's balding head shone with perspiration as he drew Elizabeth out onto the floor and said with a touch of anxiety not formerly apparent, "You're shaking, and I can't say I'm surprised, my dear. I've never seen those two so sharply at odds. Whatever the circumstances, I apologize that the situation occurred in my house. They don't like each other, but Jason and Simon are both my friends, and I'm sure they both regret the incident as much as I do. I hope you'll forgive us."

"Of course."

Elizabeth glanced toward the terrace doors as Jason emerged and walked toward the bar. She breathed a sigh of relief when Simon came out a few moments later. She held her breath when the dance ended and Willard delivered her back to Simon's side.

His expression stiff, Simon said softly to his stout friend, "I think it would be best if we left now."

"That isn't necessary, Simon."

Simon countered apologetically, "Of course, it is, Willard. I hope you'll excuse us."

Simon glanced heatedly toward the bar, where Jason stood with his back facing them. Simon's thoughts clearly readable in his expression, he took Elizabeth's arm and said, "Are you ready to leave?"

Unable to voice her reply, Elizabeth nodded.

Helping her into the carriage minutes later, Simon patted her hand and said, "I'm sorry the evening ended before you could accomplish what you came here for."

"I'm the one who's sorry. I hope I haven't caused you any embarrassment with your friends."

"Embarrassment? No. The person who should be embarrassed is Jason Dodd."

Elizabeth noted that despite his denial, Simon's hand was sweating, and the expression on his face said otherwise as they proceeded back to the Easton Hotel in silence.

Standing outside in the shadows of the wide stone porch, Jason watched Simon's carriage pull away. The knot inside him tightened at the thought of Elizabeth confined in the intimate space with Simon.

Jason turned back toward the party abruptly and raised his chin with determination. Sam Johnson was waiting for him inside, and it was time for him to pay attention to more important matters.

As for Elizabeth, he had warned her. The rest was up to her.

Chapter Five

Sylvia Blair Huntington walked briskly along the cluttered, thickly populated streets of lower Manhattan. She drew her lightweight coat more closely around her, hoping its superior quality did not attract undue attention as she walked past tenement buildings where bedding and bawdy women hung out of unscreened windows with equal abandon; along sidewalks where street vendors of all types hawked their wares; across a street where delivery wagons and carriages impeded traffic, causing shouting matches that echoed on the humid air; and where children vainly begged pennies from commonly dressed pedestrians moving among the stalls. All were conversing in divergent languages or accents that bore no resemblance to the cultured English that she spoke.

Sylvia remembered, however, when she had been one of those ragged bumpkins hanging onto her mother's apron while the weary woman shopped among other desperate women. And she remembered resolving that she would one day put this street and everything on it behind her.

Sylvia Blair.

Sylvia smirked.

She had chosen that name carefully and had vowed she would erase from her memory the name with countless syllables that her mother had scribbled on the immigration lists upon entering the country. She had been successful in that regard. She was now Sylvia Blair Huntington.

It was time for the next step.

Sylvia looked up at the tenements as she passed. They hadn't changed much, except for deterioration due to time and neglect. A smile tugged at her lips as she noted the address she sought and started up the steps.

Sylvia was no longer smiling as she trudged up the indoor staircase toward yet another floor, past hallways echoing with the cries of babies and rancid with the smell of stale food. She paused breathlessly when she reached the fourth floor, almost gagging at the more abominable odors that permeated the area. She walked briskly forward when she spotted the number 403, and knocked heavily on the door.

Nothing.

Determined not to have climbed the endless staircase in vain, Sylvia knocked more loudly. She frowned when a voice from within asked, "Who is it?"

Still breathless, she responded, "You're expecting me."

The door opened slowly and Sylvia frowned into the dimly lit interior as she looked at a small, unimpressive, balding man and said, "Are you Milton Stowe?"

"No, I never heard of him." The response in cockney English was succinct.

"This is room four oh three, isn't it?"

"That's right."

"I was told I could find Milton Stowe here. A mutual friend named Otto directed me here."

"Otto. Oh, that's different. Come on in. Otto told me to expect somebody, but I didn't expect it to be no woman."

Waiting until the man had closed the door behind her, Sylvia scrutinized him disparagingly from head to toe, then said, "Otto told you what I need to have done, didn't he?" At his nod, she said, "But I have to say it doesn't look like you're the man for the job."

"I don't look like I can take care of it, huh?" The fellow smiled, revealing surprisingly even, white teeth. "That's where you're wrong. I've got the knack of fitting in wherever I travel, and for doing my job quickly and quietly."

"You'd need to travel for this—to Galveston, Texas."

The man shrugged. "I traveled across an ocean to get here. A few more miles ain't a problem just as long as I get well paid for it."

"Otto told you how much I'll pay."

"Two thousand dollars—half now and half when I come back with the job done."

119

Sylvia nodded. "Otto told me you're the best, and it doesn't matter to you who the person is that I want you to take care of."

"I am the best, and it don't make no difference to me at all who or what I have to do."

"It has to look like an accident. You'll have to stay in Galveston until you learn the person's routine well enough so that nobody will suspect anything." She paused. "That condition is paramount. I won't pay you the remainder of your fee otherwise."

"Don't worry about it. I've done it all before. You can pay me the first half now."

Sylvia laughed. "I'm not that much of a fool. I'll give you part of the advance now. I'll buy the ticket to Galveston and give you the rest when we meet in two days' time at the train station just before you leave."

His turn to laugh, Milton Stowe said, "I guess you ain't as dumb as you look."

Her expression turning into a sudden snarl, Sylvia snapped, "I'm not dumb at all, and you'd best remember that!" Noting that her response had had the desired effect, Sylvia reached into her reticule and withdrew a picture. She handed it to him and said, "Just to make sure you don't make any mistakes ... study this picture."

Sylvia noted the rise of the fellow's wiry brows as he said, "A woman, and a real good-looker, too."

"Does that make a difference?"

"Not to me."

Sylvia nodded. "Two days. Remember, I'll meet you at the train station with the tickets to Galveston and the first half of the payment at noon. I'll also give you this person's most recent address."

"That's fine with me. By the way, what's the name I'll be looking for?"

"The name?" Sylvia's smile flashed for the first time as she replied, "Her name is Elizabeth Huntington."

"He thinks he got away with it...." Still as agitated as he had been the previous evening when Jason Dodd openly challenged his proprietary manner with Elizabeth at Willard Spunk's party, Simon paced his spacious office. He glanced at Bruce, who sat on his leather office chair. Bruce's expression was noncommittal as Simon continued to rant, "But he's wrong. He doesn't know it yet, but he signed his own death warrant the moment he danced Elizabeth out onto that terrace."

"Don't go off the deep end, boss." Speaking for the first time, Bruce brought Simon's pacing to an abrupt halt as he continued, "Everybody knows about the run-in you had with Dodd. If something should happen to him now, somebody would be sure to look in your direction."

"Do you really think I'm a fool?" Simon's expression darkened. "I won't allow Jason Dodd to threaten my position in Galveston. No, I'm prepared to wait, but I'll get my chance, and when I do—"

Anxious to change the subject, Bruce interrupted, "In the meantime, what about that Huntington woman?"

"Elizabeth?" Simon felt the familiar tightening

121

in his groin that the thought of her always elicited. He nodded. "She was embarrassed by Jason Dodd's behavior, and she was worried about its effect on my reputation. She feels partially responsible, which makes her feel indebted to me. That Easton Hotel where she's staying—it's a rat's nest. It offends my sensibilities. Besides, it's entirely too public to suit my intentions. I need to get her out of that place … to somewhere more conducive to the type of intimacy I intend with her."

Appearing to consider Simon's statement, Bruce shook his head. "Where were you thinking of … I mean a place that's private enough so you can feel free to enjoy yourself with her?"

"Adeline Beaufort's house is empty. She left me her key while she's visiting her sister in Chicago. She'll be gone for six months, at least, and she said she felt safe leaving the key in my hands because she knew I would watch out for the place as if it were my own. If she weren't such a rich old hag, I might have refused so blatant an imposition, but it now happens to suit my needs perfectly. After all, Adeline's house is lovely … and isolated … and so large that sounds are lost in it."

"You're right." Bruce nodded. "But the house is so big that the Huntington girl might not want to stay there by herself."

"I will, of course, provide dear Elizabeth with a servant to handle her needs."

"A servant?"

"Frieda Kline will be suitable."

"Oh, that woman." Bruce grimaced.

"I don't like her either, but Frieda will do anything if the price is right, and to be honest, she enjoys my little peccadilloes."

Bruce paused in response, then asked unexpectedly, "Are your plans for Elizabeth Huntington really worth it, boss? Whit Hawk got away when you hesitated too long. If anybody realizes who she is—"

"Nobody will! I'll see to that." Simon walked a few steps closer to Bruce to stand glaring down at him hotly as he continued, "And nobody … *nobody* … is going to rob me of my pleasure with Elizabeth Huntington—most especially Jason Dodd. I'll see him dead first!"

Shrinking back in his chair under the heat of Simon's malignant passion, Bruce said with a shake of his head, "I ain't never seen you so—"

"Determined?" Simon nodded. "Yes, I'm determined. I'll see Elizabeth this afternoon. We'll talk … and she'll move into Adeline Beaufort's house tonight."

"I'm fine where I'm living now … really, Simon."

Seated across from Simon in the luxury of the Seamont Hotel restaurant, where they were having lunch, Elizabeth attempted again to reassure Simon as she said, "I know the accommodations at the Easton Hotel aren't as luxurious as they are here, and that they don't appear to be suitable to my needs, but I assure you they're fine. I've made a few acquaintances who watch out for my welfare there, and since my adopted mother's solicitor paid for my room in advance, it would be foolish for me to leave."

"Elizabeth, money doesn't matter where your safety is concerned."

"I'm perfectly safe."

"I don't believe it, considering the trash that frequents that place."

"Some of the fellows there may seem unsavory, but most are good men down on their luck. They've been very respectful to me."

"And the others?"

"I ignore them."

"That won't do, Elizabeth. I'm worried about you, and to be truthful, a few influential persons in the city have asked me why you're staying at a place like the Easton. They wonder why I haven't taken steps to establish you in a better location."

Simon inwardly smiled, seeing victory within his grasp as Elizabeth appeared distressed by his reply.

She hesitated and then responded, "I don't want my circumstances to reflect on you, Simon, but ... to be honest ... I have a limited amount of money, and I won't ask my adoptive mother to advance me more. She's already been more than generous. I'm determined to make do with what I have."

"I could, of course, advance you the funds you'll need."

"No." Elizabeth frowned. "Thank you, but no."

His acting talents coming to the fore, Simon said, as if suddenly struck with the thought, "There is another alternative, Elizabeth. There's a house in a respectable district that I've been asked to look after while the owner is visiting up north." He shrugged. "To be honest, it's been a chore for me to keep watch on it. If you'd agree to establish temporary residence there, you'd be doing both the owner and me a favor, and you'd settle your present problem, too."

Elizabeth shook her head uncertainly. "I don't know...."

"Of course, Adeline maintains a servant in the house during her absence. Your residence there would also eliminate my need to supervise the woman."

"I wasn't hesitating because I wondered if a servant was included with your offer, Simon."

"I know, but you'd be doing me a favor, after all—by eliminating my concern about the house and your welfare while you're in Galveston."

"You have been so helpful and so selfless...."

"It's been my pleasure. I know how important your search is to you."

Elizabeth unconsciously sighed. "In that case, how can I refuse?"

A flush of triumph brightened Simon's smile. "I'll come with my carriage to move you out of the Easton this evening."

Frowning, Jason walked through the doorway of the Easton Hotel. He was no longer dressed like the dandy of the previous evening. Nor was he wearing the formal jacket and trousers he was sometimes forced to wear in Galveston. Instead, he wore a comfortably worn cotton shirt and trousers, with a bandanna tied loosely around his neck in a casual version of a tie. His hat had often shielded him from the rain as well as the sun, and his hand-tooled leather boots had served him equally long and well, completing an outfit that left no doubt as to the man he was. All that was missing was the gun he normally strapped around his hips when on the trail, which he wore only occasionally in the city of Galveston. Dressed as he was, he would have been indistinguishable from the other patrons filling the lobby and adjacent barroom if not for his unusual height and breadth of shoulder. He was well aware, however, that he was not dressed for making a polite call on a woman. The lateness of the hour only compounded the inappropriateness of the call. The evening was already in full swing in the vicinity of the Easton Hotel, and Elizabeth was probably safely ensconced in her room upstairs with her door securely locked behind her.

That last thought tightened Jason's frown. He had not forgotten Elizabeth's entrance into the Easton Hotel that first day and the male interest she had stirred. She seemed to believe she had found what she was looking for in Simon Gault. He knew better. Keeping him sleepless throughout the long, previous night was his realization that she did not.

He had been unable to avoid reviewing his behavior at Willard's Spunk's party. He had finally admitted to himself that his warning about Gault didn't appear credible in light of the respect most guests at the party showed the man. Also clear was the fact that in losing his temper as he did, he had only made things worse.

If he hadn't arranged to meet Sam Johnson at the party so they might try to impress upon the members of the consortium that Houston posed a true threat to Galveston's future, he would have left shortly after seeing Simon exit the affair with Elizabeth. As it turned out, the members of the consortium had given Sam's and his concern little more than polite attention, leaving him with the feeling that the evening had been a complete waste of time.

Yet it wasn't the failure of his and Sam's arguments that gnawed at his peace of mind. He had spent the afternoon following up on the last-minute details involved in the sale and shipping of his herd from the Galveston railroad terminal. He had forced down some supper and had even attempted to pass a leisurely evening with some friends before admitting to himself that he needed to speak to Elizabeth again—to make sure she understood that she was involved with a man whose dark side was a real threat to her.

Why did he care?

The answer he had sought to deny was obvious. It lay in the heady image of Elizabeth's natural, unsuspecting beauty; in the memory of her lingering scent and tantalizing body heat as they had stood together in the shadows of the terrace; in the angry assault of her hazel eyes sparking with green fire.

But first things first.

Winding his way through the crowded lobby, Jason ascended the staircase and approached Elizabeth's room. His frown darkened as he knocked on the door. When there was no response, he knocked again. The knot inside him tightened when he glanced down to see there was no light shining underneath the doorway.

"She's gone."

Jason turned abruptly toward the bowlegged, gray-haired fellow standing behind him. The old man stared at him belligerently and repeated, "I said, she's gone. You're too late if you came here to stop them."

Jason shook his head, disconcerted. "Them?"

"She left with that Simon Gault about a couple of hours ago—bag and baggage. I didn't get no chance to tell her it was a mistake, or I would've. Elizabeth is a nice girl … too nice for the likes of him."

"What are you talking about?"

"Are you deaf or something? I said Elizabeth left with that Gault fella. I helped carry her bags down to his carriage and I heard them talking about Elizabeth going to live at Adeline Beaufort's place for a while because the Beaufort woman was visiting up north. Gault was saying she'd be better off there—safe and all—and that he'd see to it that she had everything she needed."

The old man shook his head. "It didn't make no difference to him that I was looking out for Elizabeth here, that I made sure every one of them fellas downstairs kept his distance." He grumbled, "I never did like the looks of Simon Gault. I heard things about him, and I don't trust him one bit."

His jaw tight, Jason responded, "Well, I guess she got what she came here for."

"Now you're talking crazy! Elizabeth ain't found out nothing at all about her family that she was separated from when she was younger. Thanks to Gault's advice, she ain't found nobody who recognized her pendant, either."

"Her pendant?"

The old man scrutinized him more closely. "You're Jason Dodd, ain't you? Elizabeth told me how you drove off that drunk the first day she came, and I did some asking around about you. From what people had to say, you was trustworthy enough, and I figured you was Elizabeth's friend. Now I'm beginning to wonder if I was wrong, being as you don't know nothing about her pendant."

Jason said tightly, "I'm Elizabeth's friend, all right."

The old man considered his response. "If she didn't tell you about her pendant, that's probably Gault's doing. He told her not to show that pendant to anybody because somebody might use it to take advantage of her. He said to depend on him and he'd help her find her family."

"Find her family …?"

"The crest on her pendant made her think she'd be able to get some information about them here in Galveston, but I got my doubts about that—especially with Gault helping her."

Silently cursing his stupidity, Jason replied, "You said Gault took her to Adeline Beaufort's place?"

"That's where he told his driver to go."

"When did they leave?"

"A few hours ago." The old man's cheek twitched revealingly. "I didn't like it much, but there wasn't nothing I could do about it."

"I may agree with Gault that this hotel isn't the best place for Elizabeth to be, but not for the same reason he did. For the record, I don't like Gault, either, and I'm going to make sure Elizabeth learns the truth about him."

"Well, it's about time somebody besides an old man who's half-crippled did something to help Elizabeth."

Jason asked abruptly, "What did you say your name is?"

"Everybody just calls me Charlie."

"Well, you can stop worrying, Charlie. I'll take care of straightening all this out."

"When?"

"Right now."

Jason turned toward the staircase without seeing Charlie's satisfied smile.

Doing her best to avoid Frieda Kline's penetrating stare, Elizabeth walked into the living room of Adeline Beaufort's sumptuous home. Set back from the road more than five hundred feet, the house was magnificent in its proportions and opulence, although almost obscured by the heavy foliage surrounding it. A massive living room and dining room dominated a first floor also boasting a library, a mahogany-paneled den, and a butler's pantry and generous servants' quarters off a spacious, well-stocked kitchen. Several luxurious bedrooms were located off an endless hallway that appeared to stretch for miles on the second floor. Simon had instructed his driver to carry her baggage into Adeline's master suite, an extravagantly decorated series of rooms that made her feel uncomfortable for too many reasons to enumerate. Protesting, she had told him she preferred a simple guest bedroom and had argued politely with Simon for several minutes as he had attempted to persuade her otherwise. She knew she had somehow displeased him with her insistence on the smaller quarters, but she could not fathom the reason.

Having established herself in a guest bedroom, she had finally found it necessary to tell Simon that she was weary and ready to turn in. She'd hoped he would take the hint and leave—and she sensed she had displeased him again. It was his kiss on departing, however, when he again grazed her lips while kissing her cheek, when he held her a fraction too long and too close, that made her truly uncomfortable.

Unfortunately, she was presently alone in the massive structure with only the annoying Frieda for company. Short and dark with a small-eyed, intense gaze, the woman stood in what appeared to be her habitual stance—her back curved while wringing her hands with a strange, almost gleeful expression that put Elizabeth in mind of a rodent.

"Is there anything you want, Miss Elizabeth? The kitchen is fully equipped. Maybe you'd like me to prepare a bath for you?"

"No, that won't be necessary." The thought of the small, weasel-like woman standing ready with a towel as she stepped out of the tub sent a chill down her spine. Elizabeth added, "Thank you anyway. I think I'll just turn in."

Appearing unwilling to allow their conversation to end, Frieda added, "Mr. Gault is such a nice man … and so well respected. You're fortunate that he's taken an interest in you."

"Yes, I know."

"He has his choice of women in Galveston, you know. He's the most sought-after bachelor the city has to offer."

"That's nice."

"Most women would do anything to gain his favor."

Elizabeth did not respond.

"They all cater to his smallest whim."

"That's unfortunate, isn't it?" Elizabeth responded coldly. "A woman should always value her worth. She shouldn't base it on her appeal to any man."

Frieda's small eyes narrowed as she responded, "Mr. Gault is certainly worthy of special consideration. He's wealthy and powerful enough to do anything he wants for a woman who is willing to accommodate him."

"I suppose that's true, but in Mr. Gault's case, he's a gentleman, and I'm sure he wouldn't expect a woman to 'accommodate him' unduly."

Frieda smiled unexpectedly, a hideous sight that exposed crooked, yellowed teeth as she said, "But a man is a man, after all. He does like being catered to. I suppose a smart woman would do well to remember that."

Losing patience with the game they appeared to be playing, Elizabeth said sharply, "Not *this* smart woman!"

Elizabeth turned away abruptly and said over her shoulder as she headed for the stairs, "I'm going to bed now. The rest of the evening is yours to do with as you like. Good night."

Appearing dissatisfied with being dismissed so brusquely, Frieda persisted, "You're sure you don't want anything from the kitchen, miss?"

Elizabeth responded succinctly as she started up the staircase, "I'm sure."

"What time would you like me to wake you in the morning?"

Elizabeth replied with barely restrained annoyance, "I'll wake myself. I'll also bathe myself, dress myself, and make my own breakfast when I get down to the kitchen. Good night, Frieda."

Elizabeth could not be certain, but she was almost sure she heard the woman snicker as she reached the second floor and turned toward her room.

Jason knocked heavily on the front door of Adeline Beaufort's home. He glanced around him as he waited for a response, noting that the evening had darkened, and that except for a few lights that lit the interior of the house, it was almost invisible from the road. He had been greatly relieved to see that Simon's carriage was not waiting outside when he arrived, but he realized that did not guarantee

Elizabeth was alone. Simon was crafty. He kept his private life private. It wouldn't do to let his carriage remain outside any woman's residence in open declaration of where he had spent the night, when it was just as easy to order his driver to return for him the next morning.

That thought in mind, Jason knocked harder. He drew back a step when the door was opened by a small, wizened woman who eyed him from head to toe before demanding harshly, "What do you want here?"

Annoyed by her manner, Jason replied, "I'd like to speak to Miss Huntington."

"Too late." The woman almost snickered. "Miss Huntington has retired for the evening. She's not seeing anybody this late—most especially a man who hasn't the sense to dress properly when he comes to visit a lady."

"Really? I'd prefer that you ask Elizabeth whether she'll see me instead of making the decision for her."

"I told you, she's retired for the evening, and she doesn't want to be disturbed."

"We'll see about that." Pushing back the door, Jason strode past the servant and said, "Are you going to tell her I'm here, or should I tell her myself?"

"Get out right now! If you don't, you'll answer to Mr. Simon Gault. You know who he is, don't you?"

Jason started toward the staircase as he mumbled, "Yes, I know who Simon Gault is."

"Wait! Stop!" The woman grabbed onto his

arm. Her talonlike fingers dug into his shirt as she said, "You can't go up there. Miss Huntington has retired."

Shrugging himself loose, Jason started up the stairs as the servant added harshly, "Miss Huntington is Mr. Gault's guest. He'll make sure you regret breaking in here."

Jason continued up the staircase. Unsure exactly where Elizabeth's room was located, he became certain that he was going in the right direction when the servant shouted, "Wait! Stop! Mr. Gault will be furious!"

Jason was halfway up the staircase when a voice from the upper landing called out, "What's going on down there, Frieda?"

And then he saw her.

Dressed in a simple cotton night shift that allowed only a vague outline of the womanly slenderness underneath it, her unbound hair glittering in the flickering semilight, and her perfect features reflecting her concern, Elizabeth leaned over the railing. She went rigid when she saw him. She asked coldly as he continued his approach, "What are you doing here?"

Her heart pounding despite the composed demeanor she sought to maintain, Elizabeth backed up unconsciously as Jason reached the landing and approached her. It occurred to her that he appeared somehow taller and more daunting in casual dress than in formal attire. His cotton shirt was open at the collar, exposing his muscular neck and a trace of dark hair on his chest. His shoulders looked broader in the thin cotton shirt he wore, his waist and hips narrower in trousers that fit snugly against the long length of his powerful legs. And those eyes that pinned her …

Refusing to retreat another step as he towered over her, she said, "I asked you what you're doing here."

Jason's gaze intensified before he responded, "I might ask you the same question."

"You might, but it's none of your business."

"It's more my business than you realize."

Frieda interrupted their exchange, forestalling Elizabeth's tart reply when she called out shrilly, "I'm going to get Mr. Gault right now if you don't leave!"

"No, you aren't!" Elizabeth's reply was adamant. "This is none of Mr. Gault's business, and I'm perfectly capable of handling this matter myself."

"That sounds familiar."

Turning briefly toward Jason's mumbled comment, Elizabeth looked back at Frieda when the woman insisted annoyingly, "Mr. Gault would want to know!"

"Whether he would or not, I'll handle this myself."

"But—"

"You may go to bed now, Frieda."

"Mr. Gault said—"

"*I* said … you may go to bed."

Waiting only until Frieda turned stiffly toward the maid's quarters, Elizabeth looked back at Jason to see amusement flash across his stern expression as he commented, "That's telling her. But you do know she'll run right to Gault as soon as she gets a chance tomorrow."

"I don't really care what she does."

"Or what Gault thinks?"

"I'm not obliged to explain my personal actions to Simon."

"You're not? Is that why you're here as his 'guest' instead of staying at the Easton?"

Elizabeth replied slowly, "Please correct me if I'm wrong, but aren't you the person who barged into my affairs the first day I arrived in Galveston and told me I should find a more respectable place than the Easton Hotel to stay?"

"I didn't tell you to jump from the frying pan into the fire."

"Really? Is that what I did? I also remember that you told me to find a man with a fatter wallet."

Elizabeth saw the irritation that crossed Jason's features before he said, "I was wrong when I said that. I was tired and I was irritated at being distracted from important business."

"I distracted you?"

"Among other things."

Elizabeth felt a slow heat rise to her cheeks as Jason continued, "I went to the Easton tonight to try again to convince you that you are making a mistake aligning yourself with Gault. You weren't there, and I talked to Charlie."

"Charlie …"

He paused, and then said, "All right, I admit

that I jumped to conclusions when I saw you at the Easton that first day. I figured there was only one reason a woman like you would be traveling alone to a place like Galveston. I didn't know you were trying to locate your family."

"You didn't ask."

"Or about the pendant."

Elizabeth went still. She restrained an automatic inclination to raise her hand to the bodice of her nightshift to confirm that her pendant was still concealed underneath as she said, "Charlie told you about it?"

"He did. Why didn't *you* tell me?"

"As I said, you didn't ask."

"You knew I would help you if I had known."

"How would I have known that?"

"You might've guessed from the way I came to your aid at the Seamont restaurant."

"You came to my aid the same way you went to the aid of that redheaded … woman. You seemed to believe we were two of a kind."

Jason snapped back with unexpected defensiveness, "There are some people who might consider it an insult if I really did think of you in the same way, but I'm not one of them. Chantalle is an extraordinary woman, and I'm proud to call her a friend."

"Are you? I suppose that says a lot about you."

"I think it does."

A knot twisted painfully tight inside her at Jason's defense of the redheaded Chantalle, and Elizabeth shrugged. "Whatever—you came to apologize for your mistaken presumption about me. I accept your apology, so you can leave now."

Jason stepped closer. His expression was tight as he searched her face. His gaze lingered briefly on her lips when he said, "Do you really want me to leave right now?"

A rush of heat surged along Elizabeth's spine. She struggled against an overwhelming dryness in her throat and a trembling that began inside her as she finally managed, "You have nothing else to say that interests me."

"I don't think that's true. If nothing else, you're not sure if I'm telling the truth about Gault or you wouldn't have sent Frieda away."

"I sent Frieda away because I won't let anyone tell me what to do, especially someone like her."

Jason reached out unexpectedly to touch the delicate chain that held her pendant secure underneath the bodice of her nightshift. He whispered, "It's important for you to believe me, Elizabeth. I want you to believe me."

Unwilling to let him see how his touch affected her, Elizabeth replied, "I suppose you think I should trust you."

"That's right."

"I should believe everything you said to me, about Simon being a Yankee collaborator during the blockade."

"Yes."

"Even if he says the same thing about you."

"He's lying. I never worked with the Yankees."

139

"Simon has been very generous. He wants to help me."

"Among other things."

"Stop that!" Angry at her own confused emotions, Elizabeth said, "Stop implying that Simon has an ulterior motive for bringing me here!"

Gripping her arms unexpectedly, his dark eyes burning into her, Jason held her fast as he said, "All right, I'll stop if you can honestly tell me that Gault doesn't make you uncomfortable in some way, that you didn't originally resist coming to this isolated spot and relented only because he pressured you into it, and that you resent being watched by a shrill witch who reports directly to him."

"It's not that way! Frieda is employed by the owner of this house."

"I don't think so." And when Elizabeth challenged him with a glance, he added, "Would you keep a servant like Frieda in your house?"

Elizabeth shuddered at the thought.

"You just answered my question."

"I … I don't know what you're talking about."

"Yes, you do. And you didn't deny that Gault pressured you into coming here … that you resent having Frieda here watching you." Jason said earnestly, "Elizabeth … you can't deny that there's something inside you that makes you believe me."

Jason's warmth enveloped her; the deep roll of his voice mesmerized her; his overwhelming male aura drew her toward him. Suddenly aware of the danger in the escalating heat between them, Elizabeth shook herself free of Jason's grip. She stepped back, hoping to conceal her breathlessness as she said, "It would be an obvious lie if I told you anything else right now other than that I don't really know what to believe. The only thing I'm presently sure of"—Elizabeth took a breath—"is that I want you to leave."

"I don't want to leave."

"I asked you to leave now."

Suddenly realizing that if she didn't move at that moment, if she didn't escape the growing intensity between them, she would be lost, Elizabeth turned abruptly and said, "All right, if you won't leave, then I will."

Elizabeth struggled to control her shuddering as she turned away from him and walked rigidly back toward her room.

She did not look back to see Jason standing stunned and motionless in her wake.

The semilight of the upstairs hallway flickered in a silence broken only by the echoing sound of Elizabeth's bedroom door clicking shut behind her. Myriad emotions rampant inside him, Jason stared at the closed door. How had it come to this … that Elizabeth should wish to escape him when all he had intended was to keep her safe? How had he ended up making her wary of him when all he really wanted …

Jason took a stabilizing breath. His own feelings aside, Elizabeth was still in danger from Gault. He had to make her accept that truth.

Determined, Jason walked deliberately toward

Elizabeth's bedroom. He knocked. When she did not answer, he pushed the door open and walked inside. He halted abruptly at the sight of Elizabeth standing near the dresser. The lamplight behind her illuminated her form, casting the unmistakable outline of her naked slenderness against the billowy folds of her nightshift. He swallowed tightly, scrutinizing her expression ... the shadowed planes of her beautiful face; her wide-eyed, uncertain gaze; the delicate curve of her cheek; and her mouth ... those soft, full lips that were trembling. He took a spontaneous step toward her, the desire to cover those trembling lips with his own almost more than he could restrain. He halted abruptly when Elizabeth raised a small gun into view and pointed it in his direction. Her hand was shaking as she whispered, "I asked you to leave, and you didn't. Now I'm telling you to leave."

When he did not reply, Elizabeth continued haltingly, "Don't assume that I don't know how to use this gun, because I do. I'm a very good shot."

"You don't need that gun as a defense against me, Elizabeth," Jason said softly, "I came here to apologize to you, and to try to make you believe me when I say I only have your best interests at heart."

"Simon's words."

"Simon's a liar. I'm not."

Elizabeth did not reply.

"I want you to believe me, Elizabeth."

"And I want you to go." Jason heard the desperation that entered Elizabeth's voice when she whispered, "Don't make me use this gun. I'll regret it, but I'll do it if I have to."

"Elizabeth …"

Jason heard the warning click of the hammer as Elizabeth pulled it back and said, "I'll ask you only one more time."

Aching inside, Jason replied, "All right, I'll go … but I want you to promise me you'll remember what I said."

"I won't promise anything. I just want you to leave."

"Have it your way." Aware that further pleas were useless, Jason said, "The rest is up to you. I just hope you don't realize too late that I'm telling you the truth."

Jason turned toward the doorway without any regard for the gun in Elizabeth's hand. Outside on the front doorstep, he pulled the door closed behind him, then stood motionless as the sound of the latch reverberated in the nighttime stillness. Frowning, he walked resolutely toward his horse.

Still trembling, Elizabeth stood stock-still as the sound of the front door latch echoed up into her room. She looked down at the derringer in her hand and slowly released the hammer.

Would she have shot Jason if he hadn't left?

She took a shaky breath, suddenly unsure.

Elizabeth dropped the gun onto her dresser with distaste and climbed into the large, four-poster bed. She drew the coverlet up tight against her chin and closed her eyes, only to see Jason's image staring down at her with a gaze that was almost palpable. The echo of his voice touched a spot down deep inside her as his question returned to haunt her.

Do you really want me to leave right now?

She knew what she had responded, but …

She was sure of only one thing. She had come to Galveston with a purpose in mind. She needed to accomplish it and leave quickly … before it was too late.

Chapter Six

Simon struggled to control his anger as he walked stealthily along the familiar back alley. Chantalle's elegant redbrick mansion—set some fifty feet off the road, with arching live oaks and brilliant oleander hedges that lent an aura of privacy even to those who chose to approach it directly—was the most elegant bordello in Galveston. Yet the house was only a shadow in the darkening twilight ahead of him where a hidden walkway, a high privacy wall, and a staircase to the second floor granted Simon the anonymity he desired.

Simon was as familiar with that back entrance as he was with the back of his own hand.

He mumbled under his breath as he neared. He knew his private room would be waiting for him there. The isolated room was in a section opposite the side of the house used by Chantalle's other patrons, and she kept it to be used by him alone. She did that because of his prestige … and for other, more practical reasons as well.

145

Simon knew, however, that Chantalle did not accommodate him or his perversions because she liked him. The truth was quite the contrary. For the most part, the redheaded madam and he merely tolerated each other for business reasons; at times their antagonism erupted in near violence. He was still furious with Chantalle for interfering in his perfect revenge on Whit Hawk—a revenge that had ended with the nudge of a derringer in his ribs that had sent him packing. She was the only woman in Galveston—or man, for that matter—who dared defy him. He despised her because she had glimpsed a side of him that he had kept carefully hidden from others, and she despised him because of the "dirty little secrets" she was compelled to conceal.

It amused him that Chantalle believed her intimate knowledge of him kept her safe from his machinations. What Chantalle did not know was that his hatred for Whit Hawk—and his own sexual perversions—were only the tip of the iceberg, and that she was safe only as long she served his purposes.

Actually, Simon had no doubt that although his respectable peers pretended ignorance, his clandestine visits to Chantalle's bordello were an open secret. He was, after all, a wealthy bachelor in the prime of life, a man with needs that other men appreciated even while they recognized that to be seen openly at Chantalle's would tarnish his sterling reputation. What they were not aware of was his addiction to the seamy side of sex that he sated in that private room at Chantalle's. It was a point of growing irritation for him that Chantalle had made it clear he would be tolerated in her house only as long as Angie—a greedy little harlot if there ever was one—enjoyed his perversions as much as he did.

What neither woman knew was that his depravity was growing out of control, that his appetite was becoming unquenchable, and that he was beginning to believe that nothing except his avid plans for the beauteous Elizabeth would be able to sate it.

Simon stepped up onto the staircase and ascended toward the back entrance of the house, his concealed anger heightening. It appeared, however, that the unyielding Elizabeth did not entertain any thoughts of that kind in his direction. A visit from the nauseating Frieda Kline that morning had confirmed that conclusion. She had reported the details of Jason Dodd's visit to the Beaufort mansion the previous evening with more enjoyment than he had deemed necessary. He remembered the wizened witch's attempt to appear disapproving when she said Elizabeth greeted Dodd with her unbound hair spilling over the shoulders of her sheer nightdress, that they exchanged only a few words before Elizabeth dismissed her, and that Dodd walked upstairs into Elizabeth's bedroom and shut the door behind them. Frieda claimed she had no idea exactly when Dodd left the house, except that Elizabeth arose exceedingly late the next morning and appeared exhausted.

Frieda's report had infuriated him. Were it not for the fact that he was determined to seduce the beauteous Hawk daughter before bringing her to her knees, he would have gone directly to the mansion and had his way with her. But that would have been too simple. He had known his satisfaction with that course of action would be merely temporary. No … only her complete subjugation would do. He needed to hear Elizabeth beg as her father had never begged. He needed to hear her plead with him alternately for mercy and then for more. He needed *total victory* over the Hawk siblings, whose only claim to the fortune their father had stolen from him—a fortune reclaimed at the cost of their father's life—was the Hawk blood that ran in their veins.

Those thoughts had produced an escalating rage that gnawed at him. Unwilling to trust himself before coming to terms with it, he had avoided Elizabeth and had barely made it through the day before his rage drove him to Chantalle's for relief.

Simon jerked the back door of the bordello open, glanced at the empty hallway, and then walked rapidly toward Chantalle's office door. He had no doubt Chantalle would be inside at that time of the evening, checking the account books that she maintained so meticulously. He listened briefly to make sure she was alone, then thrust the door open and entered without knocking.

Chantalle turned angrily toward him.

"You might try knocking next time, Simon. That is the polite way to enter a room."

"Really?" Simon's jaw was tight. He needed relief and he needed it fast. Uncertain whether he would be able to control his agitation much longer, he said, "Tell Angie I'm here."

"Why?"

"Why do you think? I certainly didn't come here to talk to you."

Chantalle stood up slowly. She straightened her shoulders, and then adjusted the deep neckline of the green satin gown molding her generous proportions when she noted Simon was staring avidly at her décolletage. Her heavily made-up features creased into a forced smile. "Angie's busy tonight."

"She won't be busy when she finds out I'm here."

"Not according to her."

"Whether you like to admit it or not, Angie enjoys my visits. As a matter of fact, she looks forward to them."

"Your last visit left her wary of you."

"That's hard to believe, but it's all right with me. I'll take Marian, then."

"No, you won't!" All trace of a smile dropped from Chantalle's handsome face. "You know Marian will always be off-limits to you."

"You persist in protecting a mewling whore who pretends to be shy and retiring … but I know better than that. I've heard how she acts with other men, and I intend—"

"You can 'intend' all you want. Marian is off-limits."

Simon's posture went rigid as he said with menacing softness, "I don't plan to leave here until I've spent as much time in my room with one of your women as I see fit. I don't care which woman it is, even if it must be you."

"Not in your wildest dreams! As far as I'm concerned—"

A sound at the entrance turned them both in its direction as the door swung open to reveal a smiling Angie standing there. Dark-haired and dressed in a gold gown that left little of her voluptuous proportions to the imagination, she looked at Simon with heavily lidded eyes and said, "Simon … I thought I heard your voice. I've been wondering when you'd come back."

Simon felt himself harden at the sight of Angie's bulging bosom as she leaned toward him, crooked her finger, and said, "Follow me, my insatiable lecher. I've learned some new tricks since the last time you visited. You won't get the best of me so easily this time."

Chantalle interrupted to say sharply, "I thought you said you'd had enough of Simon the last time he was here, Angie."

"That was last time. The truth is, nobody satisfies me like he does, and I'm not about to give him up." Angie strolled closer to Simon. She pressed herself against him as she said with growing heat, "I'm ready anytime you are."

Simon retorted, "You're an eager whore, aren't you?"

"Almost as eager as you are."

Barely maintaining control when Angie's smile became a leer, Simon turned toward Chantalle and said with a sneer, "As you can see, I'll be using my room most of the evening. Ignore whatever sounds you hear while I'm taking my enjoyment. I'll see that you're properly compensated."

Chantalle did not bother to respond when Angie took Simon's arm and drew him with her toward the door.

Lust almost overwhelming him, Simon waited only until the door of his private room closed behind them before ripping Angie's dress from her shoulders. He looked at her as she laughed and stood boldly with her white, naked breasts gleaming in the semidarkness. She was still laughing, but her breathing became ragged when he took her breasts in his hands and squeezed them roughly. Satisfied at her soft cry of pain when he bent down and bit her cruelly, Simon looked up to say, "You may not have honey brown hair and hazel eyes, or the class of the woman you're replacing in my mind, but you'll do for now."

"A substitute, am I?" Panting, Angie retorted with resolve flashing in her gaze, "We'll see."

Chantalle frowned when the echo of Simon's door closing reverberated in the silence of her office. Her stomach twisted tight inside her. She didn't like Simon Gault. She had long since accepted the fact that as a madam, she and her establishment were parts of the seamier side of Galveston life. She had told herself, however, that they were necessary parts, and had attempted to conduct her business with as much dignity as possible.

The truth was, she didn't like Angie much, either.

She knew Angie enjoyed more than an intimate relationship with Simon, and that Angie functioned without hesitation as his spy whenever it suited her purpose. But despite all the trouble she had caused, Angie saved her from making a difficult decision: denying Simon Gault entrance to her house. Chantalle endured the situation—but the depravity of it rankled.

A loud thumping from the room up the hall darkened Chantalle's frown. She hadn't needed Simon's reminder to disregard the sounds that normally came from that quarter when Simon was conducting "his business." The problem was that her tolerance was growing short.

In an effort to escape the curses, the sounds of sexual conflict, and Angie's pained murmurs, which she knew would be constant until Simon achieved his sexual gratification, Chantalle stood up abruptly and started for the door. She was halfway down the staircase to the main floor and the subdued din that would effectively block out the repulsive sounds when she saw Jason Dodd enter.

Elizabeth walked up the staircase toward her room as darkness overwhelmed twilight outside the windows of the Beaufort mansion. She had eaten sparingly of the dinner that Frieda had prepared for her. She was tired … weary to the bone of the fruitless search that she had conducted through the long, humid day.

Shrugging, Elizabeth entered her room and

152

closed the door behind her. She supposed she should have expected to be exhausted since she had slept so little after forcing Jason at gunpoint to leave her bedroom. His warning had nagged her into sleeplessness. It still echoed in her ears.

I just hope you don't realize too late that I'm telling you the truth.

And even more devastating, *Do you want me to leave right now?*

She'd had no true response to either of those statements, and she supposed the familiar nightmares of fire, smoke, and frantic cries that had followed hadn't helped. She remembered awaking abruptly, only to become terrified by the shifting shadows in the darkness surrounding her. The calming, unidentifiable voice that had soothed her fears throughout her childhood returned to encourage her with its whispered, *Fear is the enemy. Don't let it win.*

She didn't recall when she finally fell asleep, but when she finally awakened, the sun was already climbing toward its apex, and she had been furious with herself for having wasted valuable time that she should have used for her search.

The rest of the day had proved fruitless. Using the list of names that Simon had given her, she had visited several gentlemen and had explained her mission in coming to Galveston. She had even shown them her pendant, but the effort had been to no avail. They were polite and attentive, but none of them recognized the crest on her pendant—or even believed it had played a significant part in

Galveston's past. The thought dawned on her belatedly that each of the men to whom Simon had directed her were men in influential positions in Galveston, but who seemed to share the opinion that Galveston's past was not as important as its present or its future. She had decided to ask Simon about that concern when she saw him next.

Actually, she had received a message from Simon earlier, saying that important business would keep him away, and she seriously wondered if Frieda had had a part in his absence. In any case, she was relieved, especially in view of all that Jason had said about him.

It would be a subtle irony indeed, after the intense attention that Simon had paid to her concerns and the fact that she had felt it necessary to drive Jason away at gunpoint the previous evening, if neither of those men chose to step back into her life.

Elizabeth paused as she reached for her nightshift. Would she really care?

Simon's image flashed before her mind, and she frowned.

Jason's imaged followed, and her heart jumped a beat.

The question went unanswered.

Jason paused briefly in the entry hall of Chantalle's mansion. Frustrated by the recurring image that would allow him no rest, of brown hair liberally streaked with gold, of hazel eyes sparking with fire, and of full, appealing lips that relentlessly beckoned him, he had decided to do something about erasing it from his mind. After leaving the elaborate quarters that Gault had arranged for Elizabeth the previous evening, he had finally accepted the truth that if he'd had it his way, the evening would have ended far differently. The most difficult part of that realization was his feeling that despite the gun she had raised against him, Elizabeth felt the same as he did, and that she had known it would have taken only one touch of his hand to—

Jason muttered a low curse and closed the bordello door behind him. The thought that he dared not finish had haunted him throughout the day. It had interfered with his concentration when he had met with Sam Johnson. It had remained with him while he had searched the dock pubs afterward in an effort to locate Randolph Winters, one of Gault's captains during the blockade. Jason had learned the captain was disenchanted enough with Gault to speak out about his employer's betrayals. He'd had no luck in either effort, and his mounting frustration had delivered him to the place where he now stood.

Jason acknowledged the greetings of Chantalle's girls with a forced smile. Goldie, Marian, Poppie, Georgia ... most of them were old friends. They liked him, and he liked them, but he realized as he avoided Goldie's display of affection that he wasn't presently ready to accept what they had to offer.

Jason walked through Chantalle's elaborately decorated anteroom, past the numerous scarlet couches and gilded mirrors scattered around the main area, past the entrance to the card room that Chantalle maintained for her patrons and which was reputed to be the most honest game in town, and made his way to the large, well-stocked oak bar. He ordered a whiskey. He downed it in a gulp. He knew Chantalle carried only the best, because he had provided much of her liquor, along with other staples that were not readily available, during the blockade.

He smiled when Chantalle herself appeared unexpectedly beside him dressed in a green satin gown that made the most of her ample assets. She dismissed the bartender with a glance and said, "The next one's on me." When he downed the second drink with equal haste, she commented, "My liquor's good, but it's not that good. Have you got something on your mind that one of my girls can help you with, Jason?"

"As a matter of fact, I don't." Jason smiled and signaled her to pour another drink.

Chantalle refilled his glass slowly. "Keep this up and you won't make it out the door, much less to one of the rooms upstairs."

Jason heard himself say as he paused with his glass in hand, "I'm not in the mood for a trip upstairs with one of your girls."

"Really …" Chantalle raised her carefully shaped brows. "Let me see, adding two and two—the look on your face and the fact that my girls don't interest you tonight—leads me to believe you've got woman troubles."

Jason glanced up at her sharply, then emptied his glass again.

"I don't believe it. My girls all vie for your attention." Chantalle shrugged. "I've actually seen them draw straws for the chance to be the first one to approach when you come here. I never figured I'd see the day when you'd be turning them all away."

Jason considered Chantalle's comment. He supposed she was right. What was he doing there if he wasn't interested in one of her girls? He supposed he was there because his association with Chantalle during the blockade had left no doubt in his mind that she was fair-minded and decent despite her choice of occupations, that she was one of the few people who knew there was more to Simon Gault than met the eye, and that she had a sympathetic ear that did not come complete with a wagging tongue.

He responded, "Woman troubles ... caused by our friend Simon Gault."

Chantalle's lips tightened. "Speak for yourself. Simon may be your friend, but he isn't mine." She added, "Don't get me wrong, Jason; my feelings about Simon don't stop me from doing business with him."

"I suppose I can understand that to a degree, even if I don't think any reason would be good enough for me to associate with him." He continued darkly, "But you know how I feel about him. He's a criminal who cost the lives of countless seamen during the blockade. I mean to see that he pays for that. The problem is his sterling reputation and the fact that I can't locate anyone who's willing to speak the truth about him—anyone who doesn't show up dead the next day, anyway."

"Jason, that's a terrible thing to say!"

"It's true."

Chantalle frowned and replied guardedly, "Gault's benevolent exterior is a sham. That's true. His heart is as black as coal. That's true, too … but deliberate murder?" She shook her head. "He may have inadvertently caused some deaths, but I don't think—"

"I don't *think*, Chantalle. I *know*."

"If I were sure what you say is true …" Chantalle did not continue.

Jason responded to her unfinished statement, "I'll get proof of his crimes. I won't be satisfied until I do, but it's what's happening in the meantime that has me tied up in knots."

His frustration reflected in his expression, Jason tapped the bar for a refill, and Chantalle slowly poured him another drink as she cautioned, "I've already warned you once to take it easy. I don't allow drunks in here, and I like you too much to have you thrown out. I'm asking you a second time to take it slow."

Refusing to admit that his vision was already beginning to blur, Jason said abruptly, "I fell right into his hands, Chantalle; that's what's bothering me. I jumped to conclusions because I was too damned pigheaded to think past what appeared to be the obvious. Now it looks like I'm not the only one who's going to pay for my mistake."

"You're talking about a woman."

Jason asked unexpectedly, "Has anyone ever mentioned Elizabeth Huntington to you?"

"I've never heard of her. Should I have?"

"Maybe not, but since you know Gault so well—"

"What has Simon got to do with this?"

Jason replied, "Elizabeth Huntington ... young, inexperienced, too damned beautiful for her own good, and totally alone in a strange city."

Chantalle frowned. "If she's so young and inexperienced, what is she doing in Galveston alone?"

"I don't know ... determination, a stubborn streak that won't let her admit the foolishness of her actions, but when I saw her arrive at the Easton Hotel alone—"

"The Easton!"

"And when a drunk approached her in her room within fifteen minutes of her arrival—"

Chantalle shook her head. "Don't tell me."

"I told her there were better places in the city to stay if she was looking for a man with a fat wallet. The only problem was that I was wrong. She wasn't looking for a man. She was looking for her family. I might have understood if she had explained."

"Would you have believed her?"

"I don't know," Jason replied truthfully. "I was tired and out of sorts. I don't think I was of a mind to listen."

"What about Simon?"

"Simon listened. She even showed him her pendant."

"Her pendant?"

"It's a long story."

"I've got plenty of time."

"She was separated from her family when she was young. She doesn't remember much, but she has a pendant with a crest on it that she thinks might mean something—a crest with a ship that she traced to Galveston."

Chantalle went still. She then said, "Where is this young woman now?"

"Simon talked her into moving into the Beaufort mansion while Adeline Beaufort is visiting up north."

Chantalle's lips moved in a silent curse.

Jason emptied his glass.

"Go home, Jason."

"I'm not drunk."

"You soon will be. Go home before you're too drunk to give the right answer when one of my girls comes sashaying up to you. That may be what I do for a living, but I don't want to see a friend full of regrets the day after, especially when I can see that there's only one woman on his mind.

"Chantalle …"

"Go home, sleep it off, and use your head, not that male part of your anatomy that just reacts."

Frowning, Jason drew himself upright. "Are you throwing me out of your house, Chantalle?"

"Yes, for your own good … and for my own good, because I'm your friend."

Jason reached into his pocket, withdrew a few coins, and slapped them down on the bar. He then leaned forward unexpectedly and kissed Chantalle's heavily rouged cheek.

"What was that for?"

"For sending a man home because he's your friend." Jason added unexpectedly, "Tell me something, Chantalle … how did a nice woman like you end up in a place like this?"

Chantalle laughed aloud before responding, "I wasn't always old and fat." She sobered as she concluded, "But I *was* young and stupid, and sometimes there's no turning back. My mistakes still haunt me, and I like you too much to see you suffer the same ailment. So, go home and figure out a better way of handling things."

Jason stared at Chantalle for a silent moment, then started toward the exit. He paused as Georgia met him at the door and said with a pouting smile, "Leaving already, Jason? Goldie didn't do so well with you tonight, so I figured her misfortune might be my gain. Why don't we spend some time together?"

Jason pressed a coin into Georgia's soft palm as he whispered, "Thanks, darlin', but I've got something to do."

Out on the street, Jason breathed deeply to clear his head, and then headed for his horse.

Figure out a better way of handling things.

Good advice.

He was going to take it.

The door closed behind Jason, and Chantalle went briefly still. She then turned toward the poker tables, her expression set as she approached the gray-haired, heavily mustached cowpoke sitting there.

Hiram Charters's expression was composed in the same frown that she had seen on his face earlier in the evening. She glanced at the small stack of chips in front of him and watched as he slid them all toward the pot in the center of the table. She saw his almost imperceptible wince when the cards were turned over and Barney Holt claimed the winnings with a smile.

"Well, I guess that does it for me tonight. If Joe Beal ain't looking for hands at his ranch up north like they say he is, I won't be visiting this place for some time to come." He drew his rangy frame upright as he added with a wink at Chantalle when she walked up beside him, "And that would be a shame, because there are some people here that I would really miss."

Taking his arm as she drew him back toward the bar with her, Chantalle said, "I'm hoping I'd be one of those people you'd miss, Hiram, because I know I'd miss you."

Hiram patted the hand that Chantalle rested on his arm. His eyes held hers as he said more softly, "It's too bad you retired when you took on this place, Chantalle, because you sure know how to make an old man feel mighty fine."

"You're a good customer, Hiram, and you're a nice man."

Halting at the bar, Hiram watched as Chantalle signaled the bartender to fill his glass. He squinted at her assessingly, then said abruptly, "I'm nice and you're damned nice ... so what's going on?"

"Drink up and listen, because I've got a proposition for you."

"You're propositioning me?" He chuckled and downed his drink in a gulp, then said, "This I've got to hear."

"How would you like me to stake you at the table tonight for as long as you want to play?"

"Stake me? Why?"

"I need a favor."

"I hope you ain't going to ask me to kill somebody, because I'm not up to that."

"Not quite." Chantalle smiled. "Did you ever hear of the La Posada ranch?"

"Sure did. That's the ranch that Hawk fella bought a while back. I'm going to pass it on my way up north tomorrow."

"I need somebody to deliver a message to Whit Hawk … somebody I can trust to follow through quietly, without anybody else finding out."

"That would be me, all right, but you don't have to pay me. We're old friends, and I'm going that way anyhow."

"It wouldn't be payment, Hiram. It would be a case of one hand washing the other … like friends do, and it would be my pleasure."

"Well, if you put it that way, it would be my pleasure to help you out, too."

"All right, it's settled then." Signaling the bartender to refill Hiram's glass, Chantalle said, "One more drink, but that's all. I figure you need a clear head if you're going back to the table." When Hiram picked up his glass, Chantalle added, "I'll go and write my letter now, and you just sit yourself down and tell Jake I said to stake you to any reasonable amount you want to play tonight."

"Thank you, Chantalle."

Leaving Hiram with a wink and a smile, Chantalle turned toward her office. Her smile faded when she closed the office door behind her. She walked toward her desk, frowning. Jason had asked her if she had ever heard of Elizabeth Huntington. She hadn't, but the crest he had described on the young woman's pendant sounded exactly like a crest she had seen before. Whit Hawk deserved to know about this young woman. He deserved to see for himself if her crest matched the crest on his ring—the ring that was his only connection to the family he had lost. Whit had traveled all the way back to Galveston to warn her about the possible danger she might be in from one of her own girls. He deserved a similar consideration in return.

Her heart jumping a beat, Chantalle sat down at her desk and started to write.

A sneer twisting her sensuous features, Angie stood up in the darkness of the bordello room and reached for her dress. She turned sharply toward Simon as he said coldly, "Where do you think you're going? I'm not done with you yet."

"You're not, huh?" Angie forced a smile despite her silent anger. The bastard had done it again! He had pretended not to hear her when she had finally asked him to stop. He hadn't stopped until she had *begged*, until she had finally *pleaded* in desperation—and he had then climaxed, uncaring, that she was unsatiated. He was now ready to start all over again. But she wasn't. She needed a chance to compose herself so she could think of a way to beat him at his own game. And she would. She was determined.

Angie continued as she buttoned her dress, "I'm thirsty. I'm going down to the bar to get us a bottle for some refreshment."

"You wouldn't be trying to get away from me, would you, Angie?"

To the almost savage look in Simon's eyes, she replied, "Not a chance. You won the first battle, but you won't win the war."

Angie closed the door behind her to the sound of Simon's laughter. She cursed under her breath as she started down the steps toward the bar. The bastard. A poor substitute, was she? She'd fix him yet.

Standing at the bar a few minutes later, she waited for Jake to retrieve a bottle of his best brandy and the crystal glasses that Simon insisted on. The bastard thought that he—

Angie's thoughts stopped cold when she saw Chantalle enter the poker room from the other direction. She frowned when she saw the madam slip Hiram Charters an envelope that the old man shoved covertly into his pocket as Chantalle left the room. Moments later Hiram cashed in his hand and collected his chips with a smile.

Angie turned back toward Jake as he handed her the bottle and glasses. She said, "It looks like Hiram Charters was a big winner tonight."

Jake's bushy brows knit tight as he said, "What gave you that idea? From what I heard, Hiram's luck was real bad."

"I think you're wrong. He's cashing out a nice pile of chips right now."

"Oh." Jake shrugged. "You know Chantalle. I guess she felt sorry for him and figured out a way so the old fella wouldn't have to go off broke."

"What are you talking about?"

"I heard Chantalle say she'd stake him if he delivered a note to Whit Hawk at the La Posada ranch on his way up north."

"Whit Hawk?"

"You remember him. Chantalle took a shine to him."

Angie frowned, uncertain.

"Chantalle must be in a good mood tonight. First she's buying drinks for that Dodd fella and listening to him talk about some woman named Elizabeth Huntington, and then she's buying drinks for Hiram and offering to stake him if he'll do her a favor."

Elizabeth Huntington. Angie barely suppressed a smile. She knew that name, all right. Simon was obsessed with this Elizabeth woman, whoever she was. He had mumbled her name just before he had climaxed … the bastard!

Angie turned back toward the room where Simon waited.

Elizabeth Huntington and Whit Hawk … Chantalle knew everybody's secrets, and there was no doubt Simon would love to hear about this one.

She had Simon just where she wanted him.

Angie was still smiling an hour later when Simon stormed out of the room.

She counted the gold coins in her hand. Yes, she'd had Simon just where she wanted him.

The sun was rising over the horizon, a great golden sphere that lit the morning sky and the desolate Texas landscape below with bands of brilliant light. Hiram Charters smoothed his gray mustache, adjusted the brim of his hat against the glare of the sun, and nudged his mount to a faster pace along the familiar trail. He had started out before dawn in an attempt to get a head start on the day. It would take him out of his way and put him an hour or so behind to stop at La Posada, but it was a favor he was happy to do for Chantalle, especially in view of the fact that her generosity had allowed him to leave Galveston with a full stomach and his head held high.

Hiram unconsciously patted his shirt pocket, where he carried the envelope that Chantalle had given him. He was flattered that Chantalle trusted him to deliver the letter. He knew she met all types of men in her occupation, but he suspected there were few of them whom she felt she could depend on—which made him feel special. But Chantalle was special to him, too. He figured that if he had been a few years younger and if she hadn't already had an understanding with Captain Joshua Knowles, he might have set his own sights on her. They were both old enough to realize that a person made a few mistakes in life before his first gray hair came in, and he—

A gunshot reverberated loudly in the morning stillness, simultaneous with the blinding bolt of pain that stole Hiram's breath. He rocked backward in the saddle, struggling against the darkness threatening to overwhelm him. He was clutching the reins tightly in a desperate attempt to maintain his seat when the second gunshot hit him.

Hiram struck the ground with a loud crack of sound, but he felt no pain. Stunned, he lay motionless, unable to do anything but stare up at the blue morning sky. Incredulity struck him with the jolt of a third shot—when he realized with his last, fleeting breath that he would never see that blue Texas sky again.

Bruce approached Hiram's motionless body and halted his mount. He dismounted and nudged the old man with his foot to make sure he was dead before he crouched down and removed the letter from his shirt pocket. He then searched the old man, found the roll of bills he was looking for, and shoved them into his own pocket.

Standing above him, Bruce smiled. When the old man was discovered, everyone would believe he had been the victim of a robbery. Chantalle wouldn't realize until it was too late that the letter had not been delivered, and Whit Hawk wouldn't find out about the crest on Elizabeth Huntington's pendant until Simon had already satisfied his need for revenge.

His boss would be pleased.

Bruce looked down at Hiram's lifeless body and sneered, "Too bad you didn't know better than to make a deal with a whore, old man—especially a whore who thinks she's smarter than Simon Gault."

Content to leave Hiram's body to the buzzards, Bruce mounted up and kicked his horse into motion. Dressed as he was in Western gear, he was unrecognizable as Simon Gault's bespectacled clerk, and he was sure that no one would identify him even if he were seen riding away from the scene. He had taken care of his boss's business in the same way that he had done many times before. Hiram Charters had been a fool, but he knew better. There wasn't anybody who could get the best of Simon Gault.

As for himself, he was too smart to even try.

Chapter Seven

Milton Stowe opened the door of the elaborate bordello and stood momentarily in the entrance, amused by the pretension of the establishment. Then it occurred to him that he, of all people, should not find pretension amusing.

Milton paused to remove his hat and stood a moment longer to allow curious glances to get their fill. He was dressed to impress, and he was certain he had achieved the desired effect when there was a buzzing of interest among the whores. Obviously they were choosing who should approach him. He had paid dearly to achieve the effect he sought: that of a northerner with full pockets who was looking to amuse himself.

Milton's smile briefly faltered. It was not as if this job had started out particularly well, either. Sylvia Huntington, for all her arrogance, wasn't as smart as she thought she was. He had gone directly to the Easton Hotel—the address that she had provided for him—only to discover that Elizabeth

Huntington was no longer in residence there. Strangely enough, he wasn't able to obtain any information about where she had gone, except for a comment that she had been picked up bag and baggage by a carriage. Even the old man who worked there, a grouchy fellow named Charlie, had refused to comment when he casually expressed curiosity about the young woman who had caused so much attention at the hotel when she registered there a while back.

Aware that there would be no more information forthcoming, he had simply registered, dropped off his bags, and headed for the waterfront, where he figured Elizabeth would have gone to check on the *Sarah Jane*. He was well aware that she would have stood out like a sore thumb in that kind of an environment, and he had figured the local saloons would be the place to pick up current gossip about her.

Wrong.

All he had learned was that Simon Gault, apparently an important man in the area, had shown an inordinate interest in her. With that failure behind him, Milton had returned to the Easton, had dressed for the part, and had gotten directions to the best bordello in town—which was where he presently was.

A visit to a good bordello had never failed him. He knew that no rumor escaped a competent whore in a place where intimate relationships encouraged both men and women to talk freely, and where a reasonable sum would encourage whores to talk even more freely to him. He knew he would find out, one way or another, where the beauteous Elizabeth Huntington had gone. At the very least, he would spend some enjoyable hours relieving his tension.

Milton glanced again around him. He smiled at the sassy-looking blonde who attempted to approach him before she was pushed aside by a dark-haired young woman. He eyed the whore striding toward him critically. She was a voluptuous young woman with cold blue eyes that spoke her philosophy without the need for words, saying that where money was concerned, there was nothing she'd refuse to do. That intrigued him, even as he reminded himself that business was his primary concern, that his present assignment wasn't going to be as easy as he had thought it would be, and that locating the Huntington woman—despite the brief history Sylvia Huntington had provided when she'd met him with his train tickets—might be only the first hurdle to overcome.

The realization that he would need to familiarize himself with Elizabeth's daily routine in order to make her death appear an accident was another problem. But it must be surmounted if he expected to collect the sum waiting for him when he returned to New York. And he definitely intended to collect it. It had been his dream since first stepping on American soil to become independently wealthy, like so many of his countrymen who had achieved that goal in a more legitimate manner before him. Elizabeth would provide him with the working capital he needed.

"Hello. My name is Angie." The sultry brunette whore interrupted Milton's thoughts as she took his arm and drew him toward the parlor while asking casually, "You're new in town, aren't you?"

"Yes, I am."

"And you're from another country—England would be my guess."

"Right again."

"That's interesting. I've never been out of this country, but I expect to travel someday. I might even set up my own house in a place that tickles my fancy, so you can tell me all about your home while I make you *comfortable*." She winked. "I'm very good at making a man *comfortable*."

Milton smiled as Angie led him toward the bar and said, "But we'll have a drink first so you can tell me just exactly what you have in mind … how I can accommodate you. You'll find that I'm up to just about anything you can think of. As a matter of fact, I enjoy it when one of my male friends comes up with something different for a change. I suppose that's why I'm never bored here."

Milton did not respond as Angie led him up to a large oak bar and leaned intimately close, allowing him an unobstructed view of her cleavage as she said, "Order two of whatever drink you like. As I said, I'm up to anything you have in mind."

Smiling, Milton said just loudly enough so that the other whores could hear, "Two glasses of champagne for Angie and me."

He was going to enjoy this part of his work. Yet he was determined that however good Angie turned out to be, he wouldn't let her interfere with his getting his job done.

It was a given. Elizabeth Huntington was as good as dead.

Simon sat across from Elizabeth in the elegant Seamont Hotel restaurant that they so often frequented. She raised a crystal glass delicately to her mouth, and Simon barely controlled a lustful urge to slap the glass away and bend her to his base desires on the spot. But that was the least of what he had stored up for Elizabeth Hawk. Licentious hours spent with Elizabeth stretched out on the bed underneath him had begun inundating his thoughts with increasing frequency of late. Images of her as his slave, obedient to his slightest sexual whim, begging desperately for him to service her, had begun to nag at him. He was confident his sexual prowess was such that he could make them reality, but it would be different with Elizabeth. With her, he would enjoy the torment even more than the act, with her total humiliation as his goal. When he'd had his fill, he would dispense with her in whatever way appealed to him most.

No, he would not allow a Hawk to best him again.

Forcing himself to glance away in order to restore control, Simon then looked back when Elizabeth said, "I appreciate your thoughtfulness, Simon, but it really wasn't necessary for you to take me to lunch here today. I'm perfectly comfortable preparing my own lunch from the pantry at the Beaufort house, especially since I intend to replace everything I've used when I'm ready to leave. It's true that I haven't learned anything about the crest on my pendant yet, but I still have several gentlemen to talk to on the list you provided, so you needn't worry that my search is stalled."

Simon smiled benevolently as angry heat boiled inside him. *Hypocrite!* She thought she was so clever! She pretended not to want to be beholden to anyone, while making the most of every situation presented to her. She *intended* repayment— but what she did not expect was that she herself would be partial payment of a debt that had been owed to him for more years than he cared to count.

It galled him to admit, however, that he was making very little progress toward his goal at present. The unexpected entrance of Jason Dodd onto the scene had complicated matters more than he had anticipated. Taunted by the thought that Elizabeth had allowed Dodd into her room and most probably into her bed that first night at the Beaufort mansion, he had decided that it was time for desperate measures.

Simon's smile faded as he said slowly, "I'm afraid I have difficult news to tell you today, Elizabeth." At her frown, he went on. "Not about your pendant. Unfortunately, I don't have anything to report about it. However, I did get a letter from Adeline Beaufort this morning. She expects to return to Galveston sooner than expected—by the end of the week. She's bringing several guests with her, and she'll be needing the spare bedrooms to accommodate them."

"Oh … I'll leave the house immediately, of course."

"I'm so sorry. Adeline gave no indication that this trip up north would be any different from her previous trips. I had no way of knowing that her plans would change."

"Don't concern yourself, Simon. I'll … I'll pack up my things and go back to my room at the Easton."

"You'll do no such thing! The Easton is no place for a young woman like you."

"It's fine, and it's affordable."

"Nonsense. I won't hear of it. I have several guest rooms in my home. You can move your things into one of them right after lunch today. My driver will help you."

"No, thank you very much, but I couldn't."

"You're concerned about convention, of course." Simon's benevolent smile returned. "I have a housekeeper who has functioned as a chaperone for me in the past. The circumstances will be perfectly respectable."

"The thought that it might be otherwise never crossed my mind, Simon."

Inwardly insulted by her response, Simon replied, "I'll tell Horace to drive you to the Beaufort house and wait until you pack. Then he'll—"

"No, Simon, please … I can't accept your offer."

"What do you mean, you can't?" Barely controlling his rising anger, Simon replied, "It's the only sensible solution until you've satisfied yourself that you've found out as much as possible about the origin of your crest."

"I can't invade your privacy in that way."

"It's my pleasure, Elizabeth."

"If I move into your guest room, it's as much as saying I'm allowing my problems to become yours."

"That's not true; but even if it were, I wouldn't mind."

"You're too generous, Simon."

"I'm practical. Your funds are short—by your own proclamation—and the Easton Hotel isn't a favorable atmosphere for a young woman like yourself."

"I'll manage at the Easton, just as I did before."

"I couldn't rest knowing that you're merely *managing* when you could be perfectly comfortable in my home while you're in Galveston."

"Simon ..."

Simon allowed distress to touch his features as he said more softly, "Elizabeth, it isn't that you don't trust me, is it? I hope I've proved by my actions that anything detrimental Jason Dodd may have said about me is untrue."

Noting that Elizabeth was momentarily at a loss as to how to respond to his direct approach, Simon inwardly smiled. He had her where he wanted her, yet he couldn't afford to press her on that point. He'd allow her a little time to decide. She'd come around, and when she was properly installed in a bedroom in his house, intimacy would seem more natural. He'd make his move then, and however she reacted, she wouldn't be able to escape him.

Simon noted Elizabeth's relief when he said, "You don't have to decide right now. Think about it. I know you'll do the right thing. Now ..." Simon picked up the menu. "What shall we have for lunch?"

Jason took the stairs up to the second floor of Chantalle's fancy house two at a time. The sun had begun its descent past its apex when a messenger reached him at Sam Johnson's office to tell him that Chantalle wanted to talk to him.

Sam's wiry brows had shot upward a notch at the message the boy brought from the infamous madam.

Ignoring Sam's amusement, Jason had nodded and sent the boy on his way. He had then told Sam without further explanation that he'd return the following morning to finish their conversation. Out on the street within minutes, he had headed directly for the bordello.

Contrary to Sam's obvious reaction, Jason knew Chantalle's summons had nothing to do with the business of her house. He knew that her summons meant she had something important to tell him.

Jason paused to catch his breath as he stood before Chantalle's office door. He knocked sharply, frowning as he pushed open the door at her response. Chantalle stood up when he entered the room and closed the door behind him. The fact that she wasn't smiling confirmed his thoughts. "You wanted to talk to me, Chantalle?"

"Yes. I'm not sure what to make of all this, but the one thing I was relatively sure of was that you would want to be told right away." Chantalle continued, "We had a visit last night from a customer who's new to the city. I tend to dismiss Angie's bragging, for the most part, and I suppose I would've dismissed what she had to say a few hours ago if she hadn't mentioned the name Elizabeth Huntington."

Jason was instantly alert. "What does Elizabeth have to do with your new customer?"

"I don't really know." Chantalle's finely shaped brows drew into a frown. "Angie said this new fellow called himself Milton. He came in dressed up like a gentleman with a pocketful of money. She said he didn't look like much without the fancy duds that he was wearing, though, and she found out after a while that he was no gentleman—but that pocketful of money was real. She said he flashed his money pouch when he started asking questions about a woman named Elizabeth Huntington whom he was looking for. Angie said she played along, squeezing as much as she could out of him before telling him that Simon Gault's driver—another 'close friend' of Angie's—had told her Simon had moved a young woman named Elizabeth Huntington into the Beaufort mansion while Adeline Beaufort was away. She said she tested Milton by saying she could send somebody to tell Elizabeth that he was looking for her if he wanted her to, but he said that wasn't necessary. Angie said she raised her eyebrows at that, and Milton paid her a little extra not to discuss their conversation with anybody else—money wasted, I might add."

"This Milton fella ... what did he look like?"

"Angie said he was small, not much to him without that suit coat with the padded shoulders that he was wearing. She said he had more hair in his eyebrows than he had on his head, and that he had a funny English accent."

"He doesn't sound familiar."

"Angie said there was something strange about the way this Milton fella acted, and since you were upset about Elizabeth Huntington the last time we talked, I figured you'd want to know. I realize this fella couldn't have anything to do with Simon Gault or he would've known where Elizabeth was staying, which only made everything more confusing."

"You say he paid Angie not to let anyone know he was looking for Elizabeth?"

Chantalle nodded. "Who could he be, and why is he looking for her? If Elizabeth is as young and inexperienced as you say, why would someone like this Milton person travel to Galveston to find her?"

"I don't know."

Chantalle walked closer. Halting only a few feet away, she stared intently into Jason's eyes and asked, "Do you care about this young woman, Jason ... or did I make a mistake by calling you here?"

Jason hesitated briefly. Faced outright with that question for the first time, he responded gruffly, "You didn't make a mistake."

"Jason ..."

"I don't know what's going on, but one thing's for damned sure. I'm going to find out."

"And then?"

Momentarily silent, Jason finally responded, "I'll do what I need to do."

"You'll take care of it, huh?"

"I damned well will. You can depend on it."

Chantalle smiled. "I believe you." She added as Jason turned toward the door, "By the way, one of the other girls said you told her a while back that you were interested in talking to a fella named Captain Rudolph Winters."

Jason looked at her. "Do you know everything that goes on in this house?"

Ignoring his question, Chantalle responded, "One of my regulars mentioned that Captain Winters's ship docked in Galveston the day before last."

"Thanks."

"Jason ..."

Impatient, Jason turned back toward Chantalle again, only to see concern tighten her features as she added, "Be careful, you hear?"

But Chantalle's admonition was far from his mind as Jason drew the bordello door closed behind him.

Feeling shaken, Elizabeth stepped down from her rental carriage in front of the Easton Hotel and paid the driver. She had dismissed Simon's offer to drive her to her destination after lunch with the excuse that she wanted to walk for a bit, but that was far from the truth. She was so confused. Simon had been considerate of her from the first moment he'd met her. He had done nothing outright to stir her suspicion, and he had now generously offered her a room in his home for the duration of her stay in Galveston. It disturbed her that Jason's warnings about Simon had echoed in her mind throughout their conversation.

The evening when Jason pushed his way into the Beaufort mansion after discovering her true reason for coming to Galveston returned without warning to Elizabeth's mind. She recalled how she had been drawn to him despite her anger at his intrusion. She remembered how the sight of him had touched a confusing awareness inside her, how it had tied her stomach into knots of emotion, and how close she'd come to believing everything he'd said about Simon. She recollected how difficult it had been to keep Jason at a distance, how she had struggled against the intensity in his dark eyes, how narrowly she had escaped the temptation to yield to the unspoken hunger she sensed in him, and how she had barely resisted her growing certainty that Jason's touch would be magic against her skin, and that his kiss would be—

Elizabeth halted her thoughts abruptly. She couldn't allow her uncertainties to persist. Nor could she let a personal weakness affect the outcome of her investigation into the mystery of her past—a mystery that she felt a driving need to solve. She needed to talk to someone she could trust; she needed someone to tell her which of these men was speaking the truth. There was only one person in Galveston who fit that description.

Hesitating only a moment longer, Elizabeth entered the lobby of the Easton Hotel. All eyes turned in her direction, and she felt a familiar heat rise to her cheeks. She had forgotten how shabby the interior of the building looked, how the men milling there would follow her with their gazes, how the inevitable group at the bar would make no attempt to hide the fact that they were discussing her while she approached the registration desk.

Elizabeth went momentarily silent as the short clerk behind the counter looked up at her and said gruffly, "What do you want?"

She replied with a hint of hauteur, "You're not as courteous as the fellow who previously worked behind this desk."

"Yeah, well, he quit and I'm the desk clerk now." He paused to eye her skeptically from head to toe before saying, "This ain't the kind of place that caters to women like you, lady. What are you looking for here?"

Uncertain whether to take his comment as an insult or a compliment, Elizabeth replied, "I'm looking for Charlie."

"Charlie. You mean Charlie Dettweiler?"

"I mean Charlie, the older fellow who works here."

"What do you want him for?"

"That really isn't your concern, is it? If you don't mind, just tell him I'm here."

"That ain't necessary." Elizabeth turned at the sound of the familiar gruff voice. She blinked back the spontaneous tears that sprang to her eyes at the sight of the old man who stood behind her.

She swallowed tightly when he asked, "What are you doing here? I thought you was out of this place for good."

"I came back to talk to you, Charlie." She glanced around her. "Is there someplace where we can speak more privately?"

Turning toward the frowning desk clerk, Charlie said abruptly, "This lady and I are going into the storage room to talk for a few minutes, so hold your horses if you need me for anything, understand?"

Surprisingly, the desk clerk nodded, but Elizabeth could feel his eyes boring into her back as they entered the back room and Charlie closed the door behind them.

Turning toward her, Charlie said, "All right, spit it out. What's wrong?"

Her frustration spilling out in a spontaneous flow, Elizabeth told him about Simon's generosity, how he was helping her investigate the circumstances behind her pendant, about his most recent offer of a room in his spacious residence—and about his warnings concerning Jason. She hesitated, then recounted her experiences with Jason, his harsh manner at their meeting, the unflattering conclusions he had drawn about her, his attempt to redeem himself, and his persistent warnings about Simon that mirrored the same accusations Simon made against him. She concluded by stating flatly, "I don't know whom to believe, Charlie."

It occurred to Elizabeth as she waited for Charlie's reply that the old man standing opposite her looked no different from the other scruffy fellows in the lobby, with his wrinkled clothing, his sparse, uncombed white hair, and his rounded shoulders. Yet there was something about him, the way his gruffness was tempered with concern, as if he had only her best interests at heart, that made her tell him, "I need you to help me sort this out."

Silent for long moments, Charlie said abruptly, "Sit down before you fall down." Waiting until she was settled on one of the boxes nearby, he sat as well and said, "I ain't going to lie to you. I don't know either Simon Gault or that Jason Dodd fella very well, but talk around here is that Jason Dodd is a hardcase. Talk is, he don't give an inch in what he believes in, but that he's fair and honest, too, even if he ain't the most forgiving man in the world."

"Meaning?"

"Meaning Dodd don't forget a wrong when it's done him or somebody close to him. His shipping partner was killed during the blockade, and he don't bother to hide the fact that he thinks Simon Gault was responsible in some way. I don't know if that's true, mind you, but Dodd is convinced it is, and some say he ain't the type to give up. He's well thought of in Galveston by them shipping fellas, though—that consortium that runs the city. Folks say them fellas respect what he did during the blockade, what with furnishing supplies to people around here who didn't have the money to pay for them. They close their eyes to a lot of things because of that, including Dodd's open friendship with Chantalle Beauchamp."

"Chantalle Beauchamp … the madam."

"You heard of her, have you?"

Elizabeth's expression said it all.

"So you know she runs the most honest bordello in Galveston."

"If there is such a place."

"What do you mean?"

"An *honest* bordello."

Ignoring her reply, Charlie pressed, "About Simon Gault … I ain't had any contact with him myself, mind you, but I've heard stories."

"Stories?"

"Meaning gossip, I guess. Gault's well respected in the city, too, and he's as much a part of the social scene as Dodd could be if he wanted. Gault hobnobs with all them consortium fellas, what with inviting them to the big parties he throws and all. But there are some who say he ain't to be trusted. I've also heard talk about his dealings with Chantalle Beauchamp."

Elizabeth gasped. "Simon is friendly with the Beauchamp woman, too?"

"I don't think they're friendly. I think it's strictly business."

"Business?"

Flushing unexpectedly, Charlie said, "There are things that a man does … Well, I can't say no more. I suppose the only person who knows the truth of whether Gault has a special room at Chantalle's is Chantalle herself. Then there's that Captain Winters, who captained one of Gault's ships during the blockade. He seemed to have plenty to say after he

quit working for Gault and shipped out on the
Silver Dawn a while back. Talk is, Winters's ship
arrived back in Galveston, but that's all it might
be … just talk. All I can tell you for sure is that I'd
be careful about Simon Gault."

"Careful …"

"As for that Jason Dodd, folks say he's straight as
an arrow, even if he sometimes causes sparks along
the way."

Silent for a few moments, Elizabeth drew herself
to her feet and said, "Thanks, Charlie."

"I wish I could tell you more things for certain."

"You've said enough. I guess the rest is up to me."

Succumbing to impulse, Elizabeth kissed Charlie's wrinkled cheek and repeated, "Thanks."

Out on the street minutes later, Elizabeth knew
she had no choice in what she must do.

Chantalle looked up at the sound of a knock on
her door. She responded to find Angie standing in
the doorway with a hand on her hip and a half
smile on her face.

"You have to come downstairs to see this," Angie
announced.

Chantalle walked down the staircase behind the
jaded brunette, then went stock-still when she saw
the young woman standing uncomfortably in the
entry hall of the bordello. The visitor was conservatively dressed, with gold-streaked brown hair, intense hazel eyes, and a sober expression. Chantalle
remembered glimpsing her briefly once before. It
was Elizabeth Huntington.

Noting that several men from the inner room had started filtering out toward the foyer and that they were looking at Elizabeth with undue interest, Chantalle hastened her step. She dismissed them with a stern glance when she reached the foot of the stairs, then turned toward Elizabeth and said, "As you can see, you're causing quite a stir here, Miss Huntington, so I suggest we go upstairs to my office if you wish to speak to me privately."

Chantalle turned and started up the staircase without waiting for Elizabeth's assent, but she listened intently for the sound of the young woman's light step following behind. Halting only when she reached her office, Chantalle pushed open the door and ushered Elizabeth inside with a courteous, "Please sit down."

Elizabeth complied, then asked unexpectedly, "I didn't give my name to the woman who answered the door. How did you know who I am?"

Chantalle replied, "Who else could you be?"

"I don't understand."

"I saw you briefly once before in the lobby of the Seamont Hotel, but I confess I might not have recognized you if I hadn't made it my business to learn more about you."

"Why should you want to know more about me?"

"We share mutual acquaintances. I know that seems unlikely, considering your recent arrival in Galveston and my … occupation, but it's true."

Elizabeth Huntington's fair complexion colored revealingly at Chantalle's comment, allowing Chantalle to study her youthful beauty for a silent moment longer. Yes, Elizabeth Huntington was truly lovely, with her faultless features, her creamy complexion, and magnificent coloring. And she was a lady—it was obvious from her polite, proper manner despite their unusual circumstances. Chantalle could appreciate Jason's attraction to her, as well as understand Simon's lecherous intent. What she could not understand was why a mysterious fellow named Milton would pay Angie not to mention that he was looking for the young woman.

Deciding it was more prudent not to mention that fact while Jason was looking into the situation, Chantalle began cautiously, "Tell me how I may help you, Miss Huntington."

Elizabeth replied unexpectedly, "I'd be pleased to have you call me Elizabeth, if I may call you Chantalle."

"Agreed. I repeat … how may I help you?"

Frowning, Elizabeth began hesitantly, "I … I find myself in a difficult position, Chantalle. As you know, I'm new to the city."

"Yes, you came here to see if you could discover the origin of the crest on the pendant you wear— so you might find any remaining members of your family—although you're uncertain of the family names they might be using."

Aghast, Elizabeth asked, "How do you know all that?"

"I have my sources. So I'll ask again, how do you think I'll be able to help you?"

"I didn't come to you to talk about my search for my family." Elizabeth took a breath and then said flatly, "I've been advised by a friend that you are the only person who may know the truth about certain matters."

Chantalle frowned. "The truth?"

"About who … about whether I may trust—"

"If you expect me to tell you anything personal about my clients, I'm afraid I can't help you."

"I'm not asking for personal information, Chantalle. I'd just like to know what you think of those two acquaintances we seem to have in common."

"To avoid any misunderstanding, shall we use their names?"

Elizabeth took a breath. "Simon Gault and Jason Dodd."

"I see." Chantalle's frown darkened. "I know them both. Simon Gault's association with me isn't a very well kept secret in Galveston. His patronage of my house goes unacknowledged but is silently accepted by most, including the gentlemen in power in Galveston."

"So my friend explained."

Chantalle raised her carefully maintained eyebrows questioningly. She noted the desperation that entered Elizabeth's expression as the other woman went on.

"I need to know which of those two men I can trust to be truthful with me."

"And you expect me to tell you?"

"They each accuse the other of the same past crimes and personal deficiencies."

"What past crimes?"

"Collaboration with the Yankees during the blockade."

"And deficiencies?"

"Lying to me, for one."

"I've never known Jason to lie in the past. He wouldn't bother. As far as he's concerned, either you accept him as he is, or you don't."

"But Simon does lie in order to be accepted?"

"I didn't say that." Chantalle continued hesitantly, "Actually, I don't know Simon as well as I know Jason. You may take that however you like, but the truth is that my dealings with the two men are quite different."

"I understand you have … special arrangements with Simon."

"You don't really expect me to confirm or deny that, do you?"

"I was hoping you would."

"Well, you were wrong." Despising her need to keep silent about Simon's perversions, Chantalle continued, "I can tell you this. I do business with both men, but I consider Jason a personal friend. I would trust him with my life. It's up to you whatever conclusions you choose to draw from that statement."

"I was hoping that—"

"I'm sorry. That's all I can say."

Chantalle felt Elizabeth's scrutiny intensify briefly before she said, "Strangely enough, I think I understand your position, Chantalle. Thank you for being as honest as you can be with me." She hesitated a moment longer before saying, "And I

191

feel the need to apologize to you. I realize now that some of the prejudices I had against you were unfair. You're not what I expected."

"I wouldn't be so quick to make that statement."

"Well, first impressions can be deceiving."

"You mean by that, of course, the outrageous color of my hair and my rather unseemly style of dress. I'm sure you realize that a middle-aged woman in my position needs to maintain a certain image. She also needs to have matured past the image she projects if she expects to function efficiently—but you seem to recognize that, also. Truthfully, I didn't expect so much insight in a proper young woman, either."

Elizabeth shrugged. "I seem to be learning fast."

Chantalle said unexpectedly, "I wish I could have been more help to you."

Elizabeth continued her scrutiny of Chantalle for long moments before she said, "I don't think I'd be betraying a confidence.... But perhaps you know already that Jason also considers you a friend. That bothered me at first, but I can see now why he feels that way."

"I appreciate that." Aware that she had said all that she dared to say, Chantalle stood up and said by way of dismissal, "I don't suppose there is much left for us to discuss at this point, so I'll accompany you to the door."

Chantalle did not speak again until she drew the front door open and extended her hand to say, "I'm truly pleased to have met you, Elizabeth." Holding Elizabeth's hand a few seconds longer than necessary, she added in a softer tone, "Galveston is a lovely city, but it's recuperating from difficult times. You would do well to remember that and to keep in mind that people are not always what they appear to be."

Noting that two men with revealing gleams in their eyes had started toward them from the bar area, Chantalle added, "You should go now."

Chantalle waited only until Elizabeth stepped out onto the front staircase before closing the door firmly behind her. She then turned with a professional smile toward the men approaching her.

Jason frowned up at the great, golden globe of the sun as it began dropping toward the glittering sea. He had spent the afternoon attempting to find Elizabeth so he might discover why a mysterious fellow who was unwilling to tell anyone his last name would travel to Galveston specifically to find her—and why that fellow would pay a whore to keep that secret if he didn't have something to hide. He had gone to the Beaufort mansion, only to be told by a haughty Frieda that the mistress was not at home. He had then gone to the Seamont Hotel with the thought that he might find her dining there with Gault, only to be informed that they had left hours earlier. He had walked the Strand, hoping that he might find Elizabeth shopping there, but that effort had also been a waste of time.

Stumped and frustrated, he had decided to wait until evening. Elizabeth was sure to return to the

Beaufort mansion then, and he would make her listen to what he had to say.

Jason looked up again at the sun, then at the *Silver Dawn*, which lay at anchor in the harbor. Apparently Chantalle's information was correct. Captain Winters was back in port. He needed to talk to the man before he shipped out again. The death of the only sailor rumored to be willing to speak out about Gault's collaboration with the Yankees had brought an end to any cooperation Jason might otherwise have received from seamen in a similar position.

He had learned too late that Captain Winters, who was then on an extended voyage for Williams Shipping, was rumored to have left Gault's employ rather than cooperate with his employer's underhanded activities during the blockade. Jason had waited a long time for Captain Winters to return to Galveston. He could only hope the man hadn't had a change of heart in the time between. He also realized with some satisfaction that proving Gault's collaboration would strengthen the credibility of everything else he had told Elizabeth about the man.

With that thought in mind, Jason quickened his step as he approached the tall ship rocking gently at its mooring. The lack of activity on board indicated that most of the hands had gone ashore for the evening, but he knew no self-respecting captain would leave his ship totally unmanned. For that reason he was also fairly certain that Captain

Winters would be found hard at work—most likely on his shipping manifest in his cabin.

Jason's footsteps echoed hollowly against the gangplank as he boarded the ship. With no one on deck, he started down the stairs toward the captain's cabin, calling out as he did, "Captain Winters? Are you aboard?"

When there was no response, he knocked at the door and called out again, "Captain Winters?"

Jason pushed open the door to the cabin and walked inside. He halted briefly to allow his eyes to adjust to the shadowy interior, which was dimly lit by a single candle, then approached the desk. Captain Winters sat slumped forward onto its cluttered surface.

"Captain Winters—"

Jason stopped still when he saw the knife protruding from Captain Winters's back.

Jason strode closer with a hope that was quickly dashed when he saw that the gray-haired captain wasn't breathing.

Turning sharply at a sound in the corner of the room, he squinted into the darkening shadows, then muttered a startled epithet when Elizabeth stepped into view.

Her hands covered with blood, Elizabeth walked a few steps toward him and collapsed into his arms.

"Elizabeth, take a deep breath. That's right; take another one."

Responding automatically to Jason's softly spoken

commands, Elizabeth struggled to catch her breath in the darkening shadows of the cabin. Dazed, she looked up at Jason as he supported her sagging frame. She had come to see Captain Winters, the man Charlie had suggested could either confirm or refute Jason's claim that Simon had collaborated with the Yankees during the blockade. She had wasted valuable time searching for the ship, but had come aboard determined not to leave without uncovering the truth. She hadn't expected …

Feeling light-headed, Elizabeth swayed.

"Elizabeth, breathe deeply." Jason stripped his neckerchief from around his throat and said softly, "Wipe your hands. They're covered with blood. Tell me what happened here."

Hardly able to respond, Elizabeth muttered, "He's dead. Somebody killed him."

Jason repeated, "What are you doing here?"

"I tried to stop the bleeding, but it was too late. Then I heard somebody coming and I hid. I thought the killer had come back, but it was you." Elizabeth shivered as she looked up into Jason's eyes and whispered, "Why would someone kill him, Jason?"

Elizabeth felt the full heat of Jason's gaze as he said, "Winters was a naval war hero of sorts in these parts. Some people might think a Yankee woman who recently came to Galveston asking a lot of questions killed him because he was responsible for sending a few Yankee ships to the bottom of the sea."

"A Yankee woman." Elizabeth gasped. "You don't mean me!"

Snatching the bloodstained neckerchief from her hands, Jason tossed it aside and said, "I said *some* people might think that, especially if they had seen you with Captain Winters's blood on your hands."

"But you don't believe it, do you?"

"No, I think there's more to this than meets the eye. But I also think it wouldn't be wise for either of us to be found here right now."

"But—"

"We don't have time to talk, Elizabeth. We have to get out of here."

"We haven't done anything!"

"Elizabeth, listen to me!" Holding her so she would see the urgency in his expression, Jason said, "No one knows you in Galveston. No one can speak for your character. As far as anyone knows, you're a newly arrived Yankee with an implausible reason for coming to Galveston."

"My reason isn't implausible, and I'm not a Yankee. I'm …" Elizabeth felt her face drain of color as her denial trailed to a halt. She began again slowly, "Maybe you're right. Maybe I am a Yankee. I don't know for sure, but I do know that I didn't kill Captain Winters, and that you didn't either."

Jason countered tightly, "You're sure I didn't kill him? Maybe I did. Maybe I just came back to the cabin for some reason and—"

"You didn't kill him any more than I did! I'd be sure of that even if I hadn't been here when you arrived."

"All right, so I didn't kill him. But he's dead, Elizabeth, and you had his blood on your hands."

"I told you, I tried to help him, but he was already dead."

"However it happened, we need to get out of here while we still can. We can talk later."

"But Simon …"

Jason went still. "What about him? Either you trust Simon or you trust me. You can't have it both ways."

Jason's dark eyes mesmerized her. Yet it was the almost indefinable spark that Elizabeth saw in their depths that made her catch her breath. "Let's go," she responded hoarsely.

Concealed in the dockside shadows, Bruce watched as Jason and Elizabeth moved stealthily down the *Silver Dawn* gangplank and slipped from sight. He smiled with genuine amusement. He had accomplished his job efficiently, as usual. The common seaman's attire that he wore had allowed him to walk the dock unnoticed, and to lounge where he could watch the crewmen of the *Silver Dawn* exit the ship for a night's revelry ashore. Relatively certain the captain was alone, he had then boarded the ship and had gone to the captain's cabin with the pretense of looking for work. He had waited only for an excuse to move behind the unsuspecting captain before serving him his fate.

Bruce pondered that moment in retrospect. *Practice made perfect.* He had known the second the knife entered Captain Winters's back that he had struck a lethal blow. He had become adept at sensing those things.

He had stepped down onto the dock afterward to see Elizabeth Huntington in the distance. She had been walking toward the ship, but she hadn't given him a second glance. Curious what her reaction to the discovery of Captain Winters's body would be, he had stolen into the shadows after she passed him and had waited … and waited.

He had drawn back farther into the semidarkness when Jason Dodd appeared unexpectedly on the dock, heading for the *Silver Dawn* as well. He hadn't needed to wait long for Dodd's reaction.

It amused Bruce that Elizabeth Huntington and Dodd had obviously hoped to leave the area unseen. He suspected their effort was wasted. Unlike himself, who faded so easily into his surroundings, a woman like Elizabeth Huntington would never go unnoticed.

Bruce stood up and started in the opposite direction from the one Dodd and Elizabeth had taken. He was going to enjoy reporting back to Simon that he had reached the ship in time, and that he had made sure Captain Winters wouldn't ever speak out against him.

Bruce knew, however, that he would enjoy even more thoroughly the moment when he told Simon that Dodd had taken his precious Elizabeth away.

Chapter Eight

Elizabeth could not seem to still the racing of her heart as she followed the lead of Jason's horse through the spiked cordgrass. The salt marsh covering the isolated far end of Galveston Island shone with a silver hue under the full moon lighting their way. The silence was eerie, broken only by the buzzing of insects, the sounds of wildlife scurrying in the shadows, the occasional frantic fluttering of wings that indicated a night prowler was closing in on its prey, and the sound of their own horses' hooves echoing in the stillness.

Elizabeth attempted to control her shuddering. Her discovery of Captain Winters's lifeless body in his ship's cabin a few hours earlier had stunned her. She had been frozen with shock when Jason arrived unexpectedly shortly afterward and found her with her hands covered with the poor man's blood. A chill passed down her spine at the realization that traces of Captain Winters's blood still stained her hands, and that had it not been for

Jason, she might have stood there, unable to move, until the captain's body was finally discovered. She recalled that she had been somehow certain the moment that Jason turned toward her that she was safe and all would be well. She had not anticipated, however, his straightforward questions and his sober admonition that they needed to leave without being seen.

She had questioned that decision only briefly. The look in Jason's eyes had forestalled further dissent, and she had followed him blindly. Now, she still followed him blindly toward the remote section of the island where Jason had indicated they would be able to remain safely for the night without anyone finding them until he could learn more about what had happened.

Another chill raced down Elizabeth's spine. She sensed that Jason was more concerned about her safety than he was about his own. And she wondered why.

Jason turned toward her as the outline of a cabin became discernible. She waited as he motioned for her to move into the shadows, then continued toward the cabin on his own. Her breathing grew ragged when he disappeared through the cabin doorway.

Elizabeth waited, her heart pounding as she glanced nervously at the surrounding marshland and beach. Her anxious gaze became fixed on the cattails swaying in the gentle night breeze. She felt the stirring of memory, of cattails glowing in the darkness, sending a shimmering light across the sand that chased away the shadows threatening to engulf her. She heard a familiar voice echoing....

Fear is an enemy. Don't let it win.

Elizabeth released a breath that she did not realize she had been holding when Jason stepped back into sight from within the cabin and motioned her forward. His shoulders broad, his expression dark under the brim of his hat, he swept her down from the saddle the moment she reached him and slid an arm around her waist as he said softly, "I figured this cabin would be vacant. I discovered this place when I grazed my cattle briefly on the long western portion of the island, but on this far end, the grass is too coarse even for cattle, so it's practically uninhabited. Nobody knew about this place, and I occasionally enjoyed the solitude. No one will look for us here."

"Jason ... I don't understand. Why are we hiding?"

Jason's dark eyes pinned her. "Because there are too many questions that don't have answers."

When Elizabeth was obviously at a loss for a reply, Jason said, "I'm going to hobble the horses around back. In the meantime, why don't you go inside and see what you can do with the supplies in the saddlebags? It won't take me long."

Puzzled, Elizabeth nodded and turned toward the cabin. She was momentarily taken aback when she entered. She saw a crude fireplace, a table and two chairs, a bunk in the corner, and over a dry sink, a cabinet that was obviously built to hold supplies. The cabin, lit by a single lantern, appeared to be relatively clean of the debris she had expected, almost as if someone maintained it on a regular basis.

Jason's deep voice turned her toward him as he placed a bucket of water on the table and said, "I figured you'd want to wash your hands." When Elizabeth looked at her hands and took a shuddering breath, he drew her toward the dry sink and poured some of the water into a basin there. Silent as she washed her hands with a scented bar of soap and dried them on a clean towel, he continued, "Chantalle knows about this place, but nobody else does, so I figure it's safe."

Surprised, Elizabeth responded, "Chantalle knows about this cabin?"

"Which I suppose is the reason it looks as neat as it does. I told her about it, and she uses it when she wants to get away from her business for a while."

"You like her, don't you?"

"Yes, I do."

Elizabeth heard herself respond, "I do, too."

At his surprised reaction, Elizabeth related a brief account of her meeting with Chantalle, to which he responded sharply, "You shouldn't have gone there."

"You go there."

"That's different."

"Why is it different? Chantalle owns the place, and you like her."

"Chantalle can handle herself and the men who go there."

"I can, too."

Jason gripped her arms and said with tightly controlled anger, "Listen to me, Elizabeth. I didn't bring you here to discuss Chantalle, but since we are discussing her, let's get some things clear. By her own admission, Chantalle made a lot of mistakes that finally landed her where she is now. She's doing her best to live with her mistakes and go on from there. I admire her for a lot of things, but that doesn't mean I approve of her lifestyle."

"She considers you her friend."

"I *am* her friend, which is why she—" Jason halted abruptly, then, changing the subject unexpectedly, asked, "Do you know a man named Milton—a short, thin fella with bushy eyebrows and thin, graying hair? He has an English accent of some kind."

Elizabeth took a spontaneous backward step at Jason's sudden intensity. She shook her head. "No, should I?"

"Think about it. Could you have met him in New York, or on the way here? Maybe it was only a passing contact."

"No, I'm sure I didn't. I would have remembered an English accent if I had heard one. Why do you ask?"

"This Milton fella arrived in Galveston just recently—probably on yesterday's train. He's looking for you. He asked one of Chantalle's women if she knew where he could find you, and then paid her to keep quiet about it."

"Who told you that?"

"Who do you think?"

"Why didn't Chantalle tell me?"

"I told her I'd take care of it, and she trusts me to do that. She probably didn't want to panic you in the meantime. What she didn't know was that I'd find you in Captain Winters's cabin with blood on your hands."

"But ... what does it all mean?"

"That's what I need to find out before anybody makes another move."

Paling, Elizabeth suddenly clutched the pendant concealed underneath the bodice of her dress. She said breathlessly, "You don't suppose that Milton man knows about my pendant ... that he's connected with my family somehow ... that he has a grudge against them that I should know about?"

Jason's strong features went still. "I don't know, but that's why I wanted to get you out of the city until we have some time to think this over." He added, "I also think it's about time you showed me your pendant—that is, if you finally trust me enough."

The absurdity of the situation suddenly struck Elizabeth. In the space of an incredibly short time— less than a fortnight—she had run the gamut from despising this man to being comfortable with the knowledge that her life was in his hands—and she wasn't sure how or why it had happened. All she knew was that she did trust him. When his arms had gone around her in the captain's cabin, she had known instinctively that she was safe, and she had warmed to his touch in a way she had never felt before.

But she also knew that she could not afford to

allow emotion to interfere when the direction of both their lives presently appeared so uncertain. She replied simply, "Of course I trust you." She tugged at the chain around her neck and withdrew the pendant that had lain hidden against her skin. She added softly, "The truth is, in my heart, I suppose I always did."

Jason stepped closer to Elizabeth so he could study the pendant. He attempted to ignore the words she had added so quietly because of the tumult they raised inside him. He took the pendant into his palm to study it more closely. It was still warm from lying against her breast, and he resisted the inclination to close his hand around that intimate heat. Struggling with control, he noted that the pendant was delicately wrought, with a sailing ship on a whitecapped sea. He frowned at the words engraved there.

As if reading his mind, Elizabeth offered, "The Latin words mean, 'To four I give the world.' I don't know what the rest symbolizes. I was hoping someone in Galveston might be able to tell me."

"What brought you to Galveston in particular?"

"The name of the ship, *Sarah Jane*. It's written on the bow in letters so small that you can barely read them without a magnifying glass. I researched that name, and a ship christened the *Sarah Jane* shipped out of Galveston years ago. My adoptive parents found me in Texas, so Galveston seemed the best place to start finding out more about a past I can't remember."

Jason searched Elizabeth's face. Her color had paled even further while she spoke about the pendant. He longed to comfort her, to tell her all would be well because he'd make it well. Instead, he questioned softly, "Why is it so important to you to find out about your past, Elizabeth? Your past is exactly that—past. In light of what's been happening, maybe it's best that you can't remember it."

"You wouldn't say that if you knew what it was like to feel somewhere deep inside that something was missing from your life ... that maybe somebody was waiting for you somewhere, someone feeling the same sense of loss. And ... there are other things that I need to understand, things I can settle only by discovering more about who I am and where I really came from."

"What other things?"

"Nothing ... nothing." Elizabeth looked away to avoid his scrutiny, then turned back abruptly, emotion coloring her face as she said, "What are we going to do now, Jason? We can't hide here forever, waiting for something to happen."

Gripping her arms gently, Jason responded, "We're going to wait until it's safe to go back into the city, and then we're going to find out why Captain Winters was killed before either of us could talk to him about Gault, and why this Milton fella is trying to find you."

Elizabeth went rigidly still. "You're not thinking that Simon could have had anything to do with Captain Winters's death? Simon is one of Galveston's most upstanding citizens."

"If you believe that, why did you want to talk to Captain Winters?"

"Because a friend suggested that he might be able to tell me …" Going silent when she realized the contradiction in her intended reply, Elizabeth said, "But surely Simon's collaboration with the Yankees during the blockade isn't reason enough for him to have Captain Winters killed. The war is over. Yankees walk the streets freely in Galveston. None of it matters anymore."

Jason replied flatly, "It matters to me. My best friend died because of Gault's treachery."

"I'm sorry."

The ache inside him deepening, Jason responded, "I'm sorry, too, but sorry isn't enough. I'm going to prove Gault was responsible for Byron's death, and for the deaths of other loyal Confederate seamen like him. I'm going to make sure everyone knows that Gault doesn't deserve Galveston's admiration because he was a traitor to the city and to the Confederate cause he supposedly espoused."

Jason paused before continuing, "But something else has become equally important to me. I need to make sure Gault doesn't use his fictitious past glory to make someone I care about believe in him."

Elizabeth searched his expression soberly. She whispered, "That someone you care about—is it me?"

"Yeah … that someone is you."

Jason saw tears glitter unexpectedly in Elizabeth's clear eyes when she asked, "But … why do you care

after all the misunderstandings and anger between us?"

Jason sought the answer to Elizabeth's question
as he brushed a wayward strand of hair from her
smooth cheek. His heart began a heavy pounding
as he slid his hand into her loosely bound hair and
replied, "That's a question I've been asking myself
ever since I met you. I haven't seemed to be able to
get it out of my mind. I haven't been able to get
you out of my mind either, no matter how hard I've
tried. I'm thinking that answers your question
somehow, but all I know for sure right now is that
I need to show you how much I care. I want that
more than anything I've ever wanted before."

Jason drew her closer. He felt her sweet heat warm
him as he whispered, "Will you let me show you?"
At her silence, he urged more softly, "Elizabeth?"

Elizabeth made a soft, inarticulate response,
and she was suddenly in his arms. Shaken by the
intoxicating emotions coursing through him, Jason
covered her mouth with his own. His emotions
rose higher as the kiss deepened. She was sweet to
the taste, magic to the touch. Her body was soft
against his as it melded to his strength. He tightened his arms around her as her lips separated,
driving him to a frenzy of wanting her. His kisses
intensified; his caresses sought new intimacy. He
heard Elizabeth utter a sound of longing similar to
his own, and rational thought slipped away.

Hunger ... the anguish of need that grew ever
stronger ... the feeling that neither of them could

deny, that this inevitable moment had finally brought them into each other's arms ...

Disrobing, they were flesh-to-flesh at last. Sinking down onto the soft cot, they surrendered to the heated fervor of the powerful emotion they shared. Jason drew back briefly. His throat tight, he raked Elizabeth's naked wonder with his gaze. She was beautiful, perfect. Gently he spread her legs, readying her for his possession.

Tenderness laced with passion swept his senses as Jason thrust himself deep inside her, then held his breath as the glory of the moment pulsed through him. This was what he had wanted from the first moment he had seen Elizabeth. Only she could fill the emptiness inside him.

Elizabeth's heat closed around him, and the wonder of the moment swelled. His rhythmic thrusts surged deeper as she met them fully.

At the brink, Jason drew back suddenly. Shuddering, still joined to her, he searched her passion-flushed expression and whispered, "Tell me you want this, Elizabeth. It's important to me to hear you say the words."

Jason saw Elizabeth's momentary hesitation and he stilled. He watched her parted lips move wordlessly. He awaited her response. His heart hammered in his chest as she whispered, "Yes, Jason ... with all my heart."

The moment burst into culmination.

Lying silent and still in the aftermath, Jason drew himself up to look down into Elizabeth's flushed countenance. Her moist warmth was pressed tight to his. The silky length of her hair had come undone and flowed across the pillow, framing her faultless features with its shimmering brilliance. Her eyelashes were lush crescents against her smooth cheeks; her lips were parted with her uneven breaths.

Lowering his mouth to hers, he exulted in the fulfillment of the moment as he whispered simply against her lips, "This was meant to be."

"What do you mean, you don't know where they are?"

His voice a low snarl, Simon questioned his hireling hotly in the flickering shadows of his study. Bruce had returned hours earlier with the news that he had permanently silenced Captain Winters as ordered. The news that Elizabeth and Dodd had shown up individually, within minutes of each other, was unexpected. Yet it was the enjoyment he had glimpsed in Bruce's eyes when his henchman added that Elizabeth and Dodd had left together that had pushed Simon into near rage.

Simon barely controlled his anger. Bruce had made it clear that he disapproved of the way his employer had handled Elizabeth's unexpected return to Galveston. His presumptuous lackey apparently believed he could have done better if he were in charge. What Bruce did not take into account was that he was *not* in charge, and he never would be! He had already decided to deal with Bruce after he brought the Hawk affair to a final and satisfactory conclusion, but he presently needed his insolent underling too much to do away with him.

"You saw them leave the ship together, but you don't know where they went," Simon said. "As a matter of fact, you can't locate them now at all—is that what you're saying?"

Bruce responded flatly, "I didn't think you'd want me to follow them. I figured you might change your plans, that maybe you wouldn't want anything more to do with that Huntington woman after she and Dodd got so chummy."

"Chummy?" Simon laughed aloud. "I anticipate a far closer relationship with Elizabeth Huntington than being *chummy*. You knew my plans for her. You should have anticipated that I would want to know where they went."

"Well, she didn't go back to the Beaufort house, that's for sure. I checked, and Frieda doesn't know where she is. Dodd didn't take her back to his quarters, either, because I checked there, too."

"You checked the local hotels?"

"Nobody resembling them has been seen."

The grandfather clock chimed from the corner of the room, and Simon muttered, "It's late. Any further inquiries at such a late hour will only raise suspicion, but I expect you to find them tomorrow, wherever they went. Just report their whereabouts when you do, and I'll take it from there. It may be difficult salvaging the situation after your ineptitude but—"

"I ain't inept, boss," Bruce interrupted angrily. "I did what you told me to do and I did it right, just like I always do."

Biting back his spontaneous reply, Simon said,

"Then you may take the day tomorrow to do this assignment right, too. Find them! If you're asked why you're trying to locate Elizabeth, you may say that I'm concerned about her safety. That should cut short any further inquiries."

"And if I can't find her?"

"What do you mean, *if* you can't *find* her? Galveston is an island! It's less than two miles wide, and much of it is still uninhabited. How could you not find her?"

"What if she's left the island?"

"She wouldn't do that. Not her. She's too determined to find out what that pendant means."

"What if Jason Dodd—"

"What if … what if!" His temper flaring, Simon shouted, "There is no *what if!* You will find them and report back to me! I'll make sure Jason Dodd doesn't get in the way again!"

"You don't need to do that, boss. I can take care of him."

Simon took a moment to draw his emotions under control. He realized from the expression on Bruce's face that following through was a matter of pride to him.

Almost amused, Simon said levelly, "Are you sure?"

"Of course I'm sure!"

"All right. Get out of here and go home. You have a lot to do tomorrow."

Waiting until the door clicked closed behind Bruce, Simon started pacing. Cursing aloud, he stopped abruptly. What was he worried about? Nothing had really changed. Elizabeth still wanted to learn about her past, and he was still the only person able to tell her what she wanted to know. Dodd was a brief impediment in his plan, and once Bruce found him, that impediment would be removed.

Simon frowned. If Bruce failed him, he would take care of the matter himself. He was determined that Elizabeth would not escape him.

He was getting tired of waiting.

Milton Stowe's patience waned as he sat concealed in the darkness of night outside the Beaufort mansion where Elizabeth Huntington had supposedly taken up residence. Angie, eager whore that she was, had put him on the right track. Subtle inquiry had filled in the rest of the story. It appeared that Simon Gault, a very important man on the island, had taken a personal interest in Elizabeth Huntington and was helping her with inquiries about her pendant. Gault's disapproval of her residence in the Easton Hotel, obviously a place unsuitable for a respectable young woman, was the reason he had moved her into the Beaufort mansion.

Milton had been pleasantly surprised when he first saw it. The luxurious structure was more secluded than he had expected. It was all but hidden from the road by heavy foliage, and the style of the house, with its wide entrance, high windows, and broad veranda doors, suited him very well. He would have no difficulty at all if it became necessary for him to enter the house covertly in order to accomplish his purpose. That alternative, however, would be a last resort. A "fatal accident" of the type he needed to arrange in order to collect the full sum for his service would be better if it were accomplished somewhere else.

It appeared, however, that his strategy of becoming familiar with Elizabeth Huntington's daily routine in Galveston had stalled early on. He had been watching the Beaufort mansion since early in the afternoon, expecting Elizabeth Huntington to return. He was still waiting. It was late, too late for a young woman who was a stranger in town to be out alone. The only answer was that she was with a man—a complication he hadn't anticipated.

In any case, he was hungry, tired, and low on patience. Experience had taught him that if a woman didn't return by this late hour, she wouldn't be returning at all that night.

With that thought in mind, Milton stood up and stretched his stiff frame. Grateful for the full moon that lit his way, he dusted off his clothes and headed for the road. He'd come back tomorrow. A job that had appeared simple was now beginning to seem too much like work to suit him. He'd give it all a chance to work out, but he wasn't a patient man. He did not intend to wait too much longer to finish the job.

The flames soared higher. The heat intensified. The blinding smoke thickened, filling her throat as she struggled to escape. She heard agonized screams and shouts for help. She searched for the source of the cries—then realized they were her own.

She could not breathe. She could not think. She could not find her way as flaming beams fell around her and terror engulfed her.

Tears streaking her cheeks, she staggered blindly forward, uncertain of her direction, then fell to her knees. She couldn't get up.

The flames raced closer. They seared her skin, but she could no longer fight them. She was too weak.

It was the end for her. The fire was consuming her and she—

"Wake up! Elizabeth, wake up; you're dreaming."

Elizabeth awoke with a jolt to find darkness surrounding her. Shuddering, her breathing rapid, and her face wet with tears, she was momentarily disoriented. She searched the shadows for the unknown threat that haunted her.

"Elizabeth, look at me."

Elizabeth turned toward the deep voice beside her. She stared at the masculine image lit by the silver moonlight streaming through the window, and a relieved sob escaped her throat.

"It was a dream." Still trembling, Elizabeth struggled for control as she whispered, "But you're not a dream, are you, Jason?"

Frowning, Jason drew her into his embrace and held her close. Her heart pounded against his chest as he said, "You had a nightmare, but it's over and done. You're safe with me."

Elizabeth stared over Jason's shoulder at the wavering shadows. She closed her eyes without responding.

Drawing back, Jason pressed, "Elizabeth, did you hear me?"

"Yes, I'm fine ... now." Elizabeth managed a short, embarrassed laugh. "Ever since I can remember, I've had that nightmare about the fire in the orphanage where I lived before my adoptive parents found me. I suppose I should be accustomed to it by now, but each time it's as real as the last." She said unexpectedly, "I'm sorry."

"Sorry?"

Elizabeth paused before replying. Jason's heavy, dark hair was tousled from sleep, his powerful chest was bared above the coverlet lying across them, and his strong features were tight with concern. She responded, "The dream is my problem, something I have to conquer on my own. It's part of the reason I came here. I'm sorry this had to happen now ... that you had to see me like this."

Jason studied her expression more closely as he smoothed the tears from her cheeks. "If it's a problem, it's a problem we'll settle together. But it's just a dream and it's over now. Put it out of your mind. We'll talk about it tomorrow."

"I don't want to talk about it tomorrow. I can handle it myself."

"Seems to me I've heard that before." Jason scrutinized the growing determination in her expression before he said, "You said you trust me, Elizabeth."

"I do trust you."

"Then let me help you."

"Jason—"

"I can help you forget for a little while."

Elizabeth did not reply.

"Just say yes, Elizabeth."

"Yes?"

Jason's lips brushed hers with featherlight kisses. His kiss pressed gradually deeper. His tongue stroked her mouth, sending quivers down her spine. His hands touched her intimately, and tremors of desire raced through her.

Mesmerized by his loving touch, she felt her fear slip away. It was replaced by an emotion that lightened the ominous darkness and struck all thought from her mind.

She mumbled softly and Jason drew back questioningly. He whispered, "Elizabeth?"

She looked up into dark eyes that revealed tender, loving concern, and a yearning that she could not deny. Her reply came from the bottom of her heart as she responded with a single whispered word.

"Yes."

Chapter Nine

"Don't upset yourself, Aunt Ella."

Trevor stood at his aunt's bedside as the morning sun shone through the windows of her sedate New York mansion, but the atmosphere in the room was far from sunny. Ella Huntington's personal maid, Molly, had appeared frantically at his kitchen door as he had been preparing his own breakfast. He was an early riser because of the long hours demanded of him as an intern in one of the larger law firms in the city. Aware that his mother considered his position far beneath him, he avoided her complaints by attending to his own needs in the early morning hours. The last thing he had expected, however, was the sight of Molly at his door with tears in her eyes and a frantic plea on her lips.

Preferring not to awaken his mother, he had raced to his Aunt Ella's bedside to console her. His heart ached at the dear woman's distress. He had never understood his mother's barely concealed aversion to her. Aunt Ella had never been anything but kind to him. He liked Elizabeth, too. He didn't share his mother's opinion that Elizabeth was an interloper who hoped to steal his inheritance. In truth, he wanted no part of the Huntington estate. His father had refused Uncle Wilber's largesse because he knew that he had already squandered more than his share. Unlike his mother, Trevor did not feel he deserved a wealthy lifestyle just because his name was Huntington. And unlike his father, he had a vision for his future. His mother did not approve of it, but he would not allow her to deter him.

Yet he had no shield against his mother's disapproval. He knew he was not the son Sylvia Huntington had hoped for. He knew he never would be. He wished his mother would accept him for the man he was, but he could not escape the feeling that he had let her down.

His attention returning to Aunt Ella as a tear trailed down her pale cheek, he took her bony hand in his and said, "You mustn't worry about Elizabeth, Aunt Ella. You know how competent and determined she is. And she's such a lady through it all. She'll do well wherever she goes."

"But she's so inexperienced, Trevor." Another tear traveled down his aunt's wrinkled cheek. "I had a bad dream about her last night. I dreamed her life was in danger, that someone was trying to kill her."

"That's foolishness! Who would want to hurt Elizabeth? She's a beautiful young woman."

Aunt Ella's hand tightened on his. "A part of me

knows you're right, but there's another part of me that's still afraid. Perhaps I should send her a wire, just to make sure she's all right."

Squeezing his aunt's hand tighter, Trevor replied, "If that will make you feel better, of course you should do it; but you'll probably receive a letter from her soon. Even today, perhaps."

"Would you send the wire for me, Trevor? Just tell her I want to be sure she's all right. Ask her to wire me back. She'll understand. She knows … she knows how limited my time is, and she's aware how much I want her life to be settled before I go."

"Aunt Ella …" Trevor felt his throat tighten at the love so openly displayed in his aunt's gaze. His own mother had never looked at him like that. Swallowing against the lump in his throat, he said, "Of course I'll send a wire for you. I'll send it before I go to my office."

"Thank you. Thank you so much, Trevor. You always were a dear boy."

A sound in the doorway raised both their gazes toward Sylvia Huntington as she unexpectedly entered the room. Smiling stiffly, she said, "I couldn't help overhearing. Trevor will gladly send a wire to Elizabeth for you, Ella, but your concern is misplaced. Elizabeth is a very determined young woman. You needn't worry about her." She continued, "Luckily, my servant heard Trevor leave this morning. She awakened me, and I came right here. I knew there could be nowhere else where my son would rush before breakfast."

"I'm sorry. I didn't mean to disturb anyone.

Molly obviously panicked when I became upset. I must tell her not to bother you again."

"Nonsense! I'm always at your beck and call. You know that, Ella." Moving Trevor aside, Sylvia patted Ella's hand before turning back to her son to say, "You should be on your way to work now, Trevor. I'll take care of Aunt Ella."

Trevor nodded, uncertain. He bade his aunt good-bye and turned toward the door as his mother said, "Wait for me outside for a moment, dear. I have an errand for you to run for me."

Trevor had barely pulled the door closed behind him when it opened again to his mother's stern countenance. Waiting only until they had progressed a few steps down the hallway, where they would not be overheard, Sylva said harshly, "You have a weak spot for that old woman, don't you?"

Uncertain how to respond, Trevor said, "Aunt Ella's dying, Mother."

"Yes, but she'd better hold on a little longer. I'm not ready for her to go yet."

Baffled by his mother's response, Trevor frowned as Sylvia took an aggressive step toward him and commanded, "Make sure you send that telegram, you hear? Do it today … right away. I want your aunt to know you followed through. I want her to get a response from Elizabeth so she'll know everything is going exactly as that damned young woman hoped."

"Mother!"

"Just send it!"

Watching as Sylvia turned abruptly and headed back toward Ella's bedroom, Trevor shook his head. He stepped out onto the street minutes later, still bewildered by his mother's seeming change of heart.

Sylvia Huntington paused with her hand on the doorknob of Ella Huntington's bedroom door. She smiled with satisfaction. Her son was a ninny, but he would do what she told him to do. He always did. He would send the telegram to his cousin, and the avaricious snip would respond quickly for fear of disfavor that might put her inheritance in jeopardy. It would all happen quickly, before Mr. Stowe had a chance to do his work. With everything apparently going so smoothly in Galveston, Ella would be totally unprepared when an accident occurred so *unexpectedly*.

Sylvia's smile broadened. She herself would be shocked at Elizabeth's demise, of course. She would barely be able to contain her grief, but she would not ignore her responsibility to console Ella—or to remind the dying woman that only two people remained to uphold the Huntington family name.

Yes, Trevor would soon be wealthy—no thanks to his own spineless self. And *she* would soon be living the life she deserved.

Careful to remove any sign of a smile from her face, Sylvia reentered Ella's room and walked back toward the bed.

* * *

Jason awoke instantly when a shaft of light struck the cot on which he was lying. He glanced around the cabin, his arm curling protectively around Elizabeth where she slept beside him. He listened intently for any foreign sound, double-checking that the handgun was within his reach. Satisfied to hear only the echoing screech of seabirds outside the cabin as they sought their morning meal, and to discern only the faint stirring of the horses hobbled at the rear of the cabin as they foraged for food, he relaxed and turned his attention to Elizabeth.

A moment of silent awe struck him as he looked down at her sleeping face. Her silky tresses in disarray, her features void of any artifice, the delicate line of her shoulders bare above the coverlet that lay across them both, she was flawless in every detail. He supposed he would never get enough of looking at her. He remembered the evening he first saw her walk across the Easton lobby with every male eye following her. He recalled how irate he had been to see snickering cowpokes assessing her boldly. He felt years had passed since they'd spoken their first words to each other—harsh and angry words. He remembered that he had figured she'd gotten only what she had asked for when that drunk accosted her outside her room—but in spite of it all, he'd been unable just to walk on by.

He had wanted her from the first moment he saw her. He had resented the feelings she raised inside him almost as much as he had resented her irritating independence. That independence was still a point of contention with him. He knew that would never change, but it was a characteristic that annoyed him while still stirring his admiration. Elizabeth was a challenge ... one he now realized he would gladly pursue the rest of his life.

But he was only too aware that Elizabeth wasn't thinking about the rest of her life. Her past was more important to her than her future—a past that possibly put her in jeopardy.

At the moment, however, he wasn't interested in the past or the future. It was the present that set his heart pounding.

Lowering his mouth to Elizabeth's parted lips, Jason could not resist brushing them lightly ... once, twice. His mouth clung to hers as she stirred and turned toward him. Her naked breasts moved warmly against his chest. Her warm delta was hot against his hardening desire as she opened her eyes and looked at him.

Strangely powerless to speak, he stared into her heavily fringed orbs, where green sparks intermixed with gold came slowly to life. He brushed her fluttering eyelids with his lips, followed the finely sculpted line of her cheek to the lobe of her ear. He whispered unintelligibly between kisses that followed a course back to her mouth.

He caressed her breasts and lowered his mouth to their crests. Elizabeth gasped softly, and his ministrations deepened. He slid his hands down her slender hips, then followed the course with his mouth until he met the warm crevice between her thighs. He kissed it lightly, and Elizabeth gasped again. He kissed her more deeply. She made a spontaneous sound as he cupped her buttocks with his palms and raised her up more fully to him. She was honey sweet and hot to his taste, and he indulged himself thoroughly, wanting and needing as he had never hungered before.

He felt her shudder. He heard her gasp a few whispered words. He felt her quaking with the wonder of fulfillment, and he accepted her throbbing tribute freely.

Her quaking had not completely stilled when he slid himself up upon her and thrust himself into her moistness. Her loving heat stole his breath as he began moving slowly … tenderly.

The moment was almost upon him when he stopped, in tight control as he stared down again at her. He whispered, "This was meant to be. You know that, don't you, Elizabeth?"

But his question went unanswered as his control lapsed and he was thrust into sudden ecstatic fulfillment.

Still breathing heavily, Jason raised himself above her sated stillness at last. "Elizabeth?" he pressed.

He watched her eyes open. Her gaze connected with his, reaching a spot inside him untouched by any other as she responded in a whisper, "Yes … meant to be."

Milton Stowe moved stiffly in his concealed position outside the Beaufort mansion. It had occurred to him during the previous night, which he'd spent in an uncomfortable bed in the Easton Hotel, that possibly—through some stroke of luck—

Elizabeth might already have met with an accident and would never return to the Beaufort house or any other. The thought of collecting an exorbitant fee from Sylvia Huntington without any effort at all had amused him. It had been barely light when he had headed back to the spot outside the Beaufort mansion that he now occupied.

He had been watching for two hours, and he was already stiff and sore. If the Huntington woman didn't show up soon, he was going to take some steps that would force her out into the open.

Drawing back at a sign of movement at the mansion's front door, Milton saw the aged servant emerge and pull the door closed behind her. He gave a harsh snort. The old hag would never dare use the front entrance for her comings and goings if she thought anyone was around to see her. He supposed it made her feel important to exit a grand mansion as if she belonged upstairs, instead of in some small, miserable room behind the kitchen.

Milton drew back further as she neared him on the path. He barely controlled a derisive snort. She really was an ugly old witch.

Staring after her with a grimace, Milton was startled to see movement in the bushes on the far side of the courtyard. He remained still as two figures grew gradually clearer and began moving slowly toward the house. He recognized the woman from the picture that Sylvia Huntington had given him. It was Elizabeth Huntington … and damned if she didn't even look better than her photograph. He wasn't sure who the big man moving stealthily beside her was. It wasn't Simon Gault; that was for sure. The only other person he could be was a man called Jason Dodd, who was reported to have given the visiting beauty more than a normal share of attention.

Milton frowned. It appeared they had been waiting for Frieda's departure before going into the house. Why were they sneaking around as if they didn't want to be seen?

Milton watched them enter the house through the front door. The stupid servant had obviously left it open, allowing free access to anyone who might want to help himself to whatever was inside.

Thinking he might take advantage of the situation himself, Milton watched and waited.

Jason drew Elizabeth forward as they slipped through the front door of the Beaufort mansion and started toward the staircase. "Frieda was guarding the door like a bulldog the first time I came here," he said with a touch of irony, "and now she's left it open for anyone to enter."

"She's a strange person, Jason. She was accommodating in a way, but she seemed to think I should mold myself to her standards. I had the feeling that she was watching everything I did."

"She was."

"But ... why?"

"Gault arranged for her to be here."

Elizabeth went silent. What was it about Simon that so confused her? Her confusion was part of the reason she had allowed Jason to talk her into returning to the Beaufort mansion to get the list of prominent persons Simon thought she should interview about her pendant. Jason wanted to see the names of the men Simon had suggested. Jason had also said he wanted to see the paperwork she had obtained relating to the *Sarah Jane* before coming to Galveston. It had all seemed logical to her while she was lying in Jason's arms and his loving words were still echoing in her ears, but she was presently uncomfortable with the questions that inundated her mind.

Who was this mysterious person identified only by the name Milton, who was supposedly looking for her—and why didn't he want it to be general knowledge that he had come to Galveston to find her?

Had Captain Winters's body been discovered yet, and did his death really have anything to do with Jason or her?

Had anyone seen Jason and her leaving the ship, and if someone had, were the authorities looking for them?

Last but not least, why would Simon have gone to so much trouble to impress her when his prestige was such that he could have any woman in Galveston whom he wanted?

Elizabeth pushed open the bedroom door and walked inside. Everything appeared to be exactly as she had left it, and she walked directly to her suitcase and withdrew the papers Jason wanted. She halted when he said abruptly, "We might as well take your things with us. You don't have any intention of returning here to stay, do you?"

Elizabeth shook her head, frowning at the uncertainty of her future.

"Don't worry." Jason slid an arm around her and drew her against the strong wall of his body. "We'll figure this out."

We …

She looked up into Jason's dark eyes. It occurred to her that the word had a lovely sound.

Milton Stowe waited tensely outside the Beaufort mansion. Elizabeth Huntington and the big fellow were still inside. He didn't like this. They obviously suspected Elizabeth was in some kind of danger or they wouldn't be acting so furtively.

Milton searched his mind. No, *he* couldn't be the reason Elizabeth had gone into temporary hiding, unless …

Milton's lips curled with anger. Of course … Angie, the talkative whore. He had paid her well to keep silent about his inquiries, but if she were the cause of these unexpected complications, she wouldn't escape him. He'd see to that.

Angry, Milton drew back into deeper cover as the front door of the Beaufort house opened and Elizabeth emerged with her companion at her side. The big man was carrying her suitcase.

Damn! Elizabeth obviously wouldn't be coming back—another complication.

Elizabeth said something to the big fellow. Milton listened intently as the fellow replied, "Chantalle will take you in."

So that's where he was taking her. Ingenious! No

one would look for her in a bordello; but arranging an accident for her now would be all the more difficult, especially if that fellow remained close beside her.

Content that he knew their destination, Milton waited silently until the furtive couple slipped out of sight. Consternation filled his mind at the new problem facing him.

Just as he was about to follow them, Milton heard the sound of a step. He turned to see the old servant returning. Uncertain exactly what to expect, he waited as she went back inside, only to emerge a few minutes later at a run.

She was obviously disturbed to find Elizabeth's belongings gone and was rushing to report the situation to someone.

Relying on instinct, Milton followed the servant.

"What do you mean, Elizabeth's things are gone?"

Simon stared at Frieda darkly. The woman had interrupted his late breakfast. Annoyed, he'd had her ushered into his study, where she'd made her startling report.

He continued hotly, "You're telling me that not only did Elizabeth not return to sleep last night, but when you left the house to go to the market, you returned to find her suitcase and clothing gone?"

"I was only out a few minutes—to buy some eggs down the road. It was early. It never occurred to me that she might return while I was gone."

"She was obviously waiting for you to leave so she could enter the house without being seen."

"But why would she do that? She had no reason to—"

"Whatever her reason, you allowed it to happen. But I shouldn't have expected anything else." Simon said coldly, "You may leave now."

Shaken, her manner subservient, Frieda responded, "Do you want me to remain at the Beaufort house, in case she returns?"

"That won't be necessary. You may consider that your employment with me has ended."

Her breathing uneven, Frieda assessed Simon's heated expression, then left without a word.

Waiting only until the woman had cleared the doorway, Simon hissed under his breath, "Stupid witch!" Then, exiting his study, he walked back into the breakfast room and stopped his maid to direct, "Send someone for Bruce with the message that I want to see him right away." At his maid's wide-eyed stare, he exclaimed, "Right away, do you hear!"

Sitting back down at the breakfast table, Simon picked up his cup and took a sip, then slapped it back down in the saucer. "My tea has cooled," he told the maid who hurried in. He pushed away the plate in front of him and added, "My breakfast has cooled, also. Tell Mabel to throw this away and bring me something fresh." As the maid turned to do his bidding, Simon added, "Show Bruce into my study when he gets here, and make sure I'm informed as soon as he arrives."

Simon's lips twisted into a sneer as the maid hurried away. He did not bother to finish his breakfast when the shaken girl informed him a half hour later that Bruce had been ushered into his study.

Waiting only until he had closed the study door securely behind him, Simon said tightly, "Frieda just told me that Elizabeth and Dodd returned to the house while she was gone earlier this morning and removed her things—which means they're still in Galveston." He paused, then said more softly, "Dodd seems to have developed some kind of hold over Elizabeth. I don't intend to waste time on him. When you find him, dispose of him any way you can. Get rid of him for good, do you understand? I will not allow that man to interfere with my plans."

"What about Elizabeth Huntington?"

"No … she's mine. Make sure she doesn't find out that you had anything to do with Dodd's death. I'll take care of her in my own way. I won't be cheated of that!"

Bruce hesitated. His thin face drew into a frown as he said, "You're sure about that, boss? Whit Hawk managed to get away from you. I don't think—"

"I'm not paying you to do the thinking. Just do what I tell you to do. I want Jason Dodd dead, and I don't want Elizabeth Huntington touched! She'll turn to me when he's gone, and I'll deal with her then."

"I'm not so sure of that, with Captain Winters being killed and all."

"I'm a very persuasive man."

"But—"

"I said, I'll handle it!"

Bruce nodded. "Whatever you say."

Simon remained staring at the study door as Bruce pulled it closed behind him. It occurred to him that no one would suspect that Bruce, the slight, gray-haired, bespectacled fellow, was capable of such dastardly work. He supposed that Bruce's innocuous appearance was his greatest asset.

Simon unconsciously nodded. Perhaps he would keep Bruce around for a while, after all.

Chapter Ten

Chantalle sat at her office desk, her ledger spread out in front of her. She raised a hand to the upward sweep of her startlingly red hair and rubbed her weary eyes, making sure not to disturb the heavy kohl she used to draw attention from the age lines becoming increasingly prominent there. She took an uncomfortable breath. She would be glad when the day was over and she could shed the tight corset that had become necessary because of the extra pounds she had gained over the years. She supposed that was the reason she enjoyed occasionally using the cabin at the far end of the island that Jason had told her about. In seclusion, she was free to wear clothes that fit her and to leave her face free of the heavy makeup expected of a madam.

Activity in the salon below echoed up the stairs, accompanied by a loud guffaw, and Chantalle shrugged. Someone had arrived early in the day, and it appeared he was enjoying himself immensely. She could usually depend on the women in her house—Goldie, Marian, Poppie, Georgia, and Lily—to guarantee that much for her guests. As for Angie … she served her purpose. Laughter was common in her house. It was preferable to the sounds of crashing fists, an occasional problem when one of her customers spent too much time at the bar, or when tempers in the card room shot out of control.

Chantalle's thoughts moved inevitably to Whit Hawk. He had never lost control in the card room. She remembered the ring he had shown her when he'd first arrived. The sailing ship with the hawk flying above was not easily forgotten. Nor was Whit's search for the brother he hoped would be carrying the same ring, a brother he had lost track of years earlier. Whit had not found his brother at last report, but he had found the woman he loved. Chantalle had not been able to escape a certain sadness when he moved to his wife's ranch up north.

Chantalle had been stunned, then puzzled when Elizabeth Huntington arrived in Galveston with a pendant rumored to bear an exact duplicate of the crest on Whit's ring, especially since Whit had claimed that his sisters were dead. She was certain Hiram Charters would not have let her down, that he had delivered her message to Whit, yet Whit hadn't replied.

A knock on her office door interrupted Chantalle's thoughts. It opened to reveal Marian, looking tense and nervous. "Poppie saw someone approaching the rear entrance of the house. She wasn't sure if it was Simon, but I'm going to my room, just in case."

The lines on Chantalle's face deepened. Marian was no match for Simon's sadistic tastes in the bedroom, which was probably the reason he continued to seek her out. No, she'd never let him touch that young woman again.

Marian moved quickly out of the doorway at Chantalle's nod and drew the door closed behind her.

Standing, Chantalle waited.

"I thought you said Chantalle's house was no place for me."

Elizabeth followed close behind Jason as they negotiated the hidden walkway in the narrow back alley behind Chantalle's redbrick mansion. She frowned at the high privacy wall, imagining the many men who had entered unobserved, and the staircase to the second floor that afforded them the anonymity they desired.

The events of the morning had progressed quickly. They had left the Beaufort mansion and had gone directly to the office of Jason's friend Samuel Johnson. She had remained hidden while Jason went inside, certain that his friend would be there, working at first light. He had emerged with a dark frown. At her inquiring glance he had said flatly, "The authorities are looking for you in connection with Captain Winters's death."

Shocked into silence, she'd had no response.

She had been equally stunned when he told her where he was taking her. Still uncertain, she pressed, "Jason—"

He turned back toward her to say, "You're right—this is no place for you—but circumstances changed the moment I learned that the authorities are looking for you."

"I don't understand that. Why only me? You were there, too."

"Because you're the person who was seen boarding the ship, and the fellow who saw you remembered you very well."

Elizabeth considered his words.

The fellow who saw her …

Of course, a woman on the docks would be remembered, but dressed in Western wear, Jason would have been indistinguishable from any other cowpoke in the city, except for his unusual height and stretch of shoulders … or perhaps for that compelling, dark-eyed gaze underneath the worn Stetson he wore low on his forehead.

No, that wasn't true. There wasn't a woman between the ages of fifteen and fifty who would have forgotten Jason if she had seen him approaching the ship, no matter how he was dressed.

Jason continued, "Nobody will expect to find you here, and this place is more centrally located than the cabin. It's the safest place for you to be right now until I can find out more about Captain Winters's murder and this Milton person."

"But—"

"Don't worry. Chantalle will hide you."

"I don't want her to hide me. I want to go with you."

"No. That's out of the question. I can't take any chances."

"Chances?"

"Elizabeth …" Jason halted at the base of Chantalle's back staircase and slid his hands up her arms as he said softly, "It'll only be a little while. The sooner I can check on a few things, the better."

Elizabeth allowed Jason to draw her up the stairs behind him. She frowned as he pulled open the back door. His familiarity with that entrance made her uncomfortable. As if reading her mind, he said, "I made good use of this entry during the blockade—just in case you were wondering." He paused a moment to add, "You're going to find out sooner or later that I'm no stranger to this establishment, but the women here have never been more to me than casual … friends." Jason's voice dropped a notch as he added, "And you can believe me when I say there's nothing casual about the way I feel about you."

The look in Jason's eyes raised a lump in Elizabeth's throat as he drew her down the hallway. Sounds of activity echoed up the staircase as he knocked on a doorway, then pushed it open in response to a reply from within.

Chantalle was standing beside her desk, but Elizabeth could not help noticing her startled expression when Jason drew her inside, pushed the door closed behind them, and said, "I need a favor."

* * *

Milton Stowe drew back behind several large packing cases in the alleyway behind the red brick whorehouse he had visited once before. He watched, incredulous at the unexpected turn of events.

He had reacted instinctively when he had followed the old servant woman from the Beaufort house earlier. As he had expected, she'd gone directly to Simon Gault's mansion, no doubt to report that Elizabeth Huntington had come and gone during her absence, and that Elizabeth had obviously removed her belongings, too. Gault's response to her report could not have been good, judging from the old woman's expression when she left.

Milton had reviewed the situation afterward in his mind. Gault was reputed to be a power in the shipping community and was well respected in general. In the time he had spent at waterfront saloons shortly after arriving, however, he had heard that Gault was considered ruthless when he wanted something. And unless he missed his guess, Gault wanted Elizabeth.

Milton's course of action was clear. He needed to get to Elizabeth Huntington before Simon Gault got in the way.

Following his instinct as he had done before, he had gone to Chantalle's house and had arrived just as the man he assumed was Jason Dodd was exiting by the rear entrance. Dodd was alone. He had obviously left Elizabeth in the madam's care while he tended to some other pressing matter.

Gault and Dodd—both men were in his way, but

Dodd was presently the man who posed the bigger problem.

He needed to find out more about what Dodd had in mind.

With that thought, Milton waited only a few moments before taking off after him.

"Follow me."

Chantalle motioned Elizabeth forward after a cautious glance into the upstairs hallway. She walked quickly down the corridor, slid a key into a locked door, and ushered her inside.

Breathless, Elizabeth glanced around her. The bedroom was simply decorated with a quilted coverlet on the bed and white lace curtains on the two windows, which appeared to overlook the alleyway. The furnishings were minimal—a small bedstand, a mirrored dresser, a washstand, and an upholstered chair in the corner of the room. It was as far from a bordello bedroom as could be imagined.

"Surprised?"

Elizabeth turned back toward the brightly dressed madam. She replied, "I suppose I am."

"This section of the house isn't generally used for … business purposes. It remains private, for the most part, which is the reason I keep the doors locked. No one questions my reasons. They wouldn't dare, but the truth is that my entire life isn't a bordello. At least I tell myself that, and I try to reinforce that thought by making the private rooms in this house as ordinary as possible."

"Do you live in this section of the house?"

"What you're really asking is if my bedroom is as conservative as this one." Chantalle's broad smile flashed. "I suppose you'll never know. I do sleep a few doors away, though, and it's a long-standing rule that no one intrudes into this wing without my permission."

Elizabeth nodded. She then said, "I don't know what Jason was thinking when he brought me here, or how long he expects me to stay, but I will tell you one thing—it won't be long."

"I suppose Jason was worried because he doesn't know what to expect from the authorities. And, of course, there's that Milton fella." When Elizabeth attempted to reply, Chantalle held up her hand. "No, I don't give explanations, and I don't want any given to me. As far as Jason is concerned, no explanation is necessary. Jason brought you here. He wouldn't have done that if he didn't think it was necessary, and that's all I need to know."

Elizabeth replied stiffly, "Do you always accept what Jason says and does without question?"

"I've learned it's safer that way."

"For him or for you?"

"Does it matter?"

"You surprise me, Chantalle. I thought you were an independent woman accustomed to taking care of herself."

Chantalle replied, "Listen to me, Elizabeth. I *am* an independent woman, and I *do* take care of myself, but I'm also a woman who has learned that there are times when it's best just to believe in someone who has never let you down. Jason is one of the most honest men I know, and he doesn't have to give a reason when he asks a favor of me."

Chantalle paused, then added, "You may not consider me to be the best person to give you advice, but I'm going to do it anyway. It would be smart for you to remember that Jason isn't one to make unnecessary demands of anyone. If he asks you to do something, it'll most likely be to your benefit in the long run."

"That's how you've handled things in the past?"

"For the most part."

"And his decisions have served you well?"

"For the most part."

"I don't know if I can do that, just sit around and wait for him to return. I'm accustomed to handling things myself."

"Jason said you'd say that."

Elizabeth frowned. "What else did he say?"

"He said you'd wait for a little while anyway, and he'd be back in time to stop you from doing anything foolish."

Unable to restrain the tears that unexpectedly sprang to her eyes, Elizabeth said, "I don't know what's going on, Chantalle. The truth is, I'm afraid for him."

Momentarily silent, Chantalle responded, "Jason is smart. It won't be easy for anyone to get the best of him." Turning at the sound of footsteps on the stairs, Chantalle handed Elizabeth the room key and said, "Lock your door from the inside. It's safer that way."

And then she was gone.

* * *

Jason glanced at the sun, which was rapidly setting over the placid sea beyond the docks. He had spent the past few hours going from saloon to saloon, where he knew talk would be ripe about Captain Winters's recent murder. He hadn't learned much except that Captain Winters had been discovered by one of his men, and Elizabeth had been seen boarding the ship the previous evening after the men went ashore.

Jason glanced at the bartender who reached for his empty glass. He tapped the bar again for another drink and watched as the mustached fellow poured it without spilling a drop. He looked up when the bartender said, "I'm thinking you've done more than your share of drinking tonight. It ain't like you, Jason."

Jason smiled crookedly. Whitey was right. He had done more drinking that evening than he had done in the past few weeks. He was well-known at the docks, and seamen talked to him easily most times, but the conversation of the day seemed to center around Captain Winters's murder. No one was interested in discussing a curious new arrival named Milton—the man who was truly responsible for Jason's deceivingly leisurely round of the saloons.

He had become certain only of one thing: no one had connected him with Captain Winters's death, which meant that although Elizabeth had been seen boarding the ship, he had not. The authorities had no interest in him, which made his inquiries easier.

Jason turned as a conversation a few feet away grew louder.

"What do you suppose that Yankee woman was doing aboard the *Silver Dawn* then?"

"That Elizabeth Huntington ain't no Yankee!" Jason recognized the bearded seaman who was arguing with the shorter fellow. The seaman's name was John Gibbons, and he did not relent in Elizabeth's defense as he said, "I talked to her one day when she was trying to find the Barlett and Pierce warehouse right after she got to Galveston. She's a lady through and through. There's not a trace of Yankee in her!"

"You always was the type to be taken in by a pretty face."

"Yeah, well, you're talking through your hat, because you ain't never even met her."

Jason frowned when Gibbons turned toward him unexpectedly and said, "Ask Jason if I ain't telling the truth. He knows that Huntington woman. Talk is he spent some time with her at one of them fancy parties he gets invited to. Simon Gault escorted her there, and some say Jason got Gault's nose out of joint because of her—ain't that right, Jason?"

Aware that he was suddenly the center of attention at the crowded bar, Jason said, "I spent some time with Elizabeth Huntington at that party, and I liked what I saw. She's a lady, all right, but she doesn't let anybody tell her what to do. I tried that. It didn't work."

A chorus of laughter followed his comment, but the shorter seaman wasn't laughing as he said, "She took you in; that's what she did. She came here asking about her family, but I ain't so sure that was the real reason she was walking the docks." He looked askance at Jason and said, "Maybe she was extra nice to you because them high muckety-mucks at the party like you the way they do."

Jason said, "Those high muckety-mucks are the shipowners you work for. They're good men, for the most part. I figure if they like me ... fine. I was never really one of them, even when Byron and I owned the *Willow,* but that doesn't stop me from mixing with them when I feel like it."

"They liked that Yankee woman, too, I hear."

Jason took an aggressive step toward the shorter seaman with the acid tongue. He said with tightly suppressed anger, "Yeah, they did. I liked her too, and I'm telling you now, she doesn't have a vicious bone in her body."

"Well ... sounds to me like you know an awful lot about her body."

Jason lunged toward the fellow, only to feel strong arms holding him back as the bartender bellowed, "You said enough, George. Get out until you sober up or shut up!" He ordered, "Throw him out, boys!"

A few obliging men thrust George out onto the dock, and the bartender turned back to Jason. He said confidentially as he refilled Jason's spilled glass, "Seems like you ain't the only fella who was taken with that Huntington woman, Jason."

Jason responded tightly, "Is that so?"

"Yeah, a skinny little fella who said he was new in Galveston was in here a few days ago. His name was Matthew or Marshall … No, his name was Milton. He was asking about her. I couldn't quite figure it, being as he was a stranger in town and all, but just one look at him and I figured he was wasting his time if he was thinking about getting friendly with her. To my mind, he wouldn't stand a chance with any woman with a lick of sense, even if he did have full pockets. But his money was good, so I just poured and listened."

"What else did he say?"

"He perked up real fast when somebody mentioned that Simon Gault was escorting her around Galveston."

"This Milton fella didn't use his last name, huh?"

"No. And he got around the question of where he was living when one of the fellas asked. He said he was staying with a friend."

"A friend?"

The bartender gave a sarcastic snort. "That's right, but I've got my doubts that he has any. There wasn't much that was likable about him."

"And he never came back?"

"Not since. And I ain't sorry, neither. I figured that sooner or later, he'd be trouble."

Jason glanced again out the window at the darkening sky. He had been making the rounds for quite a while. He was sure Elizabeth wouldn't wait much longer for him to return. As a matter of fact, he figured she was probably pacing the floor at that moment, determined never to be left behind again.

Jason slapped his money down on the bar and said, "I'm going home, John." He grinned, "But maybe I'll stop off at Chantalle's place first."

"From what I hear around the bar, them ladies will be waiting for you, too."

"You hear that, do you?" Jason forced a laugh. "Well, there's no accounting for talk."

Jason turned toward the door. He was well aware that his step was unsteadier than he would have liked as he walked out onto the dock.

Bruce Carlton waited in the darkening shadows, unseen although he was only a few yards from Dodd as he exited the saloon and paused to steady himself. He couldn't believe his luck when a sailor who'd stopped at the office of Gault Shipping & Exchange before closing time mentioned that Jason Dodd was making the rounds of the saloons on the docks. He had known he'd never have a better chance to finish off Dodd. It had taken him a little while to locate the saloon where Dodd was drinking, but once he did, he had been content to wait.

Bruce smiled and withdrew the knife he had strapped to his belt. He unconsciously ran his thumb over the blade. Sharp as a razor and just as deadly. His smile broadened as he slid the knife back into its sheath. He would slip up behind Dodd and use his knife quickly and silently. Dodd wasn't at his best, and he'd never know what hit him. Chances were that nobody would find the body until dawn the next morning—and the boss would be a happy man.

Bruce went still as Dodd started down the dock and a short, burly seaman who had been thrown out of the bar earlier stepped unexpectedly into sight behind him. The seaman said something that turned Dodd toward him. The seaman threw a punch that caught Dodd unawares and sent him staggering backward. When Dodd straightened up, the fellow was prepared to launch himself again.

And the brawl began.

Milton Stowe watched the unexpected fight between Jason Dodd and the unknown seaman with intense interest. He was aware that a little distance away, Bruce Carlton, whom he recognized as Simon Gault's lackey, was hiding and watching the show, unaware that he was being watched as well.

Milton could not help being amused at the irony of the situation. He had followed Jason Dodd to the docks by instinct, had noted the moment when Carlton showed up and began watching Dodd covertly. His interest had grown when he saw Carlton take a knife from his belt and test its blade before sheathing it again in a way that drew him to just one conclusion: Carlton was watching Dodd with the intention of killing him—a man with the same murderous ends as his own. The only difference was that the intended victims were not the same.

Customers of the saloon began wandering out

onto the dock to watch the fight between Dodd and the sailor, many of them with drinks in hand. A single hard punch from Dodd knocked the sailor down on his back. The fellow moaned but did not get up, and the onlookers cheered. The dock went silent when Dodd took a few steps to stand towering over the vanquished seaman, then said a few harsh words before turning away from the man with contempt and dusting himself off.

The seaman drew himself groggily to his feet and slunk away as onlookers slapped Dodd on the back and joked. Most of them wandered back inside, while a few walked companionably at Dodd's side, conversing as he started back down the docks.

Milton looked at Carlton to see him wait only a few moments before slipping away in the opposite direction. He could almost read the man's mind. The perfect opportunity to finish Dodd off in the darkness had been lost. Dodd was spared for another day, but Milton had no doubt that Carlton would try again—probably on orders from his boss, who appeared to be ready to take Dodd's place with Elizabeth Huntington as soon as it was vacated.

Milton's amusement heightened. Both of those men were in for a surprise. Carlton did not realize that he had just provided the perfect opportunity to orchestrate the "accident" Sylvia Huntington demanded. Carlton would be waiting for a chance to get Dodd again. Wouldn't it be just too bad if poor Elizabeth Huntington got in the way of the attempt on Dodd's life and was killed? It could happen anywhere—on the street, on the docks ... or even in the bedroom.

An accident. Perfect.

All he had to do was wait.

Waiting was not Elizabeth's forte.

She paced the small bedroom in Chantalle's bawdy house, where she waited impatiently for Jason to return. Muffled male laughter echoed into the room from another quarter of the house, and she frowned. It did not improve her disposition to imagine why that fellow was chuckling, and she made a soft, huffing sound.

Questions had begun plaguing her. What in the world was she doing in this place, and how had she allowed Jason to talk her into waiting for him here?

A knock at the door sounded unexpectedly, and Elizabeth went still. She did not respond, although she was certain the light in the room could easily be seen underneath the doorway.

The knock sounded again; then an impatient female voice said, "Come on, open up, Elizabeth. This food is getting cold."

Elizabeth asked hesitantly, "Who is it?"

Again the impatient voice: "It's Angie. I'm the one who opened the door for you when you came to see Chantalle."

Elizabeth opened the door and saw the sultry brunette with a tray in her hand. Angie pushed past her and ordered, "Close the door. Chantalle will have a fit if you leave it unlocked."

Elizabeth frowned as she turned the key. Angie

had put the tray down and was looking at her expectantly. Elizabeth asked, "Is there something I can do for you?"

Angie laughed aloud. "I think the better question would be whether I can do anything for you."

Elizabeth scrutinized the woman boldly, then said, "Thanks for the offer, but I'm doing just fine."

"Oh, yes, I know that's true." Angie's full lips twisted with sarcasm. "Your only problems are that the authorities are looking for you, a slimy little man doesn't want anyone to know he's trying to locate you, and your boyfriend left you behind in a whorehouse saying he'd be back."

Elizabeth's eyes narrowed. "So you're trying to say …"

"I'm not saying anything, except that there are a few girls in this house who know Jason quite well, and who despite your problems wish they were you right now."

"Anything else?"

"That doesn't bother you, huh? Smart girl. A man has to get his jollies somehow, and most men know where to come to get them. Jason's no different."

"Oh, he's different, all right."

"Really?" Angie appeared amused. "Is that why he left you here while he went out gallivanting?"

Elizabeth eyed the voluptuous young woman for a silent moment, then said, "If you think you're going to get any information out of me by riling me up, you're wrong."

Angie stared at her a moment longer. "Well, maybe you're smarter than I thought you were. But being smart like you are, you don't like being penned up in this room all day."

"So?"

Angie's expression sobered as she said, "I might as well say what I came here for. First of all, Chantalle doesn't know I'm the one who brought you this tray. She told Marian to do it but I … talked her out of it. I don't intend to work in Chantalle's or anybody else's house all my life. I'm going to run a place like this one day, and I'm going to have women who really know how to keep men coming back. I figure there's only one way I'm going to manage that, so I'm making a little extra money wherever I can."

"So?"

"So, for a reasonable amount I'll get you whatever you need here, whenever you need it, and Chantalle doesn't have to know about it."

"I don't think I'll require your services."

"No? Well, just keep it in mind in case that fella of yours doesn't meet your expectations."

"He will."

"Oh, I forgot. Jason's different. He's not just out for himself like the rest of the boys."

"Look, I—"

"I don't need to hear it. I said what I came to say." Angie ordered abruptly, "Unlock the door and I'll get out. I got fellas downstairs looking for me—fellas who know they can depend on me for a good time. I'm losing money here."

Elizabeth hastened to oblige her.

* * *

"Let me in, Elizabeth."

Jason paused outside Elizabeth's door as sounds in the downstairs salon echoed up behind him. He heard the key turn in the lock and strode into the room as soon as the door cracked open, but he was not prepared for Elizabeth's gasp when she saw him.

"What happened?" Elizabeth touched his chin, where he was almost certain a bruise was rapidly forming.

He replied with an attempt at levity, "And you thought I was just out having a good time."

"I'm serious, Jason. What happened?"

Elizabeth drew him back to sit on the bed behind them, and Jason was momentarily amused as she moved quickly to the washstand and poured some water into the bowl. From the look on her face when he'd entered, Elizabeth had been primed to complain about being left behind in a locked room while he was out—a circumstance she would never find easy to accept. One look at him had obviously wiped that thought from her mind.

Jason glanced at his reflection in the dresser mirror across from the bed and winced. He looked worse than he had thought.

Back beside him, Elizabeth dipped a cloth into the water. He felt a familiar awakening at her gentle touch as she cleansed the cut over his eye. Her breath brushed his mouth when she alternately patted the swelling on his cheek and chin, and he breathed in her sweet scent. His glance dropped to her lips to see that they were tight with concern as she bathed his scraped knuckles.

"You didn't answer me, Jason," she said.

"I had a difference of opinion with a fellow who'd had too much to drink and had too much to say."

"About what?"

"I don't remember."

Elizabeth's eyes narrowed. "What did he say about me?"

"What makes you think the fight was about you?"

"I don't know. Maybe because you don't want to tell me."

Avoiding her question, Jason attempted to get his thoughts back on track as he said, "I didn't find out too much more than we already know about Captain Winters's death, but I do know that everything we heard about this Milton fellow is true. He made the rounds of the local saloons when he first arrived. He tried not to make it obvious that he was interested in locating you, but Whitey, the bartender at one of the saloons, saw right through him. What I don't know is why he's trying to find you, or who put him up to it."

Jason noted the thoughtful look in Elizabeth's eyes before she said, "Do you really think this fellow means me harm? I mean, why would anyone want to hurt me?"

"I don't know, but it's obvious that this fellow is hiding something. I wasn't in the best shape when I left Whitey's, so I figured I'd come right back here. But make no mistake about it: I'm going to find him tomorrow."

"Find him? And then what?"

"I'll talk to him … ask him some questions and see what his answers are."

"Do you think that's wise?"

Jason frowned. "I may look like I didn't do so well when that fella jumped me, but you can take my word for it that I left him on his back when I walked away."

"I'm not doubting you, Jason," Elizabeth said earnestly. "I'd never doubt you."

Jason was about to respond when she added, "I just thought it would be better if I went with you. Then maybe I could—"

"No." Jason shook his head adamantly. "It's too dangerous. This fella is after you, not me. I stand a better chance of getting him to talk if you're not there."

"But you said yourself, you're not at your best right now."

Jason took Elizabeth's hands in his. They were trembling, and his heart wrenched at her uncertainty. He said, "I'm fine now. I was a little dizzy when I left the saloon, but everything cleared up when it needed to."

"But look at you! You're battered and bruised."

"I've been worse."

"Maybe you should wait a day. Maybe you should forget the whole thing. Maybe this fella will just go away."

"He won't go away. He's been trying too hard to locate you to give up."

"But—"

"I'm fine. I'll take care of it."

Elizabeth's eyes had filled, her expression was tense, and she was clutching his hand. She did not look convinced, but strangely enough, all he wanted at that moment was … her.

Jason said softly, "I'm fine, Elizabeth."

Elizabeth's expression did not change.

Jason's gaze dropped again to her mouth as he said, "Maybe I could prove to you how fine I feel."

Elizabeth's cheeks flushed, and something broke deep inside him. Never more aware that he loved every inch of this independent, hardheaded, determined, and totally desirable woman, Jason slid her back against the bed behind them and covered her with his warmth. He whispered against her lips, "Let me show you, darlin'."

His appeal needed no reply.

Chantalle stood in the hallway outside the bedroom where Jason and Elizabeth were together. Angie, always on the alert and ready to show how smart she was, had slipped up beside her as she stood conversing with an old customer at the bar. Angie had whispered confidentially into her ear that Jason had finally returned and had gone directly to Elizabeth's room.

Aware that her relief at the news was briefly apparent in her expression, and annoyed to have revealed herself to the observant young whore, Chantalle had excused herself and walked up the stairs as casually as she was able.

In truth, Chantalle knew that she had been on edge from the moment Jason left the house. It was obvious how he felt about Elizabeth, and she knew he would not consider the danger to himself while trying to help her. She had also seen a look in Elizabeth's eye that said she was not the type to let him face danger alone.

Chantalle wanted this thing over and done, and she needed to know what Jason had discovered. She'd had too many losses in her life to gracefully sustain the loss of a friend who was important to her.

Perhaps it was time to talk to Jason about Hiram Charters and the message she had sent to Whit Hawk.

Chantalle had been about to knock on Elizabeth's door when she realized all was silent within. She frowned with concern when the sliver of light from underneath the door suddenly went dark.

At the subtle creaking of bedsprings, Chantalle released a tense breath. She turned back silently toward the staircase, certain that for the time being, Jason and Elizabeth were as safe as they ever could be.

Chapter Eleven

Elizabeth awoke slowly at the sounds of movement in the bordello bedroom. She turned toward the pillow beside hers, remembering the warmth of Jason's strong arms as they had held her through the night. She recalled the touch of his hands, the caress of his lips, the hunger he had awakened inside her, a longing that had expelled her fears and replaced them with a need only he could fill.

And he had filled it so well that she—

Elizabeth's eyes opened wide at the sudden realization that the pillow was empty—she was alone in bed.

Elizabeth snapped up to a seated position, unmindful of the coverlet that fell to her waist, exposing her breasts as she searched the early morning shadows of the room. She went still as an indistinct shadow took on a male form that started toward her. She gasped, then said, "Jason, you frightened me!"

Fully dressed, Jason brushed her mouth with his

as he sat on the bed beside her and said, "I have to admit that the sight of you sitting up in bed like that stirs an entirely different emotion in me, darlin'."

"Jason ..."

But Jason wasn't listening as his lips claimed hers again. His kiss lingered as he caressed her breasts, then lowered his head to suckle the pink crests.

Elizabeth gasped, powerless to move. Yet determined to speak, she said, "I wanted to say ... I need to tell you ..."

But her words drifted away as Jason pressed her back against the pillow to bathe her flesh with his lips. Lost in the wonder that he raised inside her, Elizabeth ran her fingers through his dark hair, then crushed him tight against her. She groaned softly when he left the delicate mounds to spread fiery kisses along the slender line of her shoulder, then moved back up to cover her mouth again with his. She separated her lips under his kiss, welcoming the spiraling heat inside her.

She heard Jason curse as he drew back from her abruptly and stripped off his clothes. She sucked in a breath as he entered her. She clutched him tight, meeting his thrusts as the anticipation built. A revealing shuddering overtook his powerful frame, and a reciprocal emotion escalated inside her as well.

She felt the moment approaching as Jason's control began slipping away, as the colors in her mind spiraled brighter, as they reached mutual climax with a sudden impassioned thrust.

Replete in the aftermath of their lovemaking,

Elizabeth lay motionless beneath Jason's muscular warmth. He raised himself above her to kiss her gently before he whispered against her lips, "I didn't intend this. You were sleeping so soundly that I didn't expect to wake you up before I left."

"Before you left?" Elizabeth opened her eyes to Jason's sober gaze.

"Only for a little while. I want to get down to the docks so I can talk to the seamen on the *Silver Dawn*. Captain Winters didn't hide the way he felt about Simon Gault's involvement with the Yankees during the blockade. Someone has to know something."

"I'll go with you."

"Elizabeth … I told you, it's too dangerous. Besides, I don't want the authorities to find you yet. If they put you in jail—"

"Jail!"

"As far as they're concerned, you were the last person to see Captain Winters alive."

"But I didn't see him alive. He was dead when I got there."

"I know that. You know that. But there's no way we can prove it yet."

"Jason—"

"Don't worry. I'll get this all straightened out, and I'll learn what this Milton person is up to, as well. Just be patient a little longer."

"I don't want to stay behind again."

"It's only for a little while."

"What does that mean, hours, days … months?"

"I wouldn't do that to you, Elizabeth." Jason's

dark eyes held hers. "I'd get you away from here ... from Galveston."

"I can't leave—not yet." Elizabeth unconsciously clutched the pendant that rested against her skin. "I came here for a reason that's important to me. I don't want to leave until I'm sure I've done all I can to find my family."

"It won't do you any good to find your family if you don't live to enjoy what you find out."

"Jason!"

"I need to make sure you're safe—can you understand that?"

"Of course, but—"

"No buts. Just do what I say. Stay here and wait. I won't let you down."

"But ..."

Elizabeth went silent when Jason's expression hardened. She watched as he got up and turned to dress. She silently marveled at the sight of him standing naked in the shadows of the room ... broad shoulders, narrow hips, powerful arms that had gripped her tightly, muscular legs that had driven him deep inside her. He turned briefly toward her as he pushed back the thick, dark hair that had fallen forward onto his forehead, and she saw his strong features soften briefly as they had when he'd held her in his arms. She recalled the sensation of winding her fingers in his hair at the height of her passion. She took a breath, feeling herself flush when her gaze slipped lower, past his flat stomach to the purely male part of him that had served them both so well. She wanted to tell him that none of the questions plaguing them needed answers, as far as she was concerned. All that mattered was the two of them. But she knew neither one of them would be satisfied to surrender issues so important to them.

Instead, Elizabeth watched as he dressed. Pushing back the coverlet she stood up beside him, frowning as he strapped on the gun belt he had started wearing when they left the cabin. She said, "Do you really need to wear that?"

Jason's glance said it all.

Studying him for a moment, Elizabeth pressed her naked length against him, and Jason slipped his arms around her in return. She did not say a word when he grabbed his hat, kissed her briefly, and walked out the doorway.

At his admonition, Elizabeth locked the door behind him, and then turned toward the washstand. She understood that Jason had to do what he felt was right. What she had not added was that there were certain things she felt she must do, too—no matter what the cost.

"So you're telling me that you missed the perfect opportunity to take care of Jason Dodd, and you just left the scene?"

Bruce removed his wire-rimmed glasses and wiped them with an unsteady hand, a nervous habit that betrayed his tension. He had been called into Simon's office at Gault Shipping & Exchange only moments after Simon arrived that morning. He had known the moment he walked through the

263

doorway that his boss's mood was foul. He responded, "There were too many people around, fellows from the saloon and all. It would've caused a problem if one of them saw me."

"I don't like excuses."

Bruce adjusted his glasses and said tightly, "I'll find him again, and I'll do what I have to do. Don't worry about that."

"I don't expect to wait, Bruce, and I don't intend to allow Elizabeth Huntington to slip through my fingers. Jason Dodd is in my way."

"I know that."

Bruce felt the heat of Simon's gaze singe him as his employer stood up behind his impressive desk and said, "Do your job. I don't need to remind you how important this is to me."

"I told you I'd take care of it, boss."

"I've instructed Billy Jerome to sit in the outer office temporarily. I've told him that you'll be in and out doing some work for me. He knows better than to ask questions, and that should free you up until you've done what you have to do."

Bruce frowned. Billy Jerome at his desk? He wasn't sure he liked that. Billy Jerome was too ambitious to suit him.

"Don't disappoint me."

Responding with new motivation, Bruce said, "Don't worry. I won't."

Bruce pulled the office door closed behind him, then stopped in his tracks at the sight of Billy Jerome already sitting at his desk. Bruce noted with tightening animosity that Billy was short, slight, wearing glasses—a younger version of himself. Billy's smile said he was just waiting for the chance to replace him.

Bruce raised his chin. That wouldn't happen.

He left the office without speaking a word.

Fully dressed, Elizabeth waited alone in her room as the sounds of waking stirred in the bordello outside her locked door. The rumbling of her stomach reminded her that she was hungry, but unlike Jason, who was free to eat whenever he liked, she needed to wait until someone delivered her food.

As if in response to her thoughts, a knock sounded on the door and a familiar voice said, "Open up, Elizabeth."

Elizabeth turned the key and was pushed aside by Angie as she entered the room with a tray in hand. Angie placed the tray on the bed and said, "Don't get me wrong. I'm not anybody's maid." She snickered. "I just enjoy seeing you sitting up here all alone, *waiting*."

Elizabeth said soberly, "I suppose you're what is normally described as a bitch."

Momentarily taken aback by Elizabeth's comment, Angie gave a short laugh. "Well, one thing I got to say for you—you ain't afraid to speak your mind."

"No, I'm not." Elizabeth's intense gaze pinned Angie as she said, "Let's talk business, Angie. You said you could get me what I want, when I want it."

Angie's gaze narrowed. "Yeah, that's what I said … as long as the price is right."

Elizabeth turned toward her suitcase. She removed a leather purse and withdrew a roll of her rapidly dwindling spending money. Angie's eyes widened as she counted off a sum slowly and asked, "Will this be enough?"

Angie replied with a raised brow, "What do you want me to do? Poison somebody?"

But Elizabeth did not smile when she replied, "Just answer yes or no."

Angie said, "Hell, yes, to whatever you want."

Still unsmiling, Elizabeth said, "The money is practically yours."

Milton cursed the early morning hour as he walked cautiously along the docks, following Dodd, who was some distance ahead. He had arisen at the crack of dawn from his miserable bed in the Easton Hotel, dressed, and made his way quickly to the rear entrance of Chantalle's bordello, where Dodd had returned after the fight on the docks. He had guessed that Dodd would be staying the night. No man with a drop of blood in his veins would let a woman like Elizabeth Huntington stay in that place to sleep alone.

It was common knowledge that Dodd and Chantalle had become friends during the blockade. He had no doubt that Elizabeth and Dodd were both hiding there. He suspected that Elizabeth Huntington was properly grateful to Dodd, too.

In any case, he had known that if he was wrong

and Dodd hadn't stayed at Chantalle's for the night, it wouldn't be too difficult to find him again. Dodd wouldn't stray far from Elizabeth Huntington, and she had nowhere else to go. He had also suspected that however comfortable Dodd had made himself with Elizabeth Huntington during the night, he would be up early and on his way. Fellows like him always got an early start. He could never understand it.

Milton halted to roll a cigarette when Dodd approached the *Silver Dawn* and began talking to one of the seamen working near the ship. Dressed inconspicuously, Milton knew no one would give him a second glance on a dock teaming with early morning activity. It occurred to him that Dodd was safe from whatever machinations Gault's lackey intended while he was out in plain sight. He had needed only a glimpse of the fellow to realize that however he intended to take care of Dodd, he would not make a direct assault. Rather, he suspected the lackey would wait until he could be assured of success by striking when no one was around, preferably with a shot in the dark, or with a knife in the back.

Milton paused at that thought, remembering the manner of Captain Winters's death. Perhaps Gault's lackey was more adept at the trade than he had realized.

Milton scrutinized the area as Dodd continued talking to the seaman. He wondered what Dodd could possibly be asking the fellow, and how he could turn this circumstance to his own benefit.

* * *

"You're sure Captain Winters had never heard of Elizabeth Huntington?"

Jason stood opposite Salty Rhymes, an old salt named for the profession he had chosen as a boy. Jason was aware that not only was Salty the first mate on the *Silver Dawn*; he was also the captain's best friend. It had been a stroke of luck to meet him on the docks, and Jason was determined to take advantage of it.

Salty brushed a bead of perspiration from his graying temple, his unshaven face sober as he said, "Captain Winters didn't know her, I'm sure. He got a glimpse of her with Simon Gault when we landed, and he told me so himself."

"What did he say?"

"He said he didn't know who she was, but he hoped Gault wasn't taking her in like he took in everybody else in Galveston. He said a pretty young woman like her didn't deserve somebody like Gault, because he'd just use her like he used all the women he was interested in."

"That's all he said?"

Salty smiled. "He said some other things, like if he had a woman like her ashore, he might never ship out again." Salty's smile faded. "I guess Captain Winters ain't never going to ship out again anyways."

Refusing to allow Salty to indulge his grief, Jason pressed, "Did you tell all this to the authorities?"

"I told them. They didn't want to hear nothing bad about Gault, of course. Then they said Gault had vouched for Elizabeth Huntington, saying that she had a wealthy background in New York City and that she had told him she came to Galveston hoping to find family she had lost touch with. The investigators said Gault told them he figured that since she thought her family had something to do with shipping, she had probably thought Captain Winters might be able to give her some information about them."

Jason nodded, aware that Gault had provided Elizabeth with the perfect excuse for visiting Captain Winters.

"What's your interest in all this, Jason?" Salty looked at Jason inquisitively. "You didn't know Captain Winters, and you ain't never been a friend of Gault's, if I remember right."

Jason responded with a touch of a smile. "I met up with Elizabeth Huntington a while back, and I thought she was too good to waste on somebody like Gault. I tried to warn her about him, but she didn't like hearing it. I figured she couldn't have had anything to do with Captain Winters's death, though—not a lady like her."

"The investigators said they just needed to ask her about the night when she went to see Captain Winters. They figured she might have seen something that would give them a hint who killed the captain. They couldn't figure where she had disappeared to."

"She might be visiting somewhere on the island," Jason said evasively. "She might not even know they're looking for her."

"Could be. Anyways, the crew and me are waiting for Williams Shipping to get us a new captain for the *Silver Dawn*. She's a fine old ship. Captain Winters would want us to take good care of her."

"Good luck, Salty." Jason extended his hand. "I hope you get a new captain as fine as Captain Winters."

Salty nodded, frowning as he turned away. Jason walked on, frowning as well. He didn't like the way things were shaping up. Gault had talked the authorities out of considering Elizabeth as a possible suspect in Captain Winters's murder. He knew Gault too well to believe he had done that without a reason. He figured Gault would use his defense of Elizabeth to make her feel indebted to him.

Jason's jaw tightened. *The bastard.* Gault would never get the chance to collect. Jason would take Elizabeth to the authorities himself and straighten things out as soon as he cleaned up the mystery about Milton.

But in the meantime, there was something he needed to do.

Elizabeth unlocked the door to her room in response to Angie's urging from the hallway. Angie slipped inside, placed a package on the bed, and said as she turned to Elizabeth, "It's done. Where's my money?"

Elizabeth counted out the amount into her hand.

Shoving the money into her pocket, Angie exhorted, "Just don't tell Chantalle I was the one who got you what you needed. I don't want no more trouble with her."

"Agreed."

Elizabeth frowned as she ripped open the package in the silence of her room minutes later. She scrutinized the contents.

The anger inside him was building as Jason walked boldly up the staircase to Gault Shipping & Exchange and entered the building. Brass railings, imported tile, thick carpeting—all to impress, but Jason wasn't clear exactly who was more impressed, Simon or the visitors for whom the ostentation was intended.

Jason approached the clerk in the outer office. Surprised when the fellow looked up at him, he said, "You're not the fella who usually sits at this desk."

"No, I ain't." The bespectacled fellow adjusted his glasses and asked, "Do you have an appointment with Mr. Gault?"

Jason almost laughed. Instead he responded succinctly, "No."

"The boss is busy. He don't want to be disturbed."

"But he's in?"

"Yeah, but like I said—"

Jason walked past the bespectacled clerk as the fellow scrambled to catch up with him, calling out, "Stop! Mr. Gault don't want to be disturbed!"

Jason pushed open the door to Gault's office and strode inside. He did not miss the revealing antipathy in Gault's expression before Simon forced a smile and said to his flustered employee, "Never mind, Billy. Mr. Dodd obviously has something that

271

he feels is important to say or he wouldn't burst in here so rudely. I'll talk to him. Close the door behind you when you leave."

When the bewildered clerk did not immediately react, Gault said more harshly, "Leave, and close the door behind you!"

Waiting only until the click of the door sounded, Gault asked, "What do you want, Dodd?"

Wondering how anyone could be taken in by the benevolent persona Gault adopted and dropped just as easily, Jason waited a moment to draw his emotions under control before responding, "I think a better question would be, What do you want—from Elizabeth?"

"What business is it of yours?" Gault hesitated, then asked, "Or maybe I shouldn't ask that question. The answer might be embarrassing to both you and Elizabeth, considering that she left the luxurious quarters I arranged for her after she spent the night with you."

"Frieda reported that to you, of course."

"I arranged for Frieda to serve Elizabeth, and she was upset."

"You arranged for her to *spy* on Elizabeth."

"Why would I do that?"

"The answer is obvious."

"Meaning?"

"Meaning you want Elizabeth and will do whatever you need to do to get her."

"Really." Gault chuckled. "Need I remind you that I'm considered the most eligible bachelor in Galveston?"

"Maybe … by some."

Simon drew back haughtily. "Elizabeth came to me for help in locating the family that she lost as a child. I sympathized with her plight and decided to help her."

"Elizabeth doesn't need your help anymore."

"I think you're wrong, especially in light of Captain Winters's murder."

"Which was very convenient for you, since Captain Winters was one of the few willing to speak out about your collaboration with the Yankees during the war."

"Not that fiction again."

"If it's fiction, why has anyone willing to speak out about it disappeared or been found mysteriously murdered?"

"I don't know what you're talking about."

Jason said with barely controlled anger, "You know, all right, but I didn't come here to talk about your collaboration, Gault. I'll prove it sooner or later, and everyone will see you for what you are."

"Fiction again."

Ignoring Gault's response, Jason said, "I came here today for one reason only—to warn you to stay away from Elizabeth."

"Really? What gives you the right to speak for Elizabeth?" Gault then added snidely, "Oh, you finally managed to convince her that I'm responsible for every crime that happened in this port in the last twenty years, is that it? When did that happen, when you started sleeping with her?"

Gault's arrogant remark broke through Jason's

control. His angry rush toward Gault halted abruptly when Gault pulled a pistol from his desk drawer and warned, "I'd dislike explaining this situation to the authorities if you make it necessary for me to pull the trigger on this gun, but you can be sure I will if I have to."

"Bastard."

"Get out! But first—give Elizabeth this message for me. Tell her that I understand her confusion, that I've explained her circumstances to the authorities and they no longer consider her a suspect in Captain Winters's murder. Tell her I'll take her back under my wing anytime she decides to shed your influence."

"Over my dead body."

Gault's cold glance was revealing.

Jason responded just as coldly, "I'm going to leave you with a something to think about, too, Gault—my promise that I'm going to make sure you get what's coming to you. And just for the record, I'm also going to make sure you don't take Elizabeth down with you."

Milton scrambled into a shadowed nook beside the staircase to Gault Shipping & Exchange, cursing as Jason exited the building unexpectedly and started back down the stairs with a face as dark as a storm cloud. He took a relieved breath when Jason turned toward the Strand without seeing him.

Milton followed, certain he would not have to wait much longer to act.

* * *

Elizabeth unlocked the door to her room and peered into the hallway. Satisfied that it was empty, she stepped out and locked the bedroom door behind her. She pulled the oversize Stetson down on her forehead, grateful that her heavy hair, tucked out of sight underneath the brim, held it firmly in place. The men's trousers and shirt that Angie had brought her were faded and worn, but they fit her loosely enough to conceal her slight figure underneath. The boots were her greatest problem; they were worn down at the heels and at least two sizes too large, causing her to walk awkwardly as she made her way toward the rear door.

Elizabeth released a relieved breath when she closed the door behind her. She unconsciously touched the outline of the small pistol in her pocket, then started down the staircase. She stepped down into the alleyway and scanned it briefly before heading toward the street. The dock was her goal. She needed to find Jason so she could prove to him that she was capable of working beside him without attracting undue attention. She had tried to explain to him that she couldn't wait safely locked up in a room while he exposed himself to the very danger that he claimed might be waiting for her. If he objected, she was just as determined to proceed alone, perhaps to contact Charlie, who seemed to have an uncanny insight into the workings of Galveston; or, as a last resort, to approach Simon himself.

Once she finally reached the docks, Elizabeth felt a stab of panic. Jason was nowhere to be found. She had walked through the heavy morning dock traffic, satisfied that she went unnoticed as she attempted to locate him. She had paused to watch the activity on the *Silver Dawn*, expecting at any moment that he would step into sight, but to no avail. She had walked past local saloons closed at that hour of the morning and had checked every other conceivable place where he might be, but had found no trace of him.

Elizabeth glanced at the sun as it made steady progress toward its summit. Jason had told her he wouldn't be long. She couldn't have missed him if he had gone back to Chantalle's—or could she? If so, he would be upset to find her gone.

A strange sense of anxiety suddenly overwhelmed her. Something was wrong.

Elizabeth turned back in the direction from which she had come.

Jason knocked at the door to Elizabeth's room, urging softly, "Unlock the door, Elizabeth."

He knocked again. After his brief contact with Gault, he had wanted to reassure himself of Elizabeth's safety. He knew she chafed at her circumstances, and he needed to emphasize to her again how important it was that she remain there until he discovered the connection between Captain Winters's death, Milton's pursuit of her, and Simon Gault—who he felt instinctively was deeply involved in everything that was happening.

Another truth was, he just needed to hold her.

Elizabeth's safety suddenly superceding all else in his mind, Jason knocked again. He heard a step and turned toward Chantalle as she approached, wearing a common cotton robe far different from any garment he had ever seen her in before. Her hair was unbound and her face was free of makeup, revealing her age as she said tensely, "What's wrong, Jason?"

Equally tense, Jason said, "I left earlier this morning and told Elizabeth to wait until I came back, but she isn't answering. Do you have another key to this room?"

"No."

His jaw tight, Jason did not wait for Chantalle's permission before he kicked at the doorknob, once ... twice ... then moved quickly inside when the door snapped open. He halted abruptly at the realization that the room was empty. In a few quick steps he moved to the bed, where Elizabeth's suitcase lay open; the contents were still carefully folded and undisturbed.

Jason turned toward Chantalle and said, "She went out, dammit! She knows how dangerous it is for her to be on the street right now." He took a breath, his heart pounding. "I have to find her."

He brushed past Chantalle, but turned back toward her when she gripped his arm unexpectedly and said, "Wait, Jason. There's something that I think you probably should know."

"She told you where she was going?"

"No. It's something else." Chantalle's thin brows drew together in a frown as she said, "I don't know if this has something to do with where Elizabeth went or not. It's about the pendant Elizabeth is wearing."

Chantalle hesitated, and Jason urged, "What about it?"

"The crest ... I knew I had seen something like it before when it was described to me. A fellow named Whit Hawk came to Galveston a little while back. He had a ring with the same crest on it. He was looking for a brother he had lost contact with who he said had the same ring. He said his father had given duplicate rings to his sons ... and pendants to his daughters."

Jason went still, then said, "And you didn't tell Elizabeth about him?"

"Whit said his sisters were both dead. The only thing I knew about Elizabeth was that she couldn't remember anything about her past, which included where she had gotten the pendant. I figured Whit should be the first person to be told. Hiram Charters was going right past the ranch on his way up north, where Whit had moved to be with his new bride, so I wrote Whit a letter and asked Hiram to deliver it to him."

"And?"

"Whit hasn't answered. I know Hiram delivered the letter. He wouldn't have let me down. I don't understand it."

Jason said tightly, "Why didn't you tell me, especially when I brought Elizabeth here?"

"I wasn't sure the pendant had anything to do with what was happening, but now I don't want to take any chances."

Silent for a moment, Jason said, "I have to find Elizabeth."

Waiting concealed in the alleyway behind the bordello, Milton felt a familiar sense of anticipation building. He had done everything right. He had gotten up early and had been there when Dodd emerged from the bordello's rear entrance. He had followed Dodd to the docks and then to Gault Shipping & Exchange. He had noted Dodd's black mood when he emerged and had sensed the time was ripe when Dodd headed back toward the bordello again. He somehow knew it wouldn't be long before the whole matter came to a head.

Startled by movement at the entrance to the alleyway, Milton drew back. His breathing hitched when he saw a slender male figure enter and start toward the bordello.

He stared harder, then realized with a jolt that the person was not a man. It was a woman. It was Elizabeth Huntington!

His heart palpitating, Milton spontaneously scrapped his previous plan, recognizing that he would never have a better chance than this to eliminate Elizabeth Huntington without suspicion. The location was isolated. Elizabeth was dressed in male clothing while approaching a bordello, and if Sylvia Huntington didn't consider a case of mistaken identity the "accident" she demanded, he'd make sure she paid him in full anyway.

The heavy pounding of Milton's heart echoed in his ears as Elizabeth drew nearer. Everything was in place. He need only wait a few minutes longer until he had a clear shot.

Milton raised his gun. He fired, elated when the force of his bullet knocked Elizabeth backward.

Milton stood up, intent on his victim. He did not see Jason step out of the doorway at the top of the bordello staircase. Nor did he see Jason fire the shot that struck him.

Milton felt only the impact of the bullet as it thudded into him, throwing him back against the packing cases where he had been concealed.

He experienced only the pain that stole his breath—the last breath he would ever take.

Halting abruptly with shock as he prepared to enter the alleyway, Bruce saw Elizabeth fall. He saw Jason fire the shot that brought the gunman down, then saw Jason rush down the bordello staircase toward Elizabeth.

Frantic to finish the job that Simon had set for him, Bruce raised his gun to fire at Jason, only to halt when Chantalle and several of her women rushed out of the bordello door behind him.

Aware that he could not risk being seen, Bruce cursed at the chance he had lost. He shuddered with dread at the thought of Simon's reaction as he slipped out onto the street.

Jason raced down the bordello staircase toward Elizabeth's still form. When he reached her, he saw that her hair had spilled out of her hat as she had fallen, her beautiful face was composed and still, and the bloodstain on her chest was rapidly widening.

Unaware that Chantalle had stumbled down the staircase behind him, or that she had ordered one of her women to race for the doctor, he ripped the neckerchief from around his neck and pressed it against Elizabeth's wound as he drew her up into his arms. Her breathing was shallow as he whispered urgently, "Elizabeth, can you hear me? Open your eyes, darlin'. Talk to me."

Jason was unconscious of his shuddering as he drew Elizabeth closer and demanded softly, "Open your eyes, dammit!"

The anger in his tone seemed to reach her where his plea had failed. Elizabeth stirred. Her eyes opened slightly as she responded in halting breaths, "I w-wanted to find you … to show you …"

Elizabeth's eyelids flickered as her voice trailed away.

Jason urged hoarsely, "Don't close your eyes, Elizabeth. Listen to me. You're going to be fine. You don't have to worry about that Milton fellow. He can't hurt you anymore."

"I'm tired.…"

"No, don't close your eyes!" Panicking, Jason lowered his face toward hers. His breath brushed her lips as he whispered, "Stay with me, Elizabeth. Please."

Elizabeth did not respond.

Jason glanced up to see Chantalle standing frozen beside him. He said brokenly, "Where's that doctor?"

"Jason ..."

Jason glanced back down at Elizabeth, startled as a smile flickered briefly across her lips, and she rasped, "G-guess you were right ... should have waited."

Jason felt Elizabeth's delicate frame jerk. He saw a look of panic flash across her face as she caught her breath. He watched helplessly as she struggled to breathe.

Motionless, still holding her in his arms, he stared at her incredulously as her breathing stilled.

Chapter Twelve

Jason unlocked the door and walked boldly into Milton Stowe's Easton Hotel room. Several days had passed since Elizabeth was shot, but the horror of it was with him still. He frowned, recalling the hopeless fury that had shuddered through him as he had carried Elizabeth up the stairs and placed her gently on the bed they had shared. He remembered talking to her gently, whispering his love for her, although he knew in his heart she could not hear him. He recalled the moment when the doctor arrived and pushed him unceremoniously out of the way as he began working over Elizabeth's still form.

Jason recalled the almost debilitating sense of helplessness that had swept over him. He remembered standing back, staring at the bloody circle on Elizabeth's chest, then the blinding rage that had suffused him when the doctor chased him out of the room.

It was then that he had gone back downstairs to search the gunman's body in order to identify him. He remembered finding the key to the Easton Hotel room in his vest and a receipt that identified the fellow as Milton Stowe. He had shoved them both into his pocket, silently vowing that he would uncover the reason behind the gunman's assault.

Taking the first step in that pursuit, Jason glanced around the room. It was empty, devoid of any personal articles except for the suitcase lying beside the door. He picked it up and tossed it on the bed, then searched it coldly, noting that everything in it appeared to be recently purchased. He halted abruptly at the sight of an envelope tucked into a pocket at the bottom of the case. His blood ran cold as he pulled it open. It contained a return railroad ticket to New York City—and a photograph of Elizabeth.

Jason's jaw locked tight as he turned the envelope over to examine it more closely. He went still when he read the return address embossed on the obviously expensive stationery. His face flushing with heat, he stuffed it into his pocket and slammed the suitcase closed. He gave the room a last cursory glance, then walked out into the hall and locked the door behind him.

His expression sober, Jason walked down the private wing of Chantalle's bordello and knocked on the bedroom door that Elizabeth and he shared. He entered at the response from within and glanced at Chantalle, who stood beside the bed where Elizabeth lay motionless. Elizabeth's eyes opened. She turned her head toward him and he smiled. Her color was ashen, her eyelids were heavy, and her lips could not seem to form words as she tried to speak, but she had never looked more beautiful to him than she did at that moment.

Jason sat on the chair beside the bed and clasped Elizabeth's hands in his. The memory of her lying in the alleyway, struggling to breathe, with a bloody circle rapidly widening on her chest, vividly returned. He recalled that he had panicked when her breathing appeared to stop, only to hear Chantalle admonish harshly, "She's unconscious. Carry her upstairs into the bedroom. The doctor will be here soon."

He remembered that except for the moments when Dr. Blake insisted he leave the room so he could work freely, he had not left Elizabeth's side until she was pronounced out of danger that morning.

"Gently, Jason." The doctor spoke to him in warning from the corner of the room, bringing Jason back to the present as he continued, "Remember, Elizabeth is still fragile."

Elizabeth countered in an unsteady whisper, "I'm fine. It's only a shoulder wound, and I'll be up on my feet in no time."

The graying physician paused as he closed his bag. Looking over his glasses, he said, "You neglected to add that you've lost a lot of blood, Elizabeth, and that a few inches lower and the shot would have been fatal."

Elizabeth ignored Dr. Blake's comment as she asked hoarsely, "Who was the fellow who shot me, Jason? Other than telling me he's dead, nobody seems to know anything."

Jason reported stiffly, "The man's name was Milton Stowe. He came from New York City."

"He was the man who was looking for me?"

"You never met the man?" Jason asked

Elizabeth shook her head. Not prepared to voice his suspicions quite yet, Jason said, "We can talk about him when you're feeling stronger, but I was thinking that, in the meantime, maybe it would be a good idea to send a wire to your adoptive mother in case she should hear something about what happened. I don't think you should tell her the whole truth, just that you were hurt in an accident, but that you're fine, and the man responsible was killed."

Elizabeth nodded. "You're probably right. She's so frail, and she's probably wondering why I haven't written. It would relieve her mind." Elizabeth paused, then said, "I'll trust you to say the right things if you'll send the wire for me, Jason. When I'm well I'll write to her myself."

Jason nodded. He watched for Elizabeth's reaction when he added as if in afterthought, "Didn't you mention you had an aunt Sylvia who lived in New York? Do you want me to notify her, too?"

Her expression more revealing than she realized, Elizabeth hesitated before responding, "Mother Ella will pass the information on to her." She added more softly, "To be truthful, Aunt Sylvia never liked me very much."

Elizabeth briefly closed her eyes, allowing Jason a moment to draw his hidden anger under control.

When the door clicked closed behind Chantalle and Dr. Blake, Jason began hesitantly, "Do you remember much about the time immediately after you were shot, Elizabeth?"

Elizabeth paused, then said, "Not too much. I remember that I couldn't breathe, but you were there ... and Chantalle. The next thing I remember is lying in bed with you sitting beside me."

"Do you remember anything else?"

Elizabeth shook her head, her brow furrowed. "Should I?"

"I did a lot of talking when I thought you were slipping away from me. I told you that I love you, Elizabeth, that my world would be empty without you in it, that I wanted you to hold on—if not for your own sake, then for mine, because I wouldn't be able to bear losing you."

Jason saw the tears that filled Elizabeth's eyes as she replied, "But they were words spoken in the heat of the moment, and you want to take them back now ... is that what you're trying to say?"

Startled at her response, Jason said, "No ... never! I knew I loved you the first minute I touched you. I fought it every step of the way, because I didn't want to be distracted from the purpose I was sworn to, but I couldn't get you out of my mind, no matter how hard I tried. I held back on how I felt, and then, somehow, you were in my arms. But seeing you lying in that alleyway, struggling to breathe, made it clear how precious every minute can be. I want to make sure you hear me when I say it this time."

Elizabeth's eyes brimmed with emotion as Jason said fervently, "I love you, Elizabeth. I want you to be with me the rest of my life. If we're both sworn to different purposes, we'll work toward them together. You've become a part of me, darlin', too big a part for me to ever let you go."

Pausing when Elizabeth did not reply, Jason said, "I don't expect you to say too much right now, but I want you to know that I'm going to find out why that fella was following you ... why he shot you ... and I'll make sure the person behind it all pays—whoever it is."

"Jason ..."

Elizabeth's face had paled. Jason noted that her breathing was quickening, and he felt a moment's apprehension. He had spoken too soon. He had pushed too hard. He said, "Don't say anything. I just want you to know that whatever your answer is, I'll take care of things just as I said. I wouldn't—"

"Yes, Jason."

Jason paused. He searched Elizabeth's pale face as he said, "What did you say?"

Elizabeth responded breathlessly, "You told me once that all I needed to say was yes. So I'm saying it. Yes."

His throat suddenly tight, Jason did not immediately respond, allowing Elizabeth to add, "In case I wasn't clear … I love you, too, Jason. Everything you said … I feel the same way."

Regaining his voice, Jason hushed her abruptly and whispered, "Rest now, darlin'. Go to sleep. I'll stay here with you."

Her eyelids heavy, Elizabeth said, "Did you hear me, Jason?"

"I heard you." Unable to resist, Jason pressed his mouth lightly to hers. He drew back reluctantly to whisper, "Just be ready to say it all again when you're better, so I can show you how I feel right now."

Elizabeth's brief smile lit his heart as she whispered, "Promise?"

Her eyes drifted closed as Jason responded with a single word filled with unspoken meaning.

"Yes."

Sylvia Huntington walked to the door to answer the knock that sounded in Ella Huntington's elegant bedroom. She glanced back at the older woman where she lay in her bed, then accepted the wire that Molly handed dutifully to her. She dismissed the young maid coldly. She had finally instilled in the servants' minds that *she* was now running the Huntington mansion, as she always should have been, and that during her sister-in-law's illness, *she* would handle all details pertaining to the Huntington estate.

Sylvia glanced at the sealed wire with disdain. It was undoubtedly from Elizabeth, an attempt to make amends for not having written as often as

Ella expected. Sylvia concealed a derisive snort. That was fine with her. Mr. Stowe obviously had not yet accomplished his purpose or he would have notified her personally by wire so she would be properly prepared when Ella received the news. Actually, although she was aware how important it was for Elizabeth's death to appear an accident, she was growing impatient. If Mr. Stowe delayed much longer, he'd be the one to receive a wire from her, telling him she was tired of waiting.

"Is that wire for me, Sylvia?"

Sylvia forced a smile at Ella's question. The old hag knew it was for her. Who else would be receiving a wire at her house?

Sylvia replied as pleasantly as she could manager. "Yes, it's for you. I'll open it for you, if you wish. It's no trouble."

"No, I'll open it." Ella held out a shaky hand, her expression brightening. "It must be from Elizabeth. Hopefully, it's good news. She said she'd wire me as soon as she discovered anything about her family." Her hand still extended, Ella said, "I do so want her to find them if she can. I ... I don't want her to be alone."

Sylvia looked at the hand Ella held out toward her. Knobby and skeletal, it bespoke age, sickness, and deterioration. The old woman needed to live only a little longer, just until Mr. Stowe could accomplish his job.

Unable to resist, Sylvia held on to the telegram a few moments more, silently tormenting the bedridden woman as she said, "Elizabeth would never be alone. She'll always have Trevor and me. We are *family,* you know.

"Of course." Ella licked her lips as she looked anxiously at the envelope in Sylvia's hand. "I'm sure Elizabeth realizes that and appreciates your concern, but she would still like to learn more about her origins. I know whatever she discovers will be a great consolation to her."

"I hope so. Of course, if the information she discovers is negative, she could always ignore it and go on from there."

"Sylvia ... please." Ella's shaking hand was still extended toward her, and Sylvia inwardly sneered. The old witch's arm would fall off before she'd relent.

Realizing she could delay no longer, Sylvia walked the few steps to the bed and placed the wire in Ella's trembling hand. She watched as the old woman tore open the envelope. Her gaze intent, Sylvia noted the moment that the expectation on Ella's face stiffened and turned into anxiety. Unable to wait a moment longer, Sylvia pressed, "What is it, Ella? What's wrong?"

Ella looked up, her color whitening. "It's not from Elizabeth. It's from someone called Jason Dodd. He says that Elizabeth has had an accident." Elation swept Sylvia's senses the moment before Ella said, "But she's all right ... fine, actually. The doctor says she'll be on her feet soon ... but the man responsible for her accident is dead."

Sylvia felt the blood rush to her head as she asked as calmly as she could manage, "What happened?"

"I don't know exactly. The wire isn't explicit, except to say that—"

"Let me read that wire!"

Sylvia snatched the telegram out of Ella's hand and read:

ELIZABETH HAD AN ACCIDENT BUT SHE IS FINE. STOP. THE MAN RESPONSIBLE IS DEAD. STOP. THE AUTHORITIES ARE INVESTIGATING PECULIARITIES IN THE CASE. STOP. THEY WILL TAKE ACTION AS SOON AS MORE INFORMATION IS OBTAINED. STOP. ELIZABETH WILL WRITE SOON. STOP. SHE SAYS NOT TO WORRY. STOP.

SIGNED JASON DODD.

Sylvia's heart pounded. Her head began a painful throbbing as she searched her mind for details. She restrained a gasp when she remembered the picture of Elizabeth that she had provided for Mr. Stowe. Could it be traced back to her?

Sylvia then recalled with breathtaking horror that she had placed Mr. Stowe's railroad tickets in an envelope embossed with her name and address—a deliberate, prideful gesture for which she would possibly pay dearly.

Sylvia dropped the wire back on the bed and turned toward the door, her mind whirling. She did not respond when Ella asked, "Where are you going, Sylvia? Is something wrong?"

Instead she pulled open the bedroom door and

walked out into the hallway. Ella called out behind her, but she did not answer. The corridor reeled around her as she recalled the sizable amount she had withdrawn from her account in order to advance Mr. Stowe the first payment. Would the authorities check her account when the other information came to light? How could she explain such a large withdrawal when she was ordinarily so niggardly? She had nothing tangible to show for it.

The pain in Sylvia's head grew deadening as she staggered forward. Her left arm had gone numb. Her left leg was dragging. She saw Trevor enter the hallway and heard him ask as he approached, "Mother, is something wrong?"

She tried to respond, but her drooping lips would not cooperate.

Her legs collapsed from under her and her heavy bulk hit the floor with a loud thud, but she felt only the tightening pain in her head as she stared up at the vaulted ceiling whirling above her.

The pain intensified.

The light faded.

Her breathing stopped.

Chapter Thirteen

Elizabeth walked briskly alongside the sunny New York thoroughfare. She had recovered from the gunshot wound she had received in that Galveston back alley, and now she struggled to dismiss it from her mind. How fully she had recovered was a point of contention between Jason and herself. He accused her of rushing her recuperation, of being too independent. She accused him of worrying too much and told him she was fine. They had argued those points right up until the moment they had boarded the train back to New York—but Elizabeth knew the arguments were based on love.

Elizabeth tucked her hand more securely underneath Jason's strong arm, grateful that they had reached their destination at last. Feeling a little anxious, she had told Jason she preferred to walk the last few blocks to her adoptive mother's mansion. She had declined to explain that she needed time to come to terms with emotions that had risen sharply when the train stopped, but she knew Jason understood when he arranged to have their luggage delivered without discussion.

Elizabeth's heart thundered as she glanced at the well-tended minigardens in front of the lofty mansions, at the cobbled streets and handsome carriages rolling past, and at the well-dressed pedestrians passing by. All bespoke a wealth that she had accepted without thought before leaving for Galveston.

Elizabeth noted that women almost without exception gave an extra, surreptitious glance at Jason when they passed. She wasn't truly surprised. Jason would stand out in any crowd with his masculine good looks and powerful size.

Glancing at him now, she noted that there was an unusual intensity about him today. She had sensed it building in him since they had learned of Aunt Sylvia's unexpected death. He had had so many questions about her aunt, about Trevor, and about her aunt's relationship to her adoptive mother. He had surprised her with his interest.

She had known she was not well enough to attend Aunt Sylvia's funeral, but she had been determined to return to New York as soon as possible, only for a little while, so she could comfort her adoptive mother and express her regrets to her cousin, Trevor. She supposed the poor fellow would be devastated, considering how Aunt Sylvia had doted on him in her own way.

She had known the moment she mentioned returning to New York that Jason had no intention of allowing her to go alone. He had barely left her side while she recuperated at Chantalle's residence.

At Chantalle's *bordello*.

Strangely, Elizabeth no longer thought of Chantalle's house in those terms. The women there had been generous with their help and concern. Chantalle had been endlessly kind and had made certain Elizabeth's life remained untouched by the business of the house. And if the sounds of *business* being transacted occasionally filtered up into her room, Elizabeth had done her best to ignore them.

Simon had made no attempt to contact her during her recuperation—or if he did, Jason had taken care of it, just as he was handling the investigation into the attempt on her life.

Elizabeth was aware that it bothered him that Milton Stowe remained a mystery. The authorities were unable to discover any reason for the man's having followed her to Galveston, or for his subsequent attack. In the time since, Jason had seemed to avoid any discussion of Milton Stowe. His concern for her safety never lapsed, however, and she could only reason that frustration kept him silent.

Elizabeth looked up again at Jason as they approached her adoptive mother's mansion. His brow was furrowed and his strong features were tense. She knew the thought that her adoptive mother would not accept his presence had never crossed his mind, because he was certain they belonged together and nothing could come between them.

They drew closer to the mansion, and Elizabeth's eyes filled.

Jason scrutinized her expression, asking, "What's wrong, Elizabeth? Are you all right?"

"I'm fine." Elizabeth swallowed as they stood at the foot of the front staircase. She said in an effort to reassure him, "I suppose I'm just anxious to see Mother Ella again." She added almost in afterthought, "And Trevor."

His frown tightening, Jason gripped her arm supportively as they ascended the steps and rang the bell.

The next few moments slipped by in a flurry of excitement as Mother Ella's old servant, Rufus, answered the door, finding it hard to conceal his delight at her return; Helga and Molly greeted her just as effusively. Her heart pounded as she climbed the staircase, finally knocked on the door to her adoptive mother's bedroom, and then entered with Jason beside her.

She knew she would never forget the moment when Mother Ella's frail arms slipped around her with a surprisingly strong grip. She wiped the tears of joy from the dear woman's pale cheeks, ignoring her own as she introduced Jason. "I want you to meet Jason, Mother Ella. He's very important to me."

Stepping forward, Jason leaned down to kiss Mother Ella's cheek. His expression was tender as he said, "I'm honored to meet you, ma'am, but Elizabeth didn't mention that she just introduced you to the man she's going to marry."

Elizabeth lost all sense of time in the flood of congratulations that gradually changed into discussions of her injury and subsequent recovery, as well as her investigation into her past and her plans for the future. Suddenly noticing that her adoptive mother's eyelids had grown heavy, she said apologetically, "I should have realized that you're tired, Mother Ella. Rest for a while. We'll be back later." She glanced at Molly, who had entered and was waiting nearby. "Molly will stay with you while I show Jason to his room."

It wasn't until Jason and she had drawn Mother Ella's bedroom door closed behind them that Jason drew her tight against him. He brushed her mouth with his before saying, "You'll show me to *my* room?"

Elizabeth returned the heat of Jason's gaze, regretting as much as he the temporary separation they would endure. Her recovery was still new, and their lovemaking—only recently renewed—had deepened in scope. There was not a night when she had lain in his arms that she had not realized the wealth of the emotions they shared. That same realization had been written in Jason's gaze and his touch, and in the heartfelt, loving words he whispered when her nightmares returned in the darkness of the night.

Her gaze reflecting her thoughts, Elizabeth stroked Jason's cheek as she said softly, "It'll only be for a little while."

The sound of a step turned Elizabeth toward the slender man who moved into sight at the end of the hallway. "Trevor," she called, and started immediately toward him. She threw her arms around him with tearful sincerity when she reached his side. "I wanted so desperately to be here with you through these terrible times. I'm so sorry I wasn't."

Elizabeth drew back to see that tears had flooded

Trevor's eyes as well, and she was filled with compassion for the gentle, thoughtful young man so dominated by his mother's avaricious jealousy. She whispered, "We're not blood relatives, but I hope you'll always consider me your friend."

Suddenly aware that Jason had come to stand rigidly beside her, Elizabeth looked up at him and said, "I want you to meet Jason, Trevor. I'm sure he'll feel the same way, too, when he gets to know you."

But Jason did not reply. Nor did he extend his hand to Trevor in greeting, a deliberate slight that Elizabeth did not expect. She was equally stunned when Trevor seemed to accept Jason's reaction as his due, and then said, "Please come with me, Elizabeth. There's something I have to show you."

Trevor did not speak again until they entered the walnut-paneled first-floor study. He said as he turned toward her, "My mother took over this room after you left and Aunt Ella was no longer able to come downstairs. It was her dream to own this house one day, you know, but I never realized how far she would go to realize that dream."

Elizabeth saw the shudder that shook him as he walked toward the desk dominating the center of the room and drew open a drawer. He withdrew a large leather folder marked with Aunt Sylvia's name, turned a page, then handed it to her. Indicating an entry in Aunt Sylvia's distinctive hand, he said softly, "I found a canceled draft when I attempted to straighten out the details of Mother's estate. It appears that she wasn't as careful as she thought she had been. Either that, or she never expected to be caught when she wrote out a draft for a round-trip ticket to Galveston and recorded it so precisely in her record book."

Elizabeth stared at the entry as she said, "A ticket to Galveston?"

"I thought it had to be a mistake, so I checked up on it. The ticket was purchased in her name to be used by a man named Milton Stowe."

Elizabeth gasped. She looked up at Jason when his strong arm slipped around her waist to steady her, but Jason's dark gaze was intent on Trevor's face. "I made it my business to find out who Milton Stowe was," Trevor continued. "When I did, it became clear why my mother had paid him to travel to Galveston."

Trevor paused, his voice choking as he said, "I don't know what to say, except I'm sorry, Elizabeth. I was always aware that I was a disappointment to my mother, but I never believed she would be driven to such excess because of it."

His genuine sorrow touched Elizabeth's heart.

She was still shaken after Trevor departed, leaving Jason and her alone in the study. Turning toward him as the truth suddenly struck her, Elizabeth said, "You already knew Aunt Sylvia had sent Milton Stowe to Galveston, didn't you, Jason?"

His expression still dark, Jason did not reply.

Elizabeth continued, "But you hid it from me. You sent that wire to Mother Ella so Aunt Sylvia would learn that Milton Stowe was dead, and you refused to leave my side while you waited for her reaction. I understand now why the news in that wire was too much for her. But even when Aunt Sylvia was gone, you believed Trevor had taken part in his mother's scheme. You came here ready to do what needed to be done."

Jason's expression eliminated the need for reply, and Elizabeth took a step toward him. "You know now that could never be true, don't you? Trevor would never have had a part in Aunt Sylvia's scheme. He's too sincere … too kind."

Jason's expression did not change, and Elizabeth explained, "Trevor was always my friend. He endured harsh treatment from his mother for standing up for me over the years. He never said the words, but I always knew he loved me, and that he loved Mother Ella in a way his mother never did. Mother Ella's time is limited, Jason. Trevor will soon have no one … only me … only us."

"No." Jason's reply was adamant. "Trevor will never be my friend. He's part of the reason that woman tried to have you killed. I'll never trust him, and I'll never forgive him for that."

Elizabeth moved closer. She whispered, "Trevor's friendship is important to me, Jason, because I know it's important to him."

"Elizabeth …"

Gasping as Jason pulled her suddenly into his arms, Elizabeth felt the emotion that shuddered through him as he said, "I love you, Elizabeth. Milton Stowe's bullet was mere inches from taking you away from me. The thought haunts me. I can forgive Trevor's ignorance, but I can't forgive him for accepting his mother's hatred for you. I never will."

Drawing back, Elizabeth said, "Then maybe you can accept Trevor's weakness ... his hope that one day he would be fully accepted by the mother who never showed him real love. I can, Jason, because I know now how much love really means."

Jason stared at Elizabeth a moment longer before responding, "Maybe ... someday."

A tear trailed down Elizabeth's cheek as she whispered, "Mother Ella must never know about any of this. If she found out, it would break her heart."

"I love you, Elizabeth," Jason whispered. "Whatever you decide will be all right with me."

Jason drew her closer then, and Elizabeth melted into his strength.

She had gone to Galveston to discover her past. She was determined to continue her search, but she consoled herself with a loving truth—that she *had* found her future, and that she knew now that it lay in the warmth of Jason's loving arms.

Epilogue

Simon Gault stared at the sultry trollop who stood boldly in the study of his elaborate mansion. He watched as she openly scrutinized the richly paneled walls, his extensive library, the thick carpet that had muffled her step, and the heavy, masculine furniture he had so carefully selected. He noted her amusement when she looked at the standing globe in the corner of the room, and his irritation rose a notch.

Angie had had the gall to actually come to his residence and demand admittance. He would not forget that intrusion into his privacy, but for the moment he asked gruffly, "It's almost twilight. Shouldn't you be getting ready to receive your customers at Chantalle's?"

"Any fella who comes to Chantalle's to see me will figure it's worth the wait until I come back."

Simon made a small scoffing sound before he responded, "Was there something you wanted here?"

Ignoring his question, Angie leaned on his desk,

allowing him full view of the ample womanly attributes made visible by the low-cut bodice of her dress. "I'm not going to be working in a place like Chantalle's all my life, you know," she said confidently. "I'm going to live in a house like this someday— a real respectable house that's apart from my business." She scoffed as if in afterthought, "But I'm not going to have one of them silly globes like yours in it."

"Is that what you came here to say?" Simon asked tightly.

"No, it isn't." Angie sat on the edge of the desk as she continued, "I haven't seen you at Chantalle's for a while. I figured I knew the reason you didn't come, with what happened in the back alley a while back, and since Elizabeth Huntington was recuperating in Chantalle's private wing with Jason Dodd glued to her side."

"What has that to do with me?"

"It wouldn't do your image any good to be associated with anything that happened at Chantalle's, but I figured you might want to know what's been going on with Jason and Elizabeth since they left Galveston."

"Should I care?"

"Everybody knows how interested you were in that independent witch."

"If you say so, but that's all irrelevant now, since they've left the city and won't be coming back."

Angie raised her narrow brows.

"You're telling me they will be coming back?"

Angie maintained her silence.

"Oh, I see." Simon's contempt for the trollop heightened. "You want to make sure that your trip here was worth your while. Well, I need to know if it will be worth my while also."

When Angie still did not speak, Simon pulled out the second drawer of his desk and withdrew a metal box. He unlocked the lid, removed a wad of paper currency, and counted out an amount.

"My information is worth more than that."

His irritation soaring, Simon counted out a few more bills, saying, "It had better be."

Waiting until Angie had snatched up the currency and shoved it into the bodice of her dress, he said, "Well?"

"First off, you're wrong. Elizabeth and Jason are coming back."

"How do you know that?"

"Simple. I sneaked into Chantalle's office and read the letter Elizabeth wrote to her. It was full of a lot of unimportant stuff, like how sick Elizabeth's adoptive mother is and all. But she wrote at the end that Jason and she had unfinished business in Galveston. She said that Jason still wants to prove you collaborated with the Yankees." Angie fluttered her eyelashes annoyingly as she added, "Of course, I know you're innocent."

Simon ignored her comment as he prompted harshly, "And?"

"And Elizabeth says that this time, Jason's going to help her with her search for her family."

"Her family?"

"Don't pretend you don't know. It's all about that pendant she wears."

Simon felt his color rise at her rebuke.

"Anyway, Elizabeth said she's not going to quit until she finds out everything there is to know about it."

Angie eyed his reaction for a moment before she stood up and said, "I knew you had a yen for that woman, although I could never understand it. I figured you'd want to know that Dodd got what you couldn't, and I also knew Chantalle would be the last person to tell you."

When Simon did not reply, Angie said, "If you're of a mind to let off some steam, it's all right for you to come visit me at Chantalle's. Jason and Elizabeth won't be staying there when they return. Elizabeth said Jason found a fine place for them to stay while they're in Galveston." She added, "And the truth is, I've been kind of lonesome for you."

Angie moved her body in a subtle, sensuous way that tightened Simon's groin. She laughed out loud at his obvious reaction, then pulled open the door and said as if in afterthought, "Oh, by the way, Elizabeth and Jason got married in New York—right in her adoptive mother's bedroom so the old lady could be there. They're man and wife. Fancy that!"

The door clicked closed behind Angie, and Simon rose angrily to his feet. He paced with fury as he reviewed in his mind the information that Angie had supplied.

So, Dodd thought he had outsmarted him. Dodd thought a simple marriage license would protect

Elizabeth from his designs. Not only was he a bastard—he was also a fool! Dodd had not even an inkling of the full story behind that damned Hawk crest, and Simon was determined no one ever would.

Returning to his desk, he sat abruptly, withdrew a key from his vest pocket, and unlocked the bottom drawer. He removed Harold Hawk's journal with a contemptuous smile. His entries over the years had described his every triumph over the greedy fool who had sought to steal the wealth and success meant to be his. They were his way of laughing in Harold Hawk's face even while he was in the grave.

Simon's smile dimmed. Unfortunately, his entries of late had recorded intentions more than successes.

He had duly recorded Elizabeth Huntington's unexpected appearance in Galveston, the fact that she was indeed a Hawk, and his plans to make her suffer his vengeance. It was time to update that entry.

The lamplight flickered, illuminating Simon's deadly expression as he picked up his pen. Scribbling in dark, angry letters, Simon recorded his solemn vow—that like her brother before her, Elizabeth Huntington had only temporarily escaped him, and that she would pay with more than her life when he won out in the end.

Don't miss the next installment
in the Hawk Crest Saga!

Hawk's Pursuit

Constance O'Banyon

a special preview

COMING OCTOBER 2006!

Jena Leigh arrived several minutes early for her appointment with Col. Madison. The heavyset man who greeted her introduced himself as Sgt. Walker. He briskly informed her that she'd have to wait a bit because the colonel was busy at the moment.

She dropped down on a hard, straight-backed chair, observing the activity in the office. The outer office was larger than the one at the *Daily Galveston* and everyone seemed busy working on documents. She supposed it took a lot of paperwork to take over a city the size of Galveston. She counted seven desks, but only four of them were occupied at the moment. There were four private offices leading off the main room—one of them had Col. Madison's name on it. Soldiers were coming and going from one office to another—she heard the scraping of chairs and the shuffling of papers— she was surrounded by men dressed in the hated blue Yankee uniforms. She was actually observing an occupying army at work.

Anger flushed her face as one of the men glanced up from his desk and winked at her. Indignant, she turned her face away from him, remembering the soldier who had harassed her the day of her arrival. She stood up and stalked to the door. Looking down the street a bit, her gaze settled on the same bakery shop she'd seen earlier. Her anger rose by degrees when she realized it had been in front of this very office that she'd been accosted. If she hadn't been scribbling notes when she arrived, she would have recognized the place.

She returned to her chair and tried to dismiss the incident because there were more important matters to attend to today. She was reading the file Dickerson had given her on Col. Madison. Irene had taught her that it was better to know as much as she could about the person she would be interviewing. He was from Baltimore, Maryland, and had been stationed in Washington D. C. at the beginning of the war. Later, he'd worked for the then Vice-President Johnson, who had since become President after the assassination of Abraham Lincoln. He had seen action toward the end of the war when he'd joined the Maryland Calvary. To her way of thinking, for a man to have held such prestigious positions, he must be of some importance, and he was probably an older man. But if he was so important, why had he been stationed at Galveston? Although Texas was proud of her port city, it certainly wasn't the hub of the state.

As time passed she became bored but resisted the urge to get up and pace the room, knowing

that would only call attention to herself. By her cal-
culations, Col. Madison had kept her waiting for
over an hour beyond their appointed time. To
keep from making eye contact with any of the men
in the room, she searched through other files Mr.
Dickerson had given her. Then she studied the
notes she'd taken about the first murdered woman
and frowned. Was it just a coincidence that both
women had been prostitutes and had been murdered and left in a deserted area, or was there
more to it than that? A shudder shook her body;
there must be a connection between the two deaths.

She drew in her breath and stared into space
trying to put the pieces together. She knew by the
instinct that had always guided her through a story
that the two of them had been killed by the same
man. She wondered why Mr. Dickerson hadn't
told her about the other woman. Perhaps it had
been another test to see if she'd put the pieces together by herself.

The heavyset sergeant glanced up at her and
smiled. "It shouldn't be too long now, miss." Several other soldiers were watching her, but she managed to look right through them. She squirmed in
her chair as another hour passed. Before, she had
been only mildly irritated, now she was irate. She
carefully weighed her options. What she should do
was walk out, which was probably what Col. Madison wanted her to do. No, she wouldn't give him
that satisfaction. And, if she left, Mr. Dickerson
certainly would not like it.

It was stifling in the building, and Jena Leigh

fanned herself with her handkerchief. She even
moved to the chair nearest to the window, but it
didn't help much since there wasn't a breeze stirring. Just when her temper was about to drive her
into action and she was preparing to storm out of
the place, the sergeant approached and motioned
for her to follow him.

Jena Leigh's footsteps were measured as she
crossed the room. What she wanted to do was give
Col. Madison a piece of her mind, but if she gave in
to that impulse, then he might very well have her
thrown out or not allow her to interview him at all.

"Sir," Sgt. Walker said as they entered the room,
"the reporter from the *Daily Galveston* is here."

The colonel had his head bent over whatever he
was working on and didn't bother to glance up at
Jena Leigh. He waved the sergeant out of the
room while he scribbled notes on a ledger. There
was a chair in front of his desk, but Jena Leigh
stood, waiting to be acknowledged. The man was
insufferable! There was no end to his rudeness.

He wore a blue frock coat with eagles on each
gilded epaulet. The coat was buttoned to regula-
tions, and she wondered how he tolerated the
heat. She could see little of his face since his head
was lowered, but his jaw was square, and his hair as
black as midnight. Her gaze rested on his hands;
his fingers were long and tapered and without
calluses—the hands of a gentleman and certainly
not the hands of the old man she had expected.
The longer he kept her waiting, the more she struggled with her anger.

* * *

Clay Madison heard movement and glanced up, confused to find a woman standing before him, demurely clasping a leather satchel in front of her. He noticed there was nothing demure about those angry golden eyes. He had no idea who she was or what she was doing there. Probably one of the many Texans who came by his office to lodge a complaint for one reason or another.

He stood. "What can I do to help you, madam?"

Jena Leigh stared into piercing eyes that were such light blue they were almost silver. "I had an appointment with you over two hours ago."

His gaze never wavered from hers. There was a harsh arrogance about him that put her immediately on guard. Like an officer commanding his troops, he nodded for her to be seated. Skepticism laced his words, and he stated blandly, "You can't be the reporter from the *Daily Galveston*."

"Oh, but I am." She dropped down on the edge of the chair, keeping her back straight, and her eyes level with his chin.

"And what is your name?" he asked, again with a commanding presence.

Her anger was now directed toward Mr. Dickerson, who obviously, for some mischievous reason of his own, had not informed this office to expect a female reporter. Jena Leigh was not about to allow this Yankee to intimidate her, or Mr. Dickerson to make a fool of her.

"I'm J. L. Rebel. And just for your information,

my time is as valuable as yours, and I don't appreciate being kept waiting."

He eased back into his chair, a smile tugging at his lips. Her name had a familiar ring to it, but he couldn't think why while he was staring at the loveliest creature he'd ever seen. "You are right, of course," he said at last. "It was rude of me to have kept you waiting. I ask your pardon."

It was a flimsy attempt at an apology, but probably the only one she was going to get from him. "Can we discuss what you've learned about Goldie Neville's murder?"

Clay was so caught up in watching her lush mouth that he didn't hear her question. She was an enchanting creature, and he was fascinated by the way her golden eyes sparked with anger, even if that anger was directed at him. "I'm sorry. What was your question?"

She ground her teeth and held on to her forbearance by a thin thread. He was making it clear that nothing she had to say was of any importance to him. "I was speaking of Goldie Neville."

"Oh, yes." His eyelids lowered. "The woman who was murdered. My office is looking into that. If we have anything of interest to your newspaper, I'll have Sergeant Walker find it and send it over to your office by dispatch."

Insufferable man, she thought. "I am doing my own investigation," she informed him. "Were you aware that there was a woman similarly murdered less than a month ago?"

That got his attention. "What are you saying?"

She let out an intolerant breath. "I'm saying," she glanced down at her notes, "that a Betsy Wilson was killed in the same way Goldie Neville was just over three weeks ago. I'm wondering if you've made any connection?"

"To my knowledge, this office was never informed of another woman being murdered."

"And why is that?"

She was beginning to irritate Clay. "Because, Mrs., or Miss Rebel, our job is not to investigate local murders unless they involve us directly."

"It's Miss," she informed him. "And if what you say is true, why has this office taken such an interest in Goldie Neville's death?"

God, he thought as he watched her raise her chin and look at him with contempt, he loved her sparkling amber eyes. She was magnificent! He might not like her attitude, but he liked everything else about her. And she was annoying as hell. He didn't much care for women who pushed their agendas, but she was no novice at her job, and she knew how to hit home with her questions. For some reason, however, he was glad to learn she wasn't married.

"In the Neville death, we were asked by local authorities to look into the matter because it took place near where one of our ships was docked." He glanced down at his own file. "It says here that this office gave our findings on the Neville death to a Mr. Goodall, thus concluding our part in the investigation."

Jena Leigh glanced back at her notes. "Would it

come under your jurisdiction if I told you Miss Neville was secretly meeting one of your own men?"

He was startled. "One of my men?"

"A Yankee, a Federalist, a Union soldier. I don't know if he was from this office—you Yankees are everywhere, aren't you?"

With practiced discipline he let her barb pass unchallenged. "How could you know that? It didn't come out in our investigation."

"Mrs. Beauchamp informed me that Miss Neville was very interested in a Yankee sergeant she was seeing."

He wondered what a woman like her would have in common with the madame. "And you think this fragment of Mrs. Beauchamp's imagination killed Miss Neville?"

She let her breath out slowly, trying to hold on to the thin thread that kept her temper in check. "Why would you assume Mrs. Beauchamp imagined the man? What would she have to gain by making such an assertion?"

"All I know is she didn't mention it to me. And I questioned her at some length."

Jena Leigh folded her notes and placed it in her case. Standing, she leaned forward with her hands on the desk so she would be eye level with him. "I can see you don't care about the death of one more soiled dove, do you? You only want to protect your own image and not get your hands dirty by delving too deeply into such a death."

Instead of being angered by her accusations, he

grinned. "A soiled dove—you mean a prostitute, don't you?"

She glared at him. "If you like. But I can tell you, I have no respect for your arm of the army. I, myself, had only been in Galveston for an hour when I was accosted by one of your soldiers, and right in front of this office."

Clay's brows came together in a frown. "Was that you? I witnessed that incident."

"Witnessed it, and did nothing about it." She was truly angry now. He'd seen what happened and had not come to her aid. "If your job is to protect your soldiers when they behave improperly, then you are succeeding admirably." She reached for her case and shielded herself with it. "I'm wasting my time here."

His gaze was steady and probing. "Sit down, Miss Rebel," he said in a troubled voice. "It's my job to see that both sides are heard and to prevent trouble before it begins. I can assure you in this office we will do everything in our power to bring peace to the region."

"What about the man who harassed me?"

"Were you hurt in any way?"

"I ... my shoulder was bruised." She watched Col. Madison frown, and the dark look in his eyes softened a bit. "I am sincerely sorry. On behalf of the Union Army, I apologize for the actions of one of our soldiers." He didn't see any reason to tell her that he'd already reprimanded the man who had harassed her.

She met his steady gaze, and her anger receded

enough for her to really look at him. Each feature was perfectly blended to make him one of the most handsome men she'd ever seen. His jaw was strong, his mouth was perfect. She stared into his eyes and found him similarly observing her. She tore her gaze from his, reminding herself why she was there. "I'm not impressed by your apology. I imagine if a man from Galveston dishonored one of your women, you would slap him behind bars fast enough. Is the man who shoved me against a wall behind bars, Colonel?"

Clay felt a bit uneasy because he should have taken sterner measures against Sgt. McIntyre. "I did speak to the man," he was forced to admit.

"So you detained him?"

He took a steadying breath. "I am trying to be patient, but you make it difficult." She infuriated him.

"In what way did you punish the man?"

"I warned him if he ever again committed such an act he would have to face the consequences."

"You did that much," she said critically. "He must have been trembling in his boots." She shook her head in disgust. "Read my column tomorrow and find out how the people of Galveston feel about your attempts to bring harmony to the community."

Sobering, Clay gave her a speculative glance. "You're a rarity, Miss Rebel, an idealist."

In Jena Leigh's way of thinking, he hadn't meant his assessment of her character as a compliment.

"I don't know how your Northern women are,

but here in Texas, we don't like being treated with such disrespect."

He was becoming more frustrated by the minute. She was a spunky lady, and she knew how to hit and keep on hitting. "Nor should you have to endure being disrespected."

They glared at each other until Jena Leigh said, "I have nothing further to ask of you. I'll wish you a good day, sir. I've taken up enough of your valuable time."

Before Clay could reply, she turned and swept out of the office, weaving her way past the desks in the outer room. He stood with the intention of going after her and shook his head, reconsidering. She was a hellion—a woman who seemed to push her way through life. A smile touched his lips. He would see J. L. Rebel again, of that he was certain—she was going to cause him trouble.

He motioned to one of the soldiers in the outer office. The young private hurried forward and snapped to attention. "Yes, sir," he said with a heavy Southern drawl.

"Where are you from, soldier?"

"West Virginia, sir."

"That explains the Southern accent."

Clay looked into puzzled hazel eyes and wondered if he'd ever been that young. "What's your name, Private?"

"Nathaniel Ellison, sir. And breaking away from Virginia was the best thing West Virginia ever did, sir."

"Private Ellison, I want you to do something for me."

The young soldier had never been singled out to do anything for one of the higher ranking officers, especially not the most important officer in the building. "Yes, sir."

"You saw the woman who just left here?"

"Yes, sir." He gulped, wondering if he was in trouble because he'd been staring at her, but who wouldn't have? She was beautiful. "I saw her leave," he managed to say in a shaky voice.

"Her name is J. L. Rebel, and she works for the *Daily Galveston.* Find out where she lives. I want you to become her shadow for a couple of days. Note where she goes, and who she talks to. But be discreet. Don't let her suspect she's being watched."

Ellison wondered what this was all about. But it wasn't his place to question the officers. "I'll be her shadow, sir, and she'll never know I'm there."

"Report back to me as soon as possible."

The young private saluted. "Yes, sir. I will, sir."

Jena Leigh paced Noah Dickerson's office, clasping the notes she'd taken earlier in the day. "I can tell you right now," she injected, "that Yankee officer was insufferable! He has one job, and one job only, and that is to keep his own men from being accused of anything outside the law. He wears blinders in regard to the people of this town." She paused to take a breath. "But I suppose that's to be expected." She shook her head in frustration. "Tell me where we go for justice. Where?"

Dickerson turned in his swivel chair so he could follow her pacing. "Will you be seated, J. L.? You're making me dizzy."

She dropped into a chair, and using the toe of her boot, moved her satchel from under her feet. "I'm sorry, but he made me so angry. I told him what happened to me in front of that office when I arrived in town, and you know what he did? He said he'd 'spoken with' the man. What does that mean?"

"What did you expect? The Yankee officers are going to look after their own first. If he said he spoke to the soldier, that's as good as you're going to get from him."

"Do you think he saw me as a threat to any of his men?"

"No. I think he saw you as a troublemaker."

"Yes, well, I can be," she admitted. "And I suppose I allowed what happened to me to color my view of him a bit; but under the circumstances, who wouldn't?"

The editor glanced down at the notes she'd handed him. Already she had gone further in her investigation than any of his other reporters. "So Mrs. Beauchamp said Goldie Neville was seeing a Union soldier."

"Yes. The woman wasn't quite what I had expected. She really cares about the people who work for her. She wants Miss Neville's killer brought to justice."

He arched a brow at her. "So you liked her?"

Jena Leigh shook her head. "I don't know her well enough to form an opinion. And she and I hardly travel in the same sphere." She leaned back and let out her breath. "I don't think we will be sharing lifelong secrets with each other."

Dickerson knew today had been hard for her. He imagined Irene Prescott had protected J. L. from the seamy side of life, and rightly so. "You may find this hard to understand, but Chantalle is well received by many people in Galveston. She's a successful businesswoman."

Jena Leigh nodded. "It's her business that I find objectionable."

"Well," he said smiling, "I can see how you would."

Jena Leigh decided it might be better to move on to the business at hand. She watched Dickerson closely as she asked, "You have already connected the Goldie Neville and Betsy Wilson murders, haven't you?"

He stared at her, stunned. "What! I hadn't thought—" He shook his head. "Where did you get such an idea?"

"Then you know about Betsy Wilson?"

"Yes, but I don't recall that there was much of a fuss made over her death. I believe we had a mention of her in the obituaries. At the time, she was just another prostitute, and no one was sure how she died."

Jena Leigh leaned her hands on his desk and leveled herself with him. "She was a human being, and she had a life until someone took it away from her in a most brutal way."

He rubbed his temples. "Who put you on this track?"

"Mrs. Beauchamp."

"She tied the two deaths together?"

"Not exactly, but I think the deaths are related."

"Not even the authorities made a connection." The glimmer of triumph beat in his heart. He could smell a big story, and it had taken this young woman to dog out what was right before them all. "Maybe I should put Armstrong on this story. He can push hard and batter through obstacles."

"Oh, no, you don't!" she said, slamming the palm of her hand against his desk. "This is my story, and I'm going to pursue it."

Dickerson had rarely had his authority challenged, and felt the hairs on the back of his neck rise. "I say who does what around here."

"Fine," she said, standing up and working her fingers into her gloves. "But Mr. Armstrong had weeks to come up with warning signs, and he didn't see them at all. It took me one day to put the pieces together."

"Simmer down, simmer down," Dickerson prompted, waving her toward the chair. "I'm not going to take it away from you unless I see you are in over your head."

Jena Leigh dropped down on the edge of the chair. "I can do this." She watched his face carefully as she asked her next question, "How far will you allow me to go as a reporter?"

"What do you mean?"

She shoved a sheet of paper across his desk. "I've written an article, and I was wondering if you would approve it for print."

He held up his hand to silence her while he read what she'd written. She watched him closely but couldn't tell what he was thinking from his bland expression. When he finished, he glanced at her. "The devil sent you to complicate my life, didn't he?"

"You'll publish it—as is?"

"You know this could mean trouble for us both?"

"I'm willing to chance it if you are. And should anyone object to the article, I'll take all the blame."

He laughed long and hard. "I'm afraid most of the risk is on my side." He tapped the paper against his palm and then handed it back to her. "Give it to Bob Steiner and tell him to set it in type."

She smiled at him, and even an old married man like Dickerson was not immune to her charms. "You could talk the devil into repenting," he said, waving her out of his office. "Go on, get this thing done." She was going to cause trouble for him—he could feel it in his bones.

"Thank you. You won't regret it."

"Yeah, yeah, yeah," he mused. "Visit me in a Yankee prison when Colonel Madison has me arrested."

Clay heard the sound of shattering glass in the outer office and rushed to find out what had happened. He stopped in his tracks just as another stone was hurled through the front window, showering glass everywhere. "What the hell!" he said, unsnapping his scabbard and moving to the door. Men in blue uniforms were either huddled behind desks to escape flying glass or flattened on the floor.

The mob of people consisted of twenty or so men and women—some shaking their fists, others spitting, and still others aiming more stones at the office. Clay's boots crunched against shards of glass, and he stepped out the front door.

"What is the meaning of this?" he asked angrily. "Who is responsible here?"

At that moment, everyone fell silent as one lone

officer faced them. But then they all tried to talk at once, and Clay couldn't understand anything they said.

"Silence!" He held his up his hand. "Speak one at a time so I can hear your complaints." He looked at one man with broad shoulders and an angry gleam in his eyes and picked him out right away as the leading instigator. He spoke directly to him. "Can you tell me the meaning of this?"

"If you'd read the *Daily Galveston*, you'd know why we're here," the man replied churlishly. "We ain't going to stand around while our women are molested by Yankee troops."

By now Clay had been joined by several of his men who were aiming their rifles at the crowd. Realizing the mob could turn ugly if he didn't take the sting out of their anger, he motioned for his men to lower their rifles. He then moved toward the man he'd singled out as the leader and stopped within inches of him. "What is your name, and what is your complaint?"

"My name's Carl, and me and these good people of Galveston want to know what you're going to do about what happened." He shoved a newspaper into Clay's hand and stepped back. "Read this and say it isn't true."

"Right now," Clay ordered, "I want you to all disperse and leave in an orderly manner. Sergeant Walker will take your name and make an appointment with any of you who want to talk about the matter in a calm manner. Otherwise, I'll be forced to take stern measures, and you won't like that."

The man named Carl reluctantly nodded, and most of the mob began moving away. Clay watched them for a moment, then motioned to Sgt. Walker to take the men's names. He was still angry when he entered the building clutching the newspaper that had been thrust at him. "Get this glass cleaned up," he told a young corporal who was frozen in place. "And get someone out here to replace that window. Right now," Clay told him.

The corporal turned to his companion, watching in awe as Col. Madison disappeared into his office. "He's a cool one. I've always thought officers sent men like us to do their grunt work. He faced down that mob singlehandedly until our men joined him out there."

"He's got nerves of iron, right enough," the other man replied. "That's why he's an officer, and we are mere corporals."

Clay spread the newspaper out on his desk, and his jaw tightened as he read:

The most trying times for mankind are not always when the dragons of war have been unleashed, but sometimes when the dragons have been put back in their box, and the usurpers of peace are turned loose on the populace of Galveston. Two of Galveston's own, Goldie Neville and Betsy Wilson, were brutally murdered, and no one at the Adjutant General's office seemed to think their deaths are a priority. I, myself, spoke to Col. Madison yesterday, and I got neither respect nor satisfaction from his answers. Another young woman, who shall remain nameless, was accosted by a Yankee soldier right in front of that office, and nothing was done about that. Do we sit back and allow the conquerors to ignore their soldiers as they insult our women? I say no! I say Betsy Wilson and Goldie Neville deserve to have their killers brought to justice. We cannot have this kind of monster walking the streets. I say we will not allow Miss Wilson's and Miss Neville's deaths to be ignored. We still have a voice, and I am willing to use mine. Good people of Galveston, are you?

Clay raised his head, fury driving him across the room, calling to Sgt. Walker. "I want you to get over to the—" he snapped his fingers, trying to think—"the *Daily Galveston*, and find J. L. Rebel. If she won't come with you willingly, place her under arrest."

"Yes, sir. Right away."

It was two hours later before Sgt. Walker reported back to Clay. "The newspaper office was closed by the time I'd arrived, and I spoke to a man called Bob Steiner. He said he didn't know where Miss Rebel lived, but I'm sure he was lying."

"Never mind. The workmen are here to put in the window. Stay until they are finished, and then you can leave. I'm leaving now."

Clay rode home, still fuming about the trouble that woman reporter had caused. He dismounted at the apartment house where he had taken a room. A young boy who worked at the boarding-house came forward to lead Clay's horse to the stable. His mind was on other matters as he pressed a coin in the young lad's hand. "Give him a good rubdown, and feed and water him."

Clay had access to his apartment by the back stairs, and his tread was angry and heavy on each step. He closed the door and stood for a moment, hands on hips, staring out the window. He still carried the image of flashing amber eyes. God, that woman was going to drive him to distraction. What had she been thinking to write such an article? For that matter, what had her editor been thinking to publish it? Galveston was a powder keg, and it wouldn't take much for it to explode into violence. Today they had narrowly escaped such an incident. Next time they might not prove to be so fortunate.

He unbuckled his gun belt and placed it on the dresser, then unbuttoned his jacket and hung it over a chair. Unfastening his shirt to the waist, he rolled up his sleeves, all the while contemplating just how he'd handle Miss J. L. Rebel. First of all, he'd demand to know her real name because she was obviously using an alias. No mother in her right mind would give her daughter such a name. And of course, he knew why she had chosen the last name of Rebel.

A soft knock fell on his door, and he moved to

open it. It was sundown, and the small stoop out-side his room was in shadows, but he could see the slender silhouette of a woman, although he could not see her features. "What can I do for you?"

"I had heard you wanted to see me. I found out where you lived, and here I am."

"J. L. Rebel." He opened the door wider and leaned against it. "You're the last person I expected to find outside my door." When she said nothing, he stepped aside and swept his hand forward for her to move past him.

Jena Leigh was reluctant to enter his apartment, but she did; however, when he would have closed the door, she stalled him. "Please leave it open. I don't want anyone to think—I would prefer you don't close the door."

"As if it would matter now, after the fact. If any-one saw you come here, they will already have drawn their own conclusions. But you are a young woman who throws caution to the wind, aren't you?"

"I know it looks that way to you," she said ner-vously. She watched him light a kerosene lamp and turn up the wick, casting soft light across the floor. The room was not at all what she'd expected. It was sparsely furnished with a bed, dresser, two chairs and a desk piled high with paperwork. The wooden floors glistened in the lamplight, and she stepped across a green braided rug. She raised her gaze to Clay and found him watching her closely. "I know it wasn't proper for me to come here tonight, but I just wanted to … to—"

"To?" he prodded.

"I heard about the riot today, and I never thought anyone would … would—"

"*Riots*," he corrected. "There were three. One at my office, one where several units are garrisoned, and a third at the quartermaster's offices."

"I never intended for that to happen."

He swept his hand forward, offering her a chair. "What did you expect?"

She remained standing. "I don't know. Not that."

Clay's gaze swept across her face. She looked so young—she couldn't be more than eighteen or nineteen. His jaw tightened. "If you aren't going to sit down, would you mind if I do? It's been a long day."

She saw the tired lines in his face, and she couldn't help but look at him as a man and not the enemy. He had been dressed formally the last time she'd seen him, and that had made him seem more formidable. He wasn't wearing his jacket, but there was still a scarlet sash about his waist. He was unrolling his sleeves and buttoning them, and her gaze went to the curly black hair on his chest before he buttoned his shirt. She jerked her gaze back to his face. "I shouldn't have come here."

He could feel her unease. "Forgive me," he said, reaching for his jacket and pulling it on. "I didn't expect company tonight, or I wouldn't have been dressed so informally." He sat down on a chair and crossed his legs, his hand resting on his highly polished boot. "I'm afraid I cannot offer you refreshments. These are only temporary quarters until I can find a suitable house, and as you see, I have only the bare minimum here."

"Think nothing of it. My only reason for being here is to make you understand that inciting a riot was not what I had in mind. And I want you to understand that Mr. Dickerson had nothing to do with it at all."

He folded his arms across his chest. "Your intentions are still not clear to me. But the hour is late, and I think we could talk about this at a more opportune time—say at my office tomorrow. Be there at nine o'clock in the morning, and we will discuss this in more detail."

"Yes, I must leave. But before I go, please tell me you understand that Mr. Dickerson had nothing to do with my column. If you must punish someone, the blame is all mine."

He was not willing to accept her noble sacrifice. She must have another motive for being there, and he thought he knew what it was. He stood, moving toward her and staring down into her face. "What should your punishment be, Miss Rebel?" His voice deepened. "Tell me, and I'll see to it."

She took a step backwards, not liking the gleam in his eyes. "Don't expect me to write a retraction, because I won't do that. Everything I said was true."

He stepped closer. "You won't write a retraction?" His gaze dipped to her trembling lips, and his voice lowered even more. "Are you sure?" Her mouth was so inviting he could hardly concentrate on what he was saying. "Very sure?"

She took another step toward the door. "Yes, I am."

He took the last step that brought him within inches of her. She smelled of some sweet exotic scent that he found enticing. Her skin looked smooth like silk, and he resisted the temptation to touch her.

Jena Leigh's head snapped up, and her gaze collided with smoldering silver eyes. Her throat closed off, and she could not utter a word. He was everything she'd ever fantasized that a man should be. Why did he have to be the enemy?

"Dare I hope that your true motive in coming here was to see me?" He touched her hand and for a moment her fingers curled around his, and then she jerked her hand away.

It took a moment for his meaning to penetrate Jena Leigh's thoughts, and she quickly stepped out the door and onto the stoop. "You're out of your mind! Apologize for that statement, right now!"

A quick smile curved his mouth. Most women would act indignant, pretend to misunderstand his meaning, or pretend to be faint and call for smelling salts. But this little hellion was demanding an apology. "What is a gentlemen to think when a lady shows up at his place without a proper chaperone?"

She backed toward the stairs, a shocked look on her face. "I would never confuse you with a gentleman." She wished she could retract her rash words because she was already in trouble with this man, and insulting him was not the way to gain his goodwill. She thought carefully, considering each word before she spoke. "I suppose any man might draw the wrong conclusion under the same circumstances." She felt her cheeks burn because he had misunderstood why she had come to see him. "I shouldn't have come here." She turned to leave, and his voice stopped her.

"I will want to see you in my office tomorrow morning. Be there on time."

She turned back to him. "Why can't you just say what you want now so I don't have to go to your office?"

He reached out and cupped her chin, tilting it up to him. "Because I can't think straight when you are this near." He watched her lips part in surprise and wondered what it would feel like to press his mouth against hers. "No, Miss Rebel, we can't talk here."

"You have no right to make demands on my time. When last we had an appointment, you kept me waiting for two hours. How do I know you won't do it again?"

"Nine o'clock," he reiterated.

She nodded. "I'll be there, but if you don't see me at that time, I'll leave."

"Miss Rebel, that wasn't a request. It was an order."

She nodded and moved to the steps.

Clay watched her descend the stairs and disappear into the shadows. He could still smell the lingering scent of her sweetness as he listened to the sound of her horse racing away. He braced his hands on the railing, still unsure about what had just happened. He was suspicious, and he supposed it came from the nature of his job. He was particularly suspicious of beautiful women and their motives. He thought of Paula, whose treachery was the rod by which he now measured all women. All women had a motive for what they did, and Miss Rebel's was probably ambition. She hadn't gained a name as a reporter without pushing beyond boundaries.

That little beauty would mean trouble for any man, or many men, if she had it in her mind to turn on her charms. Tonight she had acted nervous and embarrassed—it had been a pretty act. She had disrupted his office, incited the citizens of Galveston, and he couldn't allow her to get away with that.

Tomorrow, he would see her grovel.

Hawk's Pledge
Constance O'Banyon

Whit is a gambler by necessity, a loner by choice. Ever since the orphanage had gone up in flames, Whit Hawk has been searching desperately for what remains of his family. Instead he finds Jacqueline Douglas, a rancher in need of a good hand, a woman in need of the right man. Wildly beautiful, she is as untamed as the Texas he loves, and Whit knows that no matter what else life holds in store for him, the fiery redhead must be his.

TEXAS TR★UMPH

ELAINE BARBIERI

Buck Star was a handsome cad with a love-'em-and-leave-'em attitude that had broken more than one heart. But when he lost his head over a conniving beauty young enough to be his own daughter, he jeopardized all he valued, even the lives of his own children.

Ever since leaving his father's Texas Star ranch, the daring Pinkerton agent and his lovely partner Vida Malone made it their business to ferret out the truth. But the twisted secrets he begins to uncover after a mysterious message calls him home might be more than anyone could untangle. Saving his father will require all his cunning and courage, as well as the aid of the most exasperating and enticing woman ever to go undercover or drive a man to distraction.

TEXAS STAR

ELAINE BARBIERI

Buck Star is a handsome cad with a love-'em-and-leave-'em attitude that broke more than one heart. But when he walks out on a beautiful New Orleans socialite, he sets into motion a chain of treachery and deceit that threatens to destroy the ranching empire he'd built and even the children he'd once hoped would inherit it. . . .

A mysterious message compels Caldwell Star to return to Lowell, Texas, after a nine-year absence. Back in Lowell, he meets a stubborn young widow who refuses his help, but needs it more than she can know. Her gentle touch and proud spirit give Cal strength to face the demons of the past, to reach out for a love that would heal his wounded soul.

A Texan's Honor
LEIGH GREENWOOD

Bret Nolan has never gotten used to the confines of the city. He'll always be a cowboy at heart, and his restless blood still longs for the open range. And he's on his way back to the boundless plains of Texas to escort a reluctant heiress to Boston—on his way to pick up a woman destined to be a dutiful wife. But Emily Abercrombie isn't about to just up and leave her ranch in Texas to move to an unknown city. And the more time Bret spends with the determined beauty, the more he realizes he wants to be the man in Emily's life. Now he just has to show her the true honor found in the heart of a cowboy.

DEFIANT
BOBBI SMITH

Clint knows that although he stands reading his own epitaph, the words are true. Ever since the attack that killed his entire family, he's been dead inside. Only one thing keeps him going—the burning need to bring in the outlaws who did it.

Posing undercover to infiltrate the gang, Clint can let no one know his true identity or the fact that he was once a Texas Ranger. Not even the pretty daughter of a preacher man who bursts into the Last Chance Saloon. As far as she knows, he's a gunslinger who has no right to touch a good woman. But sometimes a man's got to break all the rules, ignore common sense to follow his heart, and get downright...*Defiant*.